Praise for Hel
FOLLOW ME

An Amazon Editors' Pick for

One of the 22 Best Erotic Novels to Read from
Marie Claire magazine

"Hardt spins erotic gold."
—*Publishers Weekly*

"Intensely erotic and wildly emotional."
—*New York Times* **bestselling author Lisa Renee Jones**

"With an edgy, enigmatic hero and loads of sexual tension,
Helen Hardt's fast-paced *Follow Me Darkly* had me turning
pages late into the night!"
—*New York Times* **bestselling author J. Kenner**

"A tour de force where the reader will be pulled in as if
they're being seduced by Braden Black, taken for a wild ride,
and left wanting more."
—*USA Today* **bestselling author Julie Morgan**

"Hot. Sexy. Intriguing. Page-turner."
—**International bestselling author Victoria Blue**

"Helen Hardt's gift for engaging storytelling and
unforgettable characters is at its full shine."
—*USA Today* **bestselling author Angel Payne**

"Christian, Gideon, and now…Braden Black."
—**Books, Wine, and Besties**

"This book is off-the-charts hot, very near scalding."
—**Books Best**

"It completely consumed me and I'm in love with the mysterious Braden. I want and need to know more about this man."
—**The Sassy Nerd Blog**

FOLLOW ME UNDER

A NOVEL

#1 *NEW YORK TIMES* BESTSELLING AUTHOR

HELEN HARDT

Entangled Publishing, LLC
10940 S Parker Road
Suite 327
Parker, CO 80134
rights@entangledpublishing.com

Amara is an imprint of Entangled Publishing, LLC.

Visit our website at www.entangledpublishing.com.

Edited by Liz Pelletier
Cover design by Bree Archer
Cover images by GSPictures/Gettyimages,
s_christina/Depositphotos
Interior design by Toni Kerr

ISBN 978-1-68281-554-0
Ebook ISBN 978-1-68281-555-7

Manufactured in the United States of America

First Edition January 2021

10 9 8 7 6 5 4

AMARA
an Imprint of Entangled Publishing LLC

Also by Helen Hardt

FOLLOW ME SERIES

Follow Me Darkly

WOLFES OF MANHATTAN

Rebel
Recluse
Runaway

STEEL BROTHERS SAGA

Craving
Obsession
Possession
Melt
Burn
Surrender
Shattered
Twisted
Unraveled
Breathless
Ravenous
Insatiable
Fate
Legacy
Descent
Awakened

For everyone who read Follow Me Darkly *and loved it.*
Get ready to go under…

Chapter One

Everything's ready for tonight. Are you?

I stare at the text from Braden.

For a moment, I'm no longer sitting with Betsy, my new friend who's known my ex-boss, Instagram influencer Addison Ames, since they were kids. Instead, I'm in some kind of time-warped vacuum, where only my phone and I exist. Betsy hasn't just told me that Braden dumped Addie for refusing to get kinky with him after something he did left her shaken. That women are a game to him. That Braden is dangerous. I'm simply alone, reading Braden's enigmatic text and anticipating what he has in store for me tonight.

But only for a moment.

When I look up, Betsy is fidgeting, clasping and unclasping her hands. She's clearly nervous. Clearly frightened that Addie will somehow find out she's telling me all this. How was Betsy ever friends with Addison Ames? High school was a while ago for them, of course. She and Addie are twenty-nine now.

I look at the text from Braden once more.

Everything's ready for tonight. Are you?

I can't feel my face. Only minutes earlier, I was alive with excitement and anticipation about tonight.

Now?

Am I feeling fear?

Not exactly.

Apprehension.

Yeah, a little, but that's not the sum of what's whirling through me.

Trepidation and nervousness, yes.

But underneath it all, flowing through my veins, is what I've felt all along.

Love.

Even after what Betsy told me—that Braden dumped Addie after she refused to do what he asked—I'm still in love with him.

I still yearn for him.

But I need answers. Big-time.

My hands clench into fists. My shoulders ache from the tension. A drum pounds in my head. I'm sitting here in the back room of Betsy's Bark Boutique—she even closed the shop to talk to me—and I'm ready to implode.

There's an explanation. There has to be. Braden is a man who volunteers at the food pantry that kept him fed when he was a child. He's a man who rescues dogs.

Betsy continues to speak, but her words are only a high buzzing sound between my ears. Her mouth moves, her lips flap, but nothing resonates in my brain.

Then her clammy palm lands on one of my fists.

"Skye?"

My lips part, but I can't force any words out. Instead, a squeak emerges.

"Skye?" she says again.

This time I bite my lower lip. The magnitude of the accusation she just lobbed against the man I love hits me with the full force of a sucker punch to the gut.

Addie passed out after one of their escapades. When she refused to get kinky with him again, he dumped her cold and broke her heart. She was never the same. It took her forever to rebuild her confidence—not until her Instagram took off, really.

"She's lying," I say. "Addison is lying."

Betsy bites her lip and starts fidgeting with her fingers again. "Maybe. All I have is what she told me. I certainly wasn't witness to what transpired between her and Braden."

"Besides, you're the one who told me that she pursued *him*. Maybe he decided she wasn't the right match for him." I can't help my pleading tone. I'm angry—frightened, even—but I won't take these emotions out on Betsy. None of this is her fault, and she's only trying to help me.

"I'm not saying anything, Skye, other than what Addison told me. I don't know if it's true, but if there was even the slightest chance it is"—Betsy shrugged, clasping her hands together—"I felt I needed to tell you. I don't want you to end up brokenhearted like she did. I betrayed a huge confidence telling you this because I care about you."

I nod. Betsy's a good person.

But Addison is *not* a good person. And I think deep down, Betsy knows it.

"I've searched everywhere on the internet, trying to uncover this"—I make air quotes—"'secret' that neither Addie nor Braden will talk about. And you're telling me the only secret is that he likes to tie women up, and she decided she didn't want to do that anymore?"

Is this supposed to surprise me? Addie's a major influencer. She has a public image of leadership, of being in charge of her life. Of course she doesn't want to be submissive.

Still…she knew about my nipple clamps. Did Braden use them on her? She must have consented, or Braden wouldn't have dominated her in any way. It's possible she submitted at first and then decided that wasn't her jam after they did something that freaked her out…

And then he dumped her?

Betsy looks away and unclasps her hands, fiddling with her fingers again before zeroing back in on my gaze and placing her palm on my fist once more. "If there is even a tiny chance of it being true, I had to tell you, Skye. I'd decided not to, but then you said you're in love with him. I can't let you get hurt."

"Braden would never hurt anyone. If he was the one who ended the relationship, he had a good reason." My words sound confident. Almost too confident. Am I trying to convince myself? If Betsy is telling the truth, was Addie refusing to do some kind of kink a good reason?

Or is this all an elaborately created lie? Betsy's not lying. She's telling me the truth as she knows it. But the "truth" comes from Addie, and she could very well have lied.

Silence looms between us, almost visible in its thickness. Finally, Betsy removes her palm from my balled-up fist.

"Please tell me I haven't made a mistake, Skye."

"You haven't. I'm just not sure what to do with this information."

"Whatever you do, please keep my name out of it."

"Of course. I give you my word."

She breathes a visible sigh of relief. Is she really that scared of Addison? After all, Addison does promotional posts for her business for free, supposedly because Betsy knows Addie basically stalked Braden ten years ago.

Unless there's more that Betsy isn't telling me…

"What else do you know?" I asked.

She pauses a few seconds, looking down at her plate.

Then, still not meeting my gaze, "Nothing. That's it."

"Betsy…"

"I've already said a lot more than I should have. Please let it go at that."

Though my stomach is full of knots, I nod. Clearly she's gone way out of her comfort zone, and she did it for me, in an effort to keep me from getting my heart stomped on. I've never felt *un*safe with Braden. He always made sure he had permission to do everything he did. I don't even have a safe word. What did he do to Addie that freaked her out? Is Addie embarrassed by all that happened? What part did she play in the whole thing? I already know she was the one who pursued him in the beginning. In fact, she went way beyond simple pursuit. She stalked him.

"Thank you for trusting me," I say.

She offers me a soft smile. "I like you. I felt I had to…"

"I know. Again, thank you."

She idly pulls a loose thread on her blouse. "What are you going to do?"

I sigh. "Honestly, I'm not sure. I do need to confront Braden about it, though."

Her eyes widen and her lips tremble.

"Don't worry," I rush to add. "You can trust me to keep your name out of it."

"Skye, that woman has eyes and ears everywhere." Betsy rises. "I hope I haven't made a mistake. I have to reopen the store. I can't afford the loss of sales." She walks out of the back room and into the shop.

I rise as well.

I'm not scared of Addison Ames.

Still, Betsy's words feel like invisible knives scraping across the top layer of my skin.

Chapter Two

My feet, seemingly of their own accord, take me to Braden's office building. I whisk past the reception desk to the elevators with the receptionist's "ma'am!" ringing in my ears.

I ignore her plea and take the elevator to the requisite floor, past the floor receptionist, and to Braden's office.

"Ma'am!"

Stiletto footsteps follow behind me, but I'm on a mission. A mission to confront the man I love.

Braden's assistant rises as I approach. "Hello, Ms. Manning. May I help you?"

"I'm here to see Braden."

"He's on a phone call at the moment."

"I'll just wait in his office. Thanks."

"I'm sorry. I can't let you disturb him."

"I won't disturb him." I keep walking, the compulsion to get to his office overwhelming me. Yes, I should stop. Yes, I should listen to the receptionist. Yes, I should do a lot of things.

"Ms. Manning—"

I stroll past her, my heart pounding as fear slides through me. I grasp the doorknob to Braden's office, turn it, but I don't go through.

Stop it, Skye. Just open the fucking door and go in.

I push the door open and enter.

Braden sits at his desk, his back to me, cell phone to his ear.

I clear my throat.

He turns, and his eyes widen.

He motions to the phone and then nods toward a chair.

I don't budge. This isn't the bedroom, despite what took place the last time I was here. I haven't given up control in this office. Besides, I couldn't sit still if I wanted to right now.

Finally, he says into the phone, "Excuse me for a moment, please." Then, to me, "Skye, I'll be with you in a few minutes. This is important."

"Are you going to dump me if I won't do what you want?"

Shit. Shit. Shit. I didn't mean to just blurt it out like that.

His countenance darkens. I've woken the beast. I should be frightened, but I'm not. I don't know whether I'm angry or sad or in love.

Yes, I do. I'm all three.

"This is important," he says again, but he shifts his gaze to my restless hands I can't stop wringing before he goes back to his call. "Hey, Ken, I'm going to have to put these negotiations on hold. Something has come up that requires my immediate attention." Braden ends his call and stands.

God, he seems even taller and more formidable than normal. He's angry. Really fucking angry.

And really fucking attractive.

"Have you really just accused me of being so shallow that I'd break things off with you if you don't do what I want in the bedroom?"

My jaw drops. "Of course not."

"You just said it."

"No, I didn't."

"Enlighten me, then."

"I…"

Shit. For someone who touts having control, I'm exhibiting a complete lack of control by forcing my way in here with a ten-year-old story I don't even know is true. This isn't close to how I rehearsed this conversation in my head. Except that it kind of is. The closer I got to Braden's building, the faster I walked and the angrier I became.

No. That's not true. The more *frightened* I became. Frightened of losing the man I love.

"Talk, then, Skye. Apparently you have a lot to say to me."

"This isn't my fault," I say. "You won't tell me what happened between you and Addison. What choice did I have other than to try to find out myself?"

Braden stares at me for what seems like a long time but is really only a few seconds. I can't read his expression, which frightens me even more.

Finally, "You have one very important choice, Skye." He walks out from behind his desk, like a Grim Reaper coming for my soul. "Your choice is to trust me."

Trust him? Trust that he didn't dump Addie because she wouldn't do what he wanted? Trust isn't my issue. I let my guard down with Braden. I gave him my control. I did so because I *do* trust him.

"Have I ever," he says, "in all our times together, made you feel unsafe in my presence?"

"Physically or emotionally?" I instantly regret the words.

"Either," he says, his voice low.

"No."

"Have I ever made you feel that I'd end our relationship if you refused anything I asked?"

"No, but—"

"Then what's this about?"

"You. And Addie. How your relationship ended."

"Still none of your business."

"It is! It is because... What if you do the same thing to me?"

"I'm rapidly losing my patience here."

I whip my hands to my hips. "What happened? What did you do to Addie?"

"We've been through this."

He's clearly had enough, but I can't force myself to stop. This is important. *We're* important. "She was never the same afterward. Were you...violent with her?"

He comes closer. Tension exudes from him. Tension... and sexual energy. "Where did you get this information?"

"I...I can't tell you."

"I see. Whoever this person is who gave you this information, does he or she have any firsthand knowledge of anything?"

"No."

"Yet you're ready to condemn me on hearsay. Be both judge and jury."

He's right.

I hang my head. "No. Not really. But it's also scary, trusting someone new."

He tilts my chin up. "Even if I told you everything that went on between Addison and me, you would never have the whole truth. There will always be parts of me that I keep completely private, just as there are parts of you that you keep completely private. You can never know the whole truth about anyone."

"That's not what I want."

He laughs then. The big, sarcastic guffaw that rings out through the entire office. "Skye, that's *exactly* what you want. You want control over every situation."

I open my mouth to respond but then shut it quickly. How can I argue? He's right. Completely.

"I shouldn't have to tell you this, but yes, I ended the relationship with Addison. I had my reasons. If that's not good enough for you, I guess we part ways now."

"There's more, Braden."

"There is no more, Skye. This conversation is over." He drops his hand.

I shiver. I'm not cold, but the authority in his voice… It makes me tremble. "She…was never the same. Not until her Instagram took off."

"I *said* this discussion is over."

I cower involuntarily.

"Do you fear me now?"

No, I don't fear him. To the contrary, my nipples tighten against the scratchy lace of my bra. A tickle surges between my legs. I part my lips absently, licking them.

"I don't fear you. But should I, Braden? Did Addie?"

"What went on between Addie and me is in the past. We were kids. Neither of us knew what we were doing. What we were getting into."

"Then why—"

He sighs then, running his fingers through his hair. "Why, Skye? Why? Why did you have to keep digging until my past touches us and what we have? Why do you want to ruin it? I've told you before that I won't talk about this. It has nothing to do with what you and I have." Braden turns and stares out his huge window, as if he's searching for answers himself. His eyes are heavy-lidded. He looks almost…sad.

I've never seen him sad. The urge to comfort him overwhelms me. I walk forward and cup one cheek.

"Braden," I say, "what happened?"

He meets my gaze, his blue eyes brimming with… Is it regret?

"Did she get hurt?" I ask.

He doesn't respond, and I know I've stumbled upon the beginning of the truth.

"Why didn't she use a safe word?"

He swipes his hand over his forehead and then rubs at his temples. "I don't know, Skye, but I wish she had."

Chapter Three

I know nothing more now than I did before.
Except that Braden regrets what happened between Addie and him. Whatever caused their breakup.

And I need to know what it is.

"I'm done talking about this, Skye," he says abruptly, the regret in his eyes morphing into his normal stoic look.

"But I—"

"I said I'm done. What's in the past has nothing to do with the present. With you and me. I love you, Skye, but I have my limits."

I warm at his admission of love. I never doubted it, but I love hearing it. Sometimes he is a little stingy with the words.

"I love you, too," I say.

"Good." He grips my shoulders. "I ought to take you violently, right here in the office. I ought to make you scream so loudly that my employees think I'm torturing you in here."

I inhale sharply. Why is this turning me on so much?

I want it. I want it all. I want his lips on mine, his hands on my body, his cock inside my pussy, pounding, pounding, pounding…

But he loosens his grip. "That's not who I am, Skye. I like having control in the bedroom. I like taking women to their limits. And yes, sometimes that involves some violence. But only with consent."

"I…give you my consent, Braden. Take me. Take me now, as violently as you want to."

"Don't think I don't want to. I'm hard as a fucking rock, but I will never take you in anger."

"But…you've been angry with me before, and we've—"

"Never *this* fucking angry, Skye. This isn't you coming in and copping to stealing a piece of useless mail. This is you going behind my back. Trying to find out something that's none of your business, that isn't even me anymore. It's you thinking I could do something…" He rubs both his hands over his forehead, his cheeks reddening.

"But I *don't* think it, Braden. I just want the truth."

"Then we have nothing more to discuss. Until you let this go, we don't have a future. Just goes to show you that I was initially right. I shouldn't do relationships."

My heart thunders. It drowns everything out until all I hear is its beat—the rapid roar that makes my soul shudder. I don't move.

I don't speak.

"Why are you standing there?" he asks. "There's nothing more to discuss, and I have work to do."

"What if I refuse to leave?"

The blue of his irises darkens. He can make me leave. I know this. He can easily call security or, for that matter, he can toss me over one shoulder and get rid of me himself. The thought of that happening shouldn't turn me on, but God, it does.

Silence penetrates the room. He doesn't move. Neither do I.

Stalemate?

Neither of us will give up control—until he stalks toward me, grabs my shoulders, and crushes his lips to mine.

My lips are already parted, and his tongue darts into my mouth. The kiss is raw and frantic. Raw and frantic and yes, angry. Anger exudes from Braden. Exudes from him and into the kiss.

My nipples press against his chest, and my whole body throbs in time with my heart. I'm wet. Wet and ready.

Then he rips his mouth from mine. "Fuck it," he says. "Take off your shirt, Skye. Take off your shirt and sit down in my chair."

I inhale a sharp breath and walk to his chair on wobbly legs. I unbutton my shirt, trying to go slowly but moving quickly because I can't wait for whatever he has planned. He didn't ask for my bra, but I remove it anyway and toss it onto the floor. My breasts are already warm and rosy, and they fall against my chest.

Braden sucks in a breath. "Damn, Skye, you have the most beautiful tits in the free world."

He unbuckles his belt, unzips his pants, and pulls out his beautiful, hard cock. "I'm going to fuck those tits, Skye. I want to come all over your chest and give you a goddamned pearl necklace."

He walks toward me and slides his dick up between my breasts. It's hot, so hot, and when the head of his erection comes toward my lips, I stick out my tongue and lick the tip.

"Fuck," he says. He pulls his dick back down and then slides it upward once more. "Crush your tits together, Skye. Crush your tits together and play with your nipples while I fuck them."

I'm wet now. So wet. As lovely as his dick feels between my breasts, I want him in my pussy. I *need* him in my pussy.

But I'm wearing jeans. Jeans and shoes and socks.

If only I'd taken all my clothes off and not just my shirt and bra.

He continues to slide his dick between my breasts, and I continue to flick my tongue over the tip with each thrust.

Then he thrusts upward harder, sliding the head of his cock between my lips. Now he's fucking my mouth, and oh my God, I want him even more than ever. I need him inside me. But I can't tell him because my mouth is full of his cock.

Thankfully, he seems to have the same idea. He takes his dick out of my mouth and pulls me up by my shoulders.

"Your jeans, Skye. Get those fucking jeans off. Now."

I glance toward the door. Is it locked? Hell, I don't care. I need Braden inside me, and I need him now.

Quickly I get rid of my offending shoes, socks, and jeans. He flips me around. "Put one knee up on the chair, Skye."

I obey, and swiftly he thrusts his cock inside me.

I let out a slow groan. Everything. Everything and nothing all at once. Braden inside me is all I need right now, and I want him closer. I look over my shoulder and grab his tie, yanking him down toward me. I thrust my tongue between his lips. He fucks me as we kiss, groaning into my mouth.

My boobs dangle, slapping against my naked chest. He breaks the kiss then and grabs both of my tits, squeezing each nipple.

I'm so ready. But I need him to touch my clit.

Wait! I have two hands. I only need one to hold my weight on the chair. I reach downward to my vulva—

"No!"

I freeze. My body still throbs; my nipples still long for

him to touch them.

"You don't get to come today," Braden says.

I bite my lower lip, moving my hand down again.

"I said no." He grabs both of my hands behind me, holding them in one of his, and then he loosens his burgundy tie and takes it off his neck. He quickly binds my wrists together behind my back. "When I say no, Skye, I mean *no*."

"You also said you wouldn't take me in anger."

For that comment, I get a swift smack on one butt cheek. The stinging warmth radiates to my pussy, making my clit throb even harder. Then he shoves his cock into me once more.

Every thrust makes me hotter. Every time he nips at my neck, I want more and more to jump off the peak. But I'm climbing, climbing, climbing…

He's still angry. I can feel it in the way he sinks into me. He doesn't play with my nipples anymore. He just fucks me.

"Damn it, Skye," he says, his voice low in my ear. "Damn what you do to me."

I let out a soft moan.

"Do you know how much I want to eat you right now? Eat all that cream out of you and suck on your clit until you come all over my face? Do you think it's any fun for me not to let you come? Do you?" He slaps my ass again. "Answer me. Damn it, answer me!"

"I… I…"

His hand comes down on my ass again.

I'm so close. So damned close, but I won't come. I can't. Not until he lets me.

He controls my orgasms. I never had one until him, and now he controls them all.

"Please, Braden. Please let me come."

As if in answer, he gives me one last hard thrust, and I

feel him releasing inside my walls.

"I fucking love you, Skye. I shouldn't, but I do."

He stays embedded inside me for a timeless moment. When he finally withdraws, he pushes a handkerchief into my hand. After I clean myself, I turn around, naked, and meet his gaze.

"That will be all," he says simply. "I had to have you once more."

"Are you kicking me out of your office?" I swallow as my heart drops. "Or out of your life?"

"Both."

Invisible fists crush my heart. I didn't think this through. In my need to know the truth—in my need to control—I exhibited an utter *lack* of control.

Braden walks back to his desk.

"I love you," I say.

"I love you, too." He clears his throat. "Love is nothing without trust, Skye."

I shudder, nodding. "You're right. I'm sorry. I do trust you, Braden. I wouldn't have gone as far as I have without trust. Please, I don't want to lose what we have."

He says nothing.

Nothing.

The clock ticks.

Has he changed his mind? Will he give me another chance?

Finally—

"Then be at my place this evening, as scheduled. Christopher will pick you up at six thirty."

I nod. "Okay."

"And Skye?"

"Yeah?"

"Be ready for anything."

Chapter Four

Be ready for anything.
I leave Braden's office quietly and murmur a quick apology to his assistant.

My heart races as I return to my apartment. I haven't checked my Instagram in hours, and that's unlike me, since I'm a new influencer and I need to gain followers daily. The news from Betsy completely unraveled me. Quickly, I respond to several comments, make a few deletions, and then check my email. Nothing that needs my immediate attention, thank God.

I have a few hours until I'm due at Braden's place. He's justifiably angry with me, and truth be told, I'm pretty damned angry with myself. Addison is a liar. Why did I even consider for one moment taking her word over the man I love? So he ended their relationship abruptly. So what?

I'll make this up to him. But how?

Search engines call out to me. But no, I will not spend the afternoon trying to uncover information on Braden and Addison. I haven't possibly left any stones unturned at this point.

I leave the apartment quickly. Without knowing where I'm going, I end up at Crystal's Closet, a local lingerie boutique. Strange. I hardly ever venture into this kind of shop. But here I am, so I browse.

And I browse.

Not for a minute do I think sexy lingerie will make up for what I did to Braden this afternoon, but maybe it will be a good start.

"May I help you find something?" a salesclerk asks.

"No, thank you."

"Okay, just let me know if you need anything." She smiles.

I return her smile and then, "Actually, maybe I do need some help, but it's kind of embarrassing."

"No need to be embarrassed. What can I help you with?"

"Something…submissive."

"We have some lovely leather bustiers near the back. Would you like to take a look?"

Warmth creeps into my cheeks. "Yes, please."

I follow the clerk to the back of the store. Not only are there leather bustiers but fishnet stockings, stiletto platform heels, and an array of toys.

Braden has his own toys, and I can't even begin to presume whether he would like any of these. I'm pretty sure he doesn't do his shopping at Crystal's Closet.

"We have some leather thongs, but I personally think a black lace thong goes better with one of these bustiers."

"I'm thinking maybe…" My cheeks are warming again. "I'm thinking maybe no thong at all."

"Good idea," she says with another smile. "I don't think most significant others would complain. What's your bra size?"

"Thirty-six C."

She grabs a bustier from the rack. "Try this one. I think it will flatter your figure."

I take the garment and head into a dressing room. I look around. Hidden cameras, anyone? I wouldn't be surprised. The stuff isn't cheap. I have my money from Susanne Cosmetics, but am I being ridiculous, contemplating spending some of it on a two-hundred-dollar leather bustier?

Will Braden even appreciate it? He likes toys, yes, but what if he decides to rip this off me like he ripped my dress?

Of course, he also replaced the dress.

I remove my blouse and bra and stare at myself in the mirror. The bustier is not a corset. I don't need help pulling strings. It has some subtle elastic to help it conform to most figures. I wrap it around myself and snap the hooks together in front. It takes me a moment to look in the mirror.

When I finally ease my eyes onto my reflection, they widen.

This is sexy. *Really* sexy.

I always have good cleavage, but this is better than the best push-up bra. The sides conform to my curves, leading to my mid-rise jeans but leaving about an inch of flesh visible.

"How's it going in there?" the salesgirl asks.

"Good," I say. "I'm going to take this one. It's perfect."

"Awesome. Do you want me to bring anything else to the dressing room?"

Fishnet stockings cross my mind. And the platform stilettos. But as I gaze again at my reflection, I realize I'll look a lot sexier in this bustier with jeans than I will tripping across the carpet in fishnets and stilettos.

"No, I think this will be all for today."

"Perfect. Just meet me at the cash register."

I stare at my reflection for a few more seconds. Two

hundred dollars is a lot of money for a garment I'll probably never wear in public. I contemplate calling Tessa, but I already know what she'll say.

Let your hair down, Skye. Have some fun.

I smile at myself.

Then I follow Tessa's advice *literally*. I pull my hair out of its ponytail, shake my head, and let it fall over my shoulders.

Yeah, this is fucking hot.

I can't wait to show Braden.

B ack at my apartment, I can't resist. I don't the bustier once more and then check my makeup, touching up my Susanne Cherry Russet lip stain. Crystal's Closet hasn't offered me any money to promote their products, but why not? Originally I thought I wouldn't wear this in public, but the coverage is adequate. Luckily, my arms are long enough to get a great shot that includes the one-inch sliver of exposed flesh between the leather and denim of my jeans. I quickly compose a post.

Check out my new purchase from @crystalsclosetboston. #sexybustier #crystalscloset #susannecherryrusset

In less than ten minutes, I'm inundated with responses.

Braden Black is a lucky man!

Great rack!

You look fabulous!

Item number please! My boyfriend will love that.

I check the tag that I've already ripped off the bustier and reply quickly with the item number as the comments and likes continue to roll in.

Again, I check my reflection in the mirror.

You're a fraud.

I gasp. Where did those words come from? I hear them in Addie's voice, though she didn't comment on my post. I'm not a fraud. Besides, this bustier is flattering. No one can deny that.

I quickly whitewash the idea from my mind, grab a jacket to cover the bustier, and head to the bakery. Braden didn't say anything about dinner, but six thirty p.m. usually means a meal. I'll take one of my favorite baguettes.

After grabbing the bread, I return to my apartment and check my post.

Damn! The thing has exploded. Nearly a thousand likes!

And comments galore. I scan them quickly, looking for potential deletions. Addie will have a field day with this one, but I don't find anything from her. Good. She's been quiet for the last several days. Clearly, she doesn't want me to block her any more than I want her to block me. We need to keep apprised of each other.

Is it possible that I could one day be as big an influencer as Addison Ames?

You're a fraud.

I ignore the words once more.

Christopher will be here soon to pick me up, so I go to my room and quickly run a brush through my hair. I love the feel of it over my bare shoulders. Will Braden like my bustier?

Then a knock on the door. I throw on my dark-brown suede jacket once more before answering it.

Christopher stands there, wearing his usual black. "Good evening, Ms. Manning."

"We've talked about this. Please call me Skye."

"Right. Skye."

"I'm ready." Then, "Oh, wait a minute. I picked up a

baguette for dinner." I grab it off the table and follow Christopher down to the Mercedes parked outside my building.

"How's Penny?" I ask him. I miss my puppy so much, but my gift from Braden has to live at his penthouse, since my place doesn't allow pets.

"Adorable as ever, though she's a handful. She's definitely keeping Sasha on her toes."

I smile. "Have you taken her on a walk?"

"Several short ones. She's only two months old, so her attention span isn't great, but she has to learn to go to the bathroom outside."

"I can't wait to see her."

We're silent for the rest of the ride. I find myself unconsciously pushing my toes against the floor in the back seat, trying to make Christopher drive faster. I'm eager to see Penny, but even more than that, I'm electrically charged to see Braden.

I can't believe I almost ruined what we have earlier today.

Be ready for anything.

Braden's words when I left his office. My nipples harden against the leather of my bustier.

Be ready for anything.

He'll probably want to punish me for barging into his office, interrupting an important phone call, and then lobbing accusations at him.

It's no less than I deserve.

Anticipation grips me as Christopher pulls into the underground parking lot of Braden's building.

It grips me as we walk to the elevator.

It grips me as we ascend to the penthouse.

It grips me as the elevator door opens into Braden's place. I expect Sasha and Penny to run to greet me.

But they don't. Where are they?

I turn to Christopher to ask, but he's not there. How does he disappear into thin air?

"Braden?" I call out tentatively.

Silence.

"Christopher? Annika? Marilyn?" He may have others who work here, but I don't know their names. "Penny? Sasha?"

Again, silence.

I sigh, walk into the kitchen, and place the baguette on the island countertop. No smells of cooking, and the stovetop is sparkling clean. I open the refrigerator door. Just basic staples, no dinner waiting to be heated. No drinks poured.

This is my punishment? No dinner? No dogs?

No Braden?

I leave the kitchen and walk to Braden's bedroom. I knock, but no one answers. So I turn the doorknob slowly and enter.

"Braden?"

Silence greets me again, so I walk into the room. I inhale. An aroma. I can't place it.

The bed is made, and when I gaze upward, I see the remnants of his harness thing have been removed. Fresh spackle and paint have been applied over the holes in the ceiling where the contraption once hung. That's the aroma. Fresh paint.

A sliver of relief surges through me. I wasn't excited about the prospect of being harnessed and suspended above Braden's bed. Clearly, though, he just had the contraption removed today. Possibly even after our meeting in his office. Why?

"Braden?" I say again.

I walk to the bathroom, which is also vacant. I open his

giant walk-in closet, but only clothes and the smell of his cedar shoe rack greet me.

Obviously he's expecting me, or Christopher would not have come for me.

"What's going on, Braden?" I say out loud.

Since the room is empty, I jerk when I actually get a response.

Chapter Five

"Come upstairs."

Braden's voice, but where is it coming from? There must be a speaker in here somewhere that I didn't know existed. Of course he probably has an intercom system; I just had no reason to look for one until now.

"Braden? Where are you?"

"Come upstairs," he says again, ominously.

I don't leave the room yet, though. I want to know where the speaker is. I flip on all the light switches and scramble around, looking in each crack and crevice for his hidden speaker. Is there a camera, too? Can he see me?

Probably. Which means he's watching me as I rustle around trying to find the source of his voice.

I stop abruptly. Not the best look. I inhale deeply, exhale, and then leave Braden's bedroom, closing the door behind me.

I walk back into the living area. The stairwell—the stairwell I've never stepped foot on—stands against the back wall like a mountain between Braden and me. I've never been to the second floor. His living room, kitchen, office, and bedroom are on the first floor, along with a couple other rooms.

What could possibly be on the second floor?

Maybe a meeting room. A large conference room, even. A home gym. Maybe a sauna and hot tub. Of course. The billionaire could have a second floor full of lots of things normal people like me wouldn't even think about.

No reason at all to be ambivalent about walking up the stairs. No reason at all.

Except…

Why does he want me to go upstairs to a large conference room or home gym?

Be ready for anything.

Certainly he didn't mean a meeting or a workout.

I read *Fifty Shades of Grey*. I already know Braden likes toys. What if he has one of those playrooms up there? And what if he wants to…

The staircase seems to pulse with a heartbeat of its own.

In tandem with my own heartbeat.

I walk toward the first step slowly. Methodically. It seems to get no nearer until the toe of my shoe actually hits the first step.

I walk upward, still slowly, but not slowly enough because I reach the top of the staircase all too soon.

A hallway looms, and when I flick on the light switch, I see pink rose petals strewn across black plush carpeting. They lead to a closed door at the end of the hallway.

Be ready for anything.

My heart thuds.

I stride forward, following the rose petals left by a phantom flower girl. Pink on black, like something sweet and innocent heading into something dark and mysterious.

I am the innocent flower girl, and that closed door ahead of me is the dark mystery I crave.

I take another step and then another—

My phone vibrates in the back pocket of my jeans.

Really? Right now?

I pull the phone out of my pocket and glance at it. Tessa. As much as I want to answer and get her advice, I decline the call. I'm in this now. Braden is expecting me, and he's warned me to be ready for anything.

I gave him control already in the darkness. Of course, I have no idea how dark he can actually get. How dark I *want* him to get.

The phone buzzes again, and again I decline Tessa's call. I turn the phone to silent and shove it back in my pocket.

I continue walking until the door stops my progress.

I run my fingertips along the varnished mahogany. The door is just like every other door in Braden's palatial penthouse. Why should I fear a door?

Should I knock?

Or go right in?

I knock lightly.

"Come in, Skye."

I inhale deeply, preparing myself for what might await me on the other side. Has Braden rebuilt his harness contraption inside this room? Will I find a leather table, complete with bindings and straps and things I can't even imagine? Will he tie me up and blindfold me, use one of those spreader bars on my legs?

And these are the only things I know about. What else might be behind the door? Things I've never heard of, never imagined in my darkest dreams.

Finally, I can wait no longer. I open the door, closing my eyes without meaning to.

"Open your eyes."

I hesitate and then open my eyes slowly. Colors greet me first. Blurred colors. There's a dark red. There's black. There's brown.

Slowly, the room comes into focus, and I gasp.

This isn't a dungeon. It's a bedroom. A beautiful bedroom.

"Do you like it?" Braden stands before me wearing navy dress pants and a white button-down, no tie. The burgundy tie I grabbed earlier today. The burgundy tie he bound me with. Did he put it back on after I left his office? I'm wet just thinking about our afternoon.

"I… I love it, but Braden…"

"It's yours."

"Mine? We already have a bedroom, Braden."

"I have a bedroom, Skye. This is *your* bedroom."

"But…I want to sleep with you."

"You will. You can sleep in my bed with me, or I'll sleep in your bed with you. But you need your own space, Skye. A closet of your own and a bathroom that's your own." He cocked his head. "I thought you'd like this. I've been working on it for a while."

"A while? We haven't known each other very long."

"I had the room. All I had to do was have it decorated. If you don't like what I've done, redo it. It's yours."

"You told me to be ready for anything tonight."

"I did."

"What about—" My stomach finishes the sentence by letting out a growl.

He chuckles. "You're hungry."

"Aren't you?"

"Yes. But not for food."

I bite my lower lip. "Where are the dogs?"

"Upstairs."

"We *are* upstairs." I look up. "There's a skylight."

"I have a third floor that takes up only part of the space of my first and second floors. That explains the skylight. My employees live up there. Christopher and Annika and a few others. They each have their own bedroom and bath."

"Marilyn?" I have to ask. Braden's personal chef is a blond knockout.

He shakes his head. "Marilyn prefers to commute."

I let out a sigh of relief without meaning to. It isn't lost on Braden. The left side of his lips quirks up.

"I suppose I should feed you," he says. "I have a lot planned for tonight, and you need your strength. I've already ordered takeout. It should be here in a few minutes."

Of course. Takeout. I should've thought of that, but I was too busy freaking out about what Braden had planned.

"Who's going to answer the door? Christopher just disappeared."

"My employees know when to make themselves scarce. I pay them very well to disappear when I want them to."

I shudder. "You said be ready for anything."

"So I did."

"I thought you meant…"

He lowers his eyelids slightly. "Oh, I did."

"But the bedroom… The thing above your bed…"

"I already told you about that. I've been meaning to get rid of it for a while, so I did."

I nod.

Braden's phone buzzes, and he takes a quick look at it. "Our meal is here and set up in the kitchen. Let's get you fed."

I nod.

"Take off your jacket," he says. "You can hang it in your closet."

My jacket. I smile slyly. I'd nearly forgotten about the bustier I'm wearing underneath. I unzip slowly, bringing the black leather into view. I shrug out of the suede and let it slip to the floor.

Braden's eyes go wild, and a groan vibrates from his chest.

I widen my grin.

He says nothing. Just grabs me and slams his mouth onto mine. He's gripping my shoulders, kissing me hard. My legs turn to jelly, but he steadies me and deepens the kiss. My nipples are so hard, and my pussy… God, my pussy… I'm wet and ready and—

He breaks the kiss and pushes me away slightly. "You look so sexy, Skye," he rasps.

"Do you like it?"

He doesn't answer in words, only in his gaze. Those fiery blue eyes devour me. If possible, my nipples get even harder.

He clears his throat as I drop my gaze to the bulge in his crotch.

And I hope we can eat quickly.

Chapter Six

We don't talk much during our meal of sashimi and tempura. Despite my hunger, I don't overindulge. I'm too excited for whatever Braden has planned. So excited, I drop my chopsticks not once but twice.

When we finally leave the kitchen, he leads me not to his bedroom but to his office.

"Take a seat." He motions to one of the leather chairs sitting across from his desk.

"Okay…" I sit down.

"I wasn't planning to have this talk tonight," he says, taking a seat behind his desk, "but your escapade earlier today seems to necessitate it."

"Okay…" I say again, not sure what to expect.

"I want you. I'm hard as a fucking rock right now, looking at you in that leather top. I could fuck you three different ways in the next three minutes. That's how much I want you."

I can't help a smile. The leather is abrading my nipples again, and I squirm against the wetness between my legs.

"Before we go any further, though, there's something

you should know about me."

"What's that?"

He lowers his eyelids slightly, searing my gaze with his. "I've never said 'I love you' to any woman before you."

Though I try to hold back my surprise, my eyes inadvertently widen.

"You find that surprising?"

"Of course I do. Look at you. You're Braden Black. Women have been falling all over you for ten years. Aretha Doyle and all the others."

He gives me a slight smile. "That doesn't mean I fell in love with any of them."

I warm all over, my skin tingling. From his smile or his words, I'm not sure. The words give me joy, but that smile… The smile I see so seldom…

Still, the words ignite me.

Braden loves me. Braden has never said "I love you" to another woman, but he said it to me.

This is big. This is *huge*.

I return the smile. "I don't know what to say. Except that I'm flattered." *And really, really happy*.

"I'm not asking you to say anything. Just listen, Skye."

I nod. "All right."

"Obviously, you can deduce that I don't say those words lightly. I don't, but I said them to you, and I said them for one reason."

I lift my eyebrows.

He gives me that slight smile again. "I meant them."

I let out a breath I didn't realize I'd been holding. A breath of relief. Again, I squirm against the tickle between my legs.

"I'm not in the habit of saying things I don't mean, Skye."

"I didn't think you were."

His smile disappears. "So when I say I don't talk about what happened between Addison and me, I mean it."

So we're back to this. I'm not surprised. I'm the one who brought it up, and now I have to deal with the fallout. Only fair.

"Good. You're not opening your mouth to fight me. I'd say that's progress."

"I'm not sure what I should say, Braden. I'll always wonder what happened between you and Addison. I'll always wonder why she changed so much after your relationship."

"You know Addison," he says. "You know what kind of person she is. Yet you can't figure out why she might tell lies about me? Or anyone else, for that matter?"

"I admit you have a point," I say.

"You of all people should know that Addison feels very strongly when she thinks she's been crossed. She comes out fighting, and she doesn't fight fair."

"Okay, I admit she accused me of trying to steal her spotlight, which I never meant to do. In fact, I can't. She's so far ahead of me, she may as well be in a different galaxy. But she never said or gave any indication that I hurt her in any way."

"No, she didn't. Right now, you don't have something she wants. Despite your quick success, she hasn't lost any of her own following. But she's watching you, Skye. I know she is."

I wrinkle my forehead. Is he talking about Addie watching my Instagram? Or does he mean something more? "How do you know?"

His gaze darkens. "Because I'm watching *her*."

My skin grows cold, as if it's been flash frozen like those chicken breasts at Sam's Club.

"I've been watching Addison for years," he says. "She's intelligent and cunning, but she does have a weakness."

I lift my eyebrows in question.

"Her vanity," he says. "Her need for attention."

"She's a hotel heiress. She's had everything given to her since she was born. Of course she's vain."

"True, and when she feels those things are threatened, she strikes."

"Why? Why did she strike against you?"

"You're as intelligent as she is, Skye. More so, in my opinion. You can answer the question yourself."

He's right. I nod. "She wanted you. I know the story, Braden. Parts of it, at least. She pursued you relentlessly and you began by rejecting her. But you eventually didn't reject her, and that's what led to—"

"You're getting perilously close to the line, Skye. I will *not* talk about these things."

"If you don't talk about them, what choice do I have but to find the information somewhere else?"

He shakes his head, scoffing. "My God, you will drive me to an early grave. You sit there, looking so delectable… Trying my patience…" He rakes his fingers through his gorgeous hair. "You have the choice to trust me, Skye. You have the choice to let this go."

I sigh. I want to fight back, find fault with his words. But I can't. He's right. What happened between him and Addison has nothing to do with him and me. The fact that Addie and I have a history also has nothing to do with him and me, other than that I probably wouldn't have met him but for Addison.

"You gave up your control to me in the bedroom. I need you to give up your control in this situation as well. As long as you insist on pressing me about Addison, there will always be an issue of trust between us. I won't be in a relationship with a woman who does not trust me."

I nod. He's right. I have to give up this fact-finding mission.

If I don't, I could lose the man I love.

The only problem? It goes against my inquisitive nature. It goes against my controlling nature.

"I'll try, Braden."

"Trying means nothing. You either do or you don't. Are you going to give up on this ridiculous quest for information? Or aren't you?"

I know which answer will get me into Braden's bed. Braden's bed is where I want to be. Already, his controlling nature is washing over me, making me hot, making me wet.

But if Braden thinks I can just give up on any quest for information, he doesn't know me very well. Any answer I give him won't matter. Because he knows me, and he knows the truth.

"Yes," I say, smiling. "I can give it up. I can try, at least."

Braden returns my smile.

"I see," he finally says. Then he stands.

He walks out from behind his desk and stands over me, like a tall mountain shielding me from the sun.

"Stand up," he commands.

I part my lips and obey him.

"God, those lips." His voice is raspy again. "I've told you how sexy you look in that leather thing."

"It's a bustier," I say, being careful not to stammer as he eyes me like I'm candy.

"You've seen me rip a dress to shreds before."

I nod.

"I don't think my fingers are strong enough to take on leather."

I nod again.

"So I'll ask you to do it." He turns to his desk, picks up

a pair of scissors, and hands them to me.

I drop my mouth into an O. I just paid two hundred bucks for this bustier. No way am I going to cut it off myself.

"Take them, Skye."

"Braden, I—"

"I said, *take them*."

My hand shakes as I reach forward and grasp the scissors. The steel is cool against my warm palm.

"Be careful," he says. "Don't nick your creamy skin."

I'm trembling. Truly trembling. I'm not sure I trust myself to have the scissors anywhere near my skin at the moment.

"Do you trust me, Skye?"

I hesitantly nod.

"Then give me the scissors."

I shakily hand them back to him. He grins and tucks the scissors above my navel, right onto the beautiful black leather.

I close my eyes. I can't help it. I love this bustier, and I paid a lot of money for it only hours ago.

"Open your eyes," he commands, his voice dark and forceful.

I hesitate.

"Now."

My eyes pop open, almost solely from the dark force in his voice.

"Watch my hands, Skye."

I drop my gaze to his hands holding the scissors. He squeezes his fingers to his thumb, cutting a two-inch slice into the leather. I can't help myself. I suck in a breath. My beautiful bustier will be in shreds before I know it. Two hundred dollars down the drain.

"Why is this so difficult for you?" he asks.

"Because I just bought it. I bought it to look sexy for you."

"And you do look sexy. Just like you looked sexy in that little black dress. And it turns me on to no end to cut this off you." He lowers his eyelids and inhales. "I'm hard as a rock, Skye. I'm angry as hell with you, but I want you so badly, I can't see straight." He slices another inch into the leather. "Do you have any idea what you do to me? I've never been so completely angry with someone and yet so turned on by her at the same time. You make me question things. Not just about myself but about life. It's...disorienting."

Disorienting? He's disoriented while he has scissors against my flesh?

Trust him.

"I never wanted a relationship," he continues, "but from the first time I saw you, scrambling to pick up a condom off the floor, your cheeks red with embarrassment, I wanted to fuck you. I hoped one fuck would get you out of my system, but I think we both know how that turned out." He slices another inch.

The steel blades are cool against the warm flesh of my abdomen. And I find, to my complete and utter surprise, that I'm getting even more turned on.

"I don't like feeling disoriented, Skye. Not at all. But somehow, I fell in love with you anyway. I had no intention to, but I did." He slices again, coming close to my breasts.

"Braden..."

He meets my gaze, his blue eyes on fire. "This is my time, Skye. My time to be in control. Don't speak again until I tell you to."

My flesh is smoldering. Even the cool blades of the scissors spark heat in me. My nipples harden and push against the leather binding them. I flash back to the nipple clamps and then to Braden's lips firm around them.

"I'm going to fuck you in here, Skye. In my home office.

And I've never fucked a woman in here. Never even wanted to. But I want to fuck you, and I want to do it now." The scissors slice up between my breasts, and the bustier falls onto the carpeted floor.

I feel no loss. Not now. Sure, my two hundred bucks are gone, but my breasts have been freed. They're already swollen and ruddy, the nipples jutting out for Braden's mouth.

Still, one thought flies through my mind. He says he's never fucked a woman in this home office.

Has he fucked other women at his work office?

My thoughts fly to the afternoon, me with a knee on Braden's leather chair, grabbing his tie and making him kiss me.

Then his dick inside me, tantalizing me…

But no climax.

He didn't let me climax.

Will he let me tonight?

"Skye?" he says.

I say nothing.

"You may speak just this once."

"What?"

He raises one eyebrow. "You look inquisitive."

"It's…nothing."

"Tell me."

"I just wondered…" *If you were going to let me come tonight.* No, I don't want to say that. Not now. "If you've ever made love to a woman in your other office. Other than me, that is."

He meets my gaze. "Yes, I have."

His answer isn't unexpected, but still it catches me off guard.

"Oh."

His expression is unreadable. "Does that disappoint you?"

"Of course it disappoints me." I keep myself from huffing like a jealous schoolgirl. He's much older than I am. Of course he's had sex with other women in his office. Why should that surprise me?

"You know you're not my first fuck, Skye."

"I know that. It's just… Shit. I don't know."

"I just told you I've never fucked anyone in this home office."

"I know. And I've totally ruined the moment, haven't I?"

"No"—his voice darkens—"you haven't."

Chapter Seven

"Take off the rest of your clothes," he says, "and then bend over the desk. Don't say a word."

I don't hesitate even for a millisecond. The jeans, shoes, and socks—the same ones I wore this afternoon in his business office—come off quickly.

Just the thought of that afternoon delight gets my body throbbing and ready.

Braden, of course, is still dressed. Seems to be his MO, and for some reason that I haven't quite figured out, I like being naked while he's still fully clothed. It sets my whole body on fire, forces my nipples to harden further, and makes my clit pulsate.

"You haven't bent over the desk," he reminds me.

I turn and obey him, leaning over the cool mahogany. Soon my body heat warms the wood.

"You look delectable," he says. "Utterly delectable."

Silk touches one of my wrists. He isn't wearing a tie. Where did it come from? The thought flees in two seconds because I don't care. He's going to bind me again, which means I won't be able to touch my clit. Am I still being punished?

"Braden…"

"Quiet," he says. "From here on, you don't speak again until I say you can."

I nod and close my eyes, laying my head on the desk.

A few seconds pass, and then Braden's warm body pushes against mine. He's taken off his shirt, and the feel of his warm chest on my back soothes me. Makes me want him even more.

Then his warm fingertips slide over my shoulder, down my side, to my ass. He moves upward then, swirling his fingers over my ass cheeks and then between them.

"You realize this body belongs to me. All of it. Even this." He pushes against my asshole.

I gasp sharply. He's talked about anal sex before, in fact even used a butt plug on me, but not in my ass.

"Don't worry," he says. "We won't go there tonight. Not until you're ready."

I breathe out a sigh of relief even as a wave of disappointment flows through me.

"I want you to relax, Skye. I'm going to eat your pussy now. I'm going to stick my face between your ass cheeks and lick every bit of sweetness out of you."

Sounds perfect. I let out a low moan. Then his tongue is between my legs, and he's lapping like a cat drinking cream. He licks my folds, seeming to deliberately ignore my clit, and then shoves his tongue inside me. A mini fuck with his mouth. My legs tremble, but my weight is on the desk, so they don't falter.

I begin climbing the peak, knowing full well I won't get to the top unless he lets me. Still, what he's doing to me feels amazing. His warm tongue slides over my pussy, and then—

I gasp when he slides it over my ass.

I like it.

It's different, and I like it. I know then that Braden will take me there someday. Not today, not tomorrow, but someday...and the idea thrills me.

His tongue leaves my flesh then, and I whimper at the loss. He replaces it with his finger, smoothing it along the crease between my ass cheeks.

"There's something very special about anal sex, Skye. There's the intimacy, of course, and the trust. Both of those things make it special, but there's something else that goes beyond intimacy and trust. You know what that is?"

He hasn't technically told me I can speak, so I simply try to shake my head against the hardness of the desk.

"It's taboo," he says. "Forbidden. And that's why I crave it. I love the forbidden, Skye."

I tremble, my cheek and chest sticking to the wood.

"Are you...frightened?"

I shake my head—as well as I can while it's pressed against a desk—but I'm not convincing myself, which automatically means I'm not convincing Braden.

"I will never force you to do anything," he says.

I open my mouth to tell him that I know that, but then I close it abruptly. He hasn't told me I can speak.

"Good girl."

His voice is warm now. I imagine him smiling.

He pushes his tongue against my asshole once more while he thrusts two fingers inside my pussy.

Damn. So close. I push my pelvis against the hard wood of his desk, desperately seeking some sort of stimulation for my clit.

To no avail.

Braden seems determined that I won't come tonight. He's also determined to keep driving me to the brink, to make me wild. It's working. I'm ripe and hot and so ready to come. I squeeze my eyes closed, trying to revel in the moment, to enjoy what he's doing to my body without wishing for an orgasm.

"You have an amazing pussy," he says. "I can't get enough of it. Your intoxicating flavor, the softness, the pinkish purple color. And God, the wetness. It's all so beautiful."

I want to answer him. I want to tell him how beautiful he is, too. Then I want to beg for a climax. But I don't. He hasn't given me permission to speak.

Which, though it bothers me, also makes me feel something contrary to what it should.

Relieved?

Perfect?

What exactly do I feel when I surrender my control to Braden, the man I love?

Liberated. I feel fucking *liberated*.

Which makes no sense, since I've given up control.

I close my eyes, reveling in his fingers and tongue sweeping over my most private parts. Then he stops. Abruptly stops, but somewhere in the haze of my emotion, I hear his belt clinking, his zipper unzipping.

Then he's inside me, pumping, pumping, pumping…

Taking me with the part of his body that gives me the most intense pleasure I've ever known. He pushes hard, thrusts harder, and finally my clit collides against the wood, beginning to create what I need—

Until he grips my hips and pulls me forward, preventing the friction I crave so badly.

He's still determined. Determined not to let me have a climax.

I whimper, and I moan. It's a loss I feel deeply, yet still he's inside me, filling me, completing me.

And he does complete me. He completes me so well.

I love you, Braden.

The words whiz through my head, landing in the back of my throat, wanting so desperately to spring forth.

I hold them back. I cannot force them out. His will over me is that strong.

His control over me no longer frightens me. No. Now, as I delight in each thrust, I realize the truth.

I desire his control. I fucking *yearn* for it. As contrary as it sounds, I find freedom in it.

Finally he releases, falling onto my bare back and groaning. A drip of sweat from his forehead trickles down my neck.

He holds himself in place for a moment, and I revel in our joining.

When he withdraws, he caresses both globes of my ass. "Every time with you is better than the last, Skye. Every damned time."

I nod. He still hasn't given me permission to speak.

"I have so many plans for us. Now that you've given me control in the darkness. But I also need your trust."

I do trust you. I wouldn't have been able to give up control if I didn't.

But again, the words stay in my head.

He hasn't given me permission to speak.

I can play this game as well as he does. I will not speak until he tells me I may, which means he also won't get the full surrender he's seeking.

Normally, he lets me speak by now. Has he forgotten his command? Doesn't matter. I will *not* speak.

"I never planned to fall in love," he says after a minute, his voice rumbling against my skin. "I don't have time for love, Skye. I probably won't be the kind of boyfriend you need or deserve. And of course, marriage is always out of the question."

Something squeezes my heart. Marriage? I'm twenty-four. I haven't given marriage a thought, but of course, somewhere in the back of my head, I figured I'd get married someday.

A sense of loss fills me. Do I want to marry Braden? His statement leaves a lump in my throat.

Still, I don't speak despite my desire to begin an argument about marriage.

We haven't known each other long. Marriage is far in the future anyway. Still, I'd like to think it's an eventual possibility.

I swallow the words and feelings and stay quiet.

"You may get dressed now," Braden says as he stands.

His warmth leaves me, and coolness drifts over my back. I rise from my position on the desk. My hips are stiff from staying bent over for so long.

My bustier is useless shreds of leather now. But I don the rest of my clothes. Now what? He still hasn't given me permission to speak, so I'm adamant.

I will not speak.

I wait.

I wait for his instructions, but instead of giving me any, he zips up his pants and buckles his belt. Stoic Braden has returned. Will he kick me out?

No, he won't. He told me he would never kick me out of his place again, and I can't see Braden breaking a promise, short of ending our relationship altogether.

Of course, he nearly ended it today at his office.

So again, now what?

I continue to wait for his instruction.

It doesn't come. Instead, he says, "I'm exhausted, and

I have an early meeting in the morning. Good night, Skye."

He leaves the office, closing the door behind him.

Be ready for anything.

This is what he planned? To abandon me? What about his earlier text?

Everything's ready for tonight. Are you?

Of course, that was before…

Now what? Am I supposed to stay here? Spend the night in his office?

No, I will not. I'm obviously free to leave. Christopher will most likely be happy to drive me home. Or I can go up to the new bedroom Braden showed me earlier. Or I can go to Braden's bedroom and snuggle up to him.

Three choices.

One problem, though.

Braden still hasn't given me permission to speak. Does he realize his error?

A grin splits my face.

Yes, he does. This is a test. A damned test.

Fine. I've never failed a test in my life, and I don't plan to start now. I can eliminate two of my choices quickly. I will not go join Braden in his bedroom, because it will be difficult not to speak there. I also won't go find Christopher and ask him to take me home, because that will require the use of my voice.

The reasoning behind him giving me my own room — tonight of all nights, when he nearly ended our relationship earlier — suddenly becomes crystal clear.

I gather the tatters of my bustier and leave Braden's office, heading into the living area and then up the stairs, the pink rose petals still illuminating the path to my bedroom.

I smile again to myself.

Braden Black, you've met your match.

Chapter Eight

I wake up to the sun streaming through the skylight in my luxurious bedroom in Braden's penthouse. Oddly, I feel better rested than I have in some time. I could say it was the expensive mattress. I could say it was the pillow that seemed to conform to my neck and head. I could say it was any number of things, all of which probably played a part.

In reality? It's the big fat fact that I passed Braden's test.

So far, anyway. How am I supposed to get through the day without speaking? I have to be able to answer the phone if someone calls with an offer. I suppose I can answer any offer with email.

I still have to get home, though. Asking Christopher to take me will require my voice. I suppose I could use the Uber app, but once the driver arrives, I'd likely have to speak.

I have to think of something. I have to *win*.

Is Braden still here? I honestly have no idea. My phone sits on the night table where I plugged it in last night. I grab it to check the time and—

A piece of white paper sits on top of a velvet jewelry box.

I put my phone down and unfold the paper.

Nice work, Skye. You may speak now. I hope you like your gift. Braden

I smile. As I suspected, Braden knew exactly what he was doing.

And I have successfully passed his test.

Apparently I also earned a reward, though his note doesn't call it a reward. He called it a gift, so I choose to see it as such. Just a gift from a man to the woman he loves. My heart swells as I pick up the box, caressing its velvety texture, and open it.

Earrings! I gasp at their beauty. They're simple ruby studs set in white gold, but the clarity is superb. I love them at once. They're understated and elegant—something I'd choose for myself.

I smile as warmth rushes over me. Braden chose something he knew I'd love. With his money, he could have bought the most ostentatious piece of jewelry, but he gave me something beautiful in its simplicity.

I stare at them for a moment, letting something sink in.

This is my first gift from Braden. Sure, he replaced Tessa's dress that he ruined, and he built me a lovely room in his home for my use, but this…

This is just because, and I love them all the more. I hastily put them on.

Braden is probably already at his office. After all, he left the note and earrings sometime before I woke up.

I look around the beautiful bedroom. He was planning to keep me from speaking, so he gave me a place where I could stay without using my voice.

Nice work, Braden.

I can't help adding inside my head… *And nice work, Skye.*

I still have a problem, though. No bra or shirt. I slept in

my birthday suit, so I get up, amble over to the closet, and open it.

It's full of a wide variety of clothing. I smile again. He thought of everything.

I shower quickly and dress in my jeans from yesterday and a shirt from the closet. Then I walk down the staircase to be greeted by Sasha and my adorable Penny. I revel in their doggy kisses and say hello to Annika, who is dusting the living room. I peek in Braden's home office, but he's not there. Shoot. I want to thank him for the earrings in person. I guess a phone call will have to do. Then I walk to the kitchen.

Marilyn is wiping up the stovetop.

"Good morning," I say.

"Good morning, Ms. Manning. What can I get you for breakfast this morning?"

"Oh. I don't know."

"Mr. Black says you can have whatever you want." She smiles. "I can whip up some pancakes or waffles. I even have fresh blueberries. Bacon, eggs, toast. You name it."

"How about some coffee?"

"You got it. Black, right?"

"Right."

She sets a steaming mug of black coffee in front of me, and I take a seat at the island.

"I guess maybe just some scrambled eggs and a piece of toast."

"Are you sure? These blueberries will make some great pancakes."

"I don't want to put you to any trouble."

"It's honestly no trouble, Ms. Manning."

"Skye, please."

"Okay, Skye." She smiles.

And I decide I like Marilyn. I wasn't so sure at first. But

apparently, she's not after Braden and he's not after her.

"Seriously, just the eggs and toast." I smile.

"Coming right up."

Christopher walks in then. "Any coffee left, Marilyn?"

"Sure. I'll get you a cup."

"Morning, Ms. Manning," he says.

"Skye," I say adamantly.

"Right, Skye." He smiles. "Will you be needing a ride home?"

"Yes, please. But not until after breakfast."

"Can I make you anything, Christopher?" Marilyn asks.

"Actually, whatever you're making right now smells great."

"Scrambled eggs and toast for Skye. It's no problem to add a few more." She takes two more eggs out of the carton.

"That'll be great." Christopher sits next to me at the island. "We can leave after breakfast."

I take a sip of coffee. "Sounds perfect. What time did Braden leave this morning?"

"Early. I took him to the airport."

I try to hide my surprise. "He said he had an early meeting."

"He does. In L.A."

Again, I mask my surprise. Why didn't he say anything? I can ask Christopher, but then it will be clear that Braden didn't tell me where he was going, and for some reason, I don't want Christopher or Marilyn to know I'm not privy to Braden's whereabouts.

"Oh," I say.

"He comes back this afternoon. He actually flew commercial this time. The jet has some scheduled maintenance."

I nod, taking another sip of my coffee. Braden didn't say anything about tonight anyway. Will I be seeing him? I have no idea.

Braden is my boyfriend—the man I love and who loves me and who left me a beautiful gift this morning—yet these two people know more about him than I do. More about his schedule, anyway.

"I'll give him a call later." I take a bite of eggs from the plate that Marilyn has set in front of me.

Christopher smiles, picks up a piece of toast, and takes a bite.

I clean my plate for show, but the eggs and toast that smelled so good while they were cooking taste like sawdust. Even the gorgeous ruby studs feel heavy on my ears.

"Thank you so much, Marilyn." I touch my napkin to my lips and stand. "I'm ready to go, Christopher."

Though I'm still irked that I didn't know Braden was going to L.A., once I'm back at my apartment, I can't wipe the smile from my face. Yeah, I'm pretty pleased with myself. I beat Braden at his own game. I know one thing, though.

The next game will be more difficult.

Why are we playing games, anyway? We're supposed to be in love. But I can't deny the enjoyment I feel now. Maybe this game is a part of that. And I won. I passed his test.

I grab my phone to thank him for the earrings, but I get his voicemail.

You've reached Braden Black. Please leave a message, and I'll return your call as soon as possible.

"Hi, Braden," I say into the phone, still unable to wipe the smile away from my lips. "It's me. Thank you so much for the ruby earrings. I love them. In fact, I'm wearing them right now. They're perfect. Call me. I love you."

I fire up my computer. A few new emails since I last checked my phone. One from Eugenie at Susanne Cosmetics.

Skye, hello!
Are you available to fly to New York first thing next week? Say the word, and I'll send you a first-class ticket. The social media marketing department is very excited about meeting you in person and discussing what we all believe will be a beneficial partnership.
Best, Eugenie

Braden rarely makes plans with me a day, let alone a week, in advance. The one exception was the Opera Guild Gala. But…he's my boyfriend. We're together. Should I check with him before I accept Eugenie's invitation?

On the other hand, this is work. This is my living now, and he didn't check with me before flying to L.A. this morning.

I quickly type a response to Eugenie accepting the invitation. The e-ticket arrives in my inbox a few minutes later.

I can't help but smile. I'm taking pictures. Granted, most of them are selfies of me wearing lip stain, but at least I'm taking pictures and getting paid for them. I'm doing what I love, and I also have time to snap the kind of photos I truly enjoy, since I'm no longer bound to a day job.

My email dings—from Tammy at New England Adventures. I scoff.

Dear Skye,
We appreciate your interest in becoming a social media spokesperson for our company. However, we unfortunately have to rescind our offer per Section 4A(3) of the contract sent to you.
Sincerely, Tammy Monroe

Nothing I didn't expect. Somehow, Addison got wind of my offer from the company and slid in to take it away from me. They weren't going to pay me much—way below what Addison asks for. So either they got a fresh infusion of cash, or Addison agreed to do their promotions for peanuts, as she would say.

Yeah, she's that petty. She's already made it known what she thinks of me becoming an influencer. I imagine it won't stop anytime soon.

Braden offered to take care of it for me, but I turned him down. If I'm going to do this, I'm going to do it on my own.

You're a fr—

My phone interrupts my thoughts. I don't recognize the number.

"Hello?"

"Is this Skye Manning?"

"Yes, it is."

"Fabulous. Good morning, Skye. My name is Heather Thomas, and I'm the manager here at Crystal's Closet Boston. In the less than twenty-four hours since you posted on Instagram wearing one of our bustiers, we've had thirty-five people come in asking to buy one."

"Goodness. I'm glad the post was good for business."

"Both good and bad for business. Now we're out of stock, but that's never a bad thing. We're just sending customers to our online store, and if things keep going strong, we'll be out of online stock by this evening."

I'm not sure what to say. Luckily, Heather continues.

"Needless to say, we're absolutely thrilled. Honestly, I had no idea one Instagram post could do so much."

"I'm glad you're happy."

"Great, because we'd love for you to do another post. Actually, a series of sponsored posts wearing the bustier."

My mouth drops open. I no longer have the bustier. Braden cut it into pieces.

"Okay… Why don't I come in and talk to you about what you're looking for?" *And also find some way to tell you that my boyfriend destroyed the garment.*

"That would be fabulous. How about lunch today?"

It's nearly eleven now. Lunch is in an hour. "Dinner might work better for me."

Except Braden might be expecting to have dinner with me. Of course, he hasn't mentioned anything about dinner. Currently he's in L.A., and though Christopher said he'd be home this afternoon, he might not have been factoring in the time difference. This is business. Why shouldn't I have dinner with Heather to discuss business?

"Dinner would be fabulous," she says. "I'll make a reservation. Do you have any preferences?"

"No, I eat most anything. Just email me the information and I'll meet you." I hastily give her my email address.

"Fabulous," she says. "I absolutely can't wait to meet you in person."

"I'm looking forward as well," I say. "Thank you so much for your call."

I end the call, mentally patting myself on the back for not using the word "fabulous." Clearly Heather's favorite word.

Dinner plans made. A girl has to eat, after all. And next week, I fly to New York.

This is all so unbelievable. Mere weeks ago, I was assistant to Addison Ames. Now I'm a budding Instagram influencer, and Braden Black is in love with me.

Fucking surreal.

Now, what to do until dinner? I change into my workout gear, grab a water bottle and one of my cameras, and head to the studio to pick up a quick yoga class. Afterward, I walk around the city for an hour, shooting candids. Next, I stop for a cup of coffee and a sandwich, do a quick post gratis, and give Tessa a call.

"You're kidding me!" she gushes. "You're going to be modeling clothes on Instagram for Crystal's Closet?"

"Not modeling," I say. "I mean, not modeling anything too risqué."

"How do you know? They may want you to model pasties and thongs."

I can't help a boisterous laugh. "I don't think so."

"What if that's what they want, though? You've got a great body, Skye."

"Thank you, but I doubt they'd want an amateur like me."

"What if that's exactly what they want?"

I gnaw on my lower lip. "I don't know, Tess. I can't exactly turn down money right now."

"Speaking of money, what is your billionaire boyfriend going to say about you exposing yourself to all of Instagram world?"

Brick in gut. I've been so excited about the opportunity that I haven't given Braden's feelings a thought…other than thinking it's his own damned fault he didn't make dinner plans with me. Did he see the Instagram post? Is that why he cut the bustier off me?

I don't share, Skye.

Though technically he's never said those words to me, I consciously know the truth of them.

Does that include looking? He had a conniption when he found me with Peter Reardon at the MADD gala.

"Braden doesn't own me," I say.

"Braden is about as alpha as you can get," Tessa says. "And I can't think of any man who will want his girlfriend posing on social media wearing next to nothing."

"It's not like I'm doing it to be noticed," I say. "I'm doing it to make money."

Tessa erupted in laughter again. "Do you have any idea what you just said?"

Brick in gut again. "Yeah, I do. Maybe I should flog myself." I laugh nervously at my own joke.

"Better yet, I'm sure Braden will be happy to flog you."

I stiffen. I haven't told Tessa about Braden's enjoyment of dominance in the bedroom. So why is her statement so prophetic?

Betsy. Betsy probably told her about Braden's tastes.

"Skye? Did I lose you?"

"No, I'm here. I'll let you know how the meeting with Heather goes."

"Where's Braden?"

"He's in L.A. today on business."

"That works out well for you. He doesn't even have to know about your little dinner with Crystal's."

Except he's supposed to be back this afternoon. But I don't say that to Tessa.

"I suppose so," I finally say. "I have to run. I need to make something presentable out of my wardrobe for a business dinner. And for a business meeting in New York next week."

"Out of your wardrobe? New York? We need to do some shopping."

Tessa's right. I have nothing to wear in New York. I wore jeans and blouses to work with Addison. And now that I work for myself? I wear whatever. The little black dress Braden had made for me or a black leather bustier…

"You just scared the shit out of me," I say to her.

"Don't be scared. This is great. It's a chance to shop."

"You know I'm not the shopaholic you are."

"If it's money you're worried about, don't. I'm the best

at finding bargains."

"True." Tessa and I are on nearly the same budget, and she always looks like a million bucks when she's spent only a hundred.

"This weekend," she says. "You're mine."

I can almost see her eyes bulging out of her head through the phone.

"We'll hit all the outlets, plus Ross and T.J. Maxx."

I don't mean to, but I groan. To Tessa, shopping is an all-day adventure akin to an amusement park. To me? It's like sitting through a bad movie. With a groping date. And popcorn without enough butter.

Tessa laughs. "We'll have fun. Just think of all the great photos you can take for your social media posts."

"No company is going to pay me to post about buying cheap clothes."

"Yeah, you're probably right." She laughs again. "We'll have fun anyway. And I guarantee you, by the time I'm done with you, you will be ready for New York and beyond."

"Great. That still doesn't help me tonight."

"Tonight's easy. Wear the bustier you bought at the store."

Except the bustier no longer exists. But I don't tell Tessa. It's too personal.

"Yeah, I'll figure something out," I say.

"Call me after dinner. I can't wait to find out what kind of deal they offer you."

"Will do."

I end the call, walk to my closet, and peruse the garments hanging there.

This is going to take some doing.

Chapter Nine

Heather Thomas is beautiful in a really unique way. She has a Morticia Addams vibe going, but it works for her. She's dressed all in black leather, even her pants, and though she isn't as naturally pale as Morticia, her red-black lipstick makes her appear that way.

She stands when the maître d' brings me to her table in the back of Union Oyster House. Funny, I haven't been here since my first dinner date with Braden. It's one of my favorites.

Once I see Heather, though, I feel like a child in my navy blue sheath and black pumps. Sure, I look professional, but Heather looks like the goddess of death.

"Skye!" She pulls me into a hug.

Okay, she's a hugger. I can deal with a hugger. But her dark look doesn't go with the whole hugging thing.

She pulls back. "My, you do look fabulous. And I have to say, you fill out our bustier like no one I know."

First thing she does is compliment my rack. Interesting start to a business meeting.

"Sit down, please." She gestures to the chair that the maître d' is holding out for me. "I just can't wait to discuss everything with you."

"Thank you. I'm looking forward to our discussion as well." I take the menu from the maître d'. Not that I need it. I know this menu by heart.

"I adore seafood," Heather says. "It's simply fabulous. You said you eat anything, so I hope you adore it as much as I do."

"I do. I didn't get such good seafood growing up."

"Oh?"

"Yeah. I grew up in Kansas, rural Kansas. Meat and corn country."

"Really?" She lifts her eyebrows. "You seem so...urban."

"I've been here since college. I went to BU and never left."

"Wonderful. Just fabulous." She closes her menu. "I've been talking to corporate, and we're very excited to have you come on board, Skye."

I force a smile. "Thank you. I appreciate your confidence in me."

"I personally think *you* are the next big influencer on the rise. I've gone back through all of your posts, and your photos for Susanne Cosmetics are just fabulous." Heather unfolds her napkin and places it in her lap.

"Thank you."

"You're so pretty, yet not in an unapproachable way. Do you know what I mean?"

I think she means I'm not Addison Ames. Which I guess is a good thing, though Addie is beautiful.

"Sure. I guess."

"Believe me, it's a compliment." Heather gestures with her hands, her black fingernails waving. "You've been on the scene for what? Two weeks at most? And people adore you. Of course, the fact that you're Braden Black's girlfriend is icing on the cake."

Icing on the cake? The whole reason anyone cares what I have to say is *because* I'm Braden Black's girlfriend. Which kind of bugs me, but since I need to make a living, I'll deal with it.

"What kind of promotions are you looking for?" I ask.

"Probably similar to what you're doing for Susanne. As you may know, Crystal's Closet has a line of cosmetics, but we don't want to compete with Susanne. We're interested in you for other product lines."

"Oh? Which ones?"

"Our clothing, of course. And our"—she raises her eyebrows—"line of sensual products for the bedroom."

My cheeks warm. "I'm not exactly sure what you mean."

Heather laughs, a chirpy laugh that doesn't go with her dark look. "Nothing too risqué. Mainly the bustier, as I said on the phone."

"I'll be perfectly honest with you, Heather," I say. "I'm not sure I'm comfortable with—"

My jaw drops as my heart starts to beat double-time.

Braden is walking toward us.

"What is it?" Heather asks.

"Braden. He's here."

"Fabulous! I'd love to meet him."

In seconds, he's standing next to the table. "Skye," he says.

"Hi, Braden. This is Heather Thomas."

Heather holds out her hand, still sitting. "It is fabulous to meet you, Mr. Black."

Braden takes her hand. "Nice to meet you as well. I hope you don't mind, but I need to steal Skye away from you for a few minutes."

"Of course not. Would you care to join us?"

"Thank you. I would love that. But first I need to talk to Skye alone."

Heather gives Braden a dazzling smile. Rather, what *would* be a dazzling smile except for her nearly black lipstick, which makes it kind of menacing. "Absolutely. Take all the time you need. I'm going to order a cocktail. Skye, would you like anything?"

"We'll both have a Wild Turkey, neat," Braden offers.

"Fabulous. I'll take care of it."

"Skye?" Braden meets my gaze, his blue eyes burning.

"All right." I stand. "Excuse me, Heather. We won't be long."

She nods, and I follow Braden out of the restaurant.

"What's going on?" he says.

I fidget a little with my hands. "Well, it's called dinner, Braden."

He's not amused. "You know what I mean."

"You and I didn't have dinner plans, so when Heather asked me to join her, I said yes."

"Christopher told you I would be home this afternoon."

"He did, but at the risk of repeating myself, you and I did not make any dinner plans."

"You told Christopher you'd call me later."

"I did. I called you to thank you for the earrings—I love them, by the way—and you didn't call me back."

His gaze burns me. "You're playing a game with me again, Skye."

Games? He really wants to go there? "Seriously? A game? I called you, Braden. You didn't return the call. And what about the game you played with me last night? Keeping me from talking?"

"That wasn't a game."

"No. It was a test." I cross my arms over my chest.

"Skye—"

"A test, Braden. That's exactly what it was. And I passed."

The tiniest beginning of a smile twitches at the corners of his lips. "You did."

I can't help a self-satisfied smile.

"And now you're paying me back."

I shake my head. "You're wrong."

A husky chuckle emerges from his throat. "I'm not wrong. You knew very well I wanted to have dinner with you tonight."

"How am I supposed to know that?"

"Christopher told you I'd be home this afternoon."

"Yes. Christopher told me. *You* didn't tell me anything, Braden. I didn't even know you went to L.A. until Christopher told me."

"Christopher only tells you what I tell him to tell you."

"And because Christopher deigns to tell me that you'll be home this afternoon, I'm supposed to assume you want to have dinner with me?"

"Don't turn this into an argument over semantics," he says. "You knew very well I wanted to have dinner with you tonight, and that's why you accepted Ms. Thomas's invitation."

"I accepted her invitation because she has work for me."

"No."

"Yes. She has work, and I need work. I'm unemployed, remember?"

"You misunderstood me. What I mean is, no, you will not be working for Crystal's Closet."

"And just why not?"

"Because…what you and I do in the bedroom is our

own business."

My jaw drops. "Braden, I would never —"

"Why do you think I cut that damned bustier off you last night?"

"Because you like ripping clothes off me. You've made that clear."

Again, the insistent smile tugs at the corners of his mouth, but he keeps it at bay. "I won't deny that, but there were easier ways of getting a leather bustier off you than cutting it with scissors."

"So?"

"So…I was making sure you wouldn't take another photograph of yourself wearing it."

So he *had* seen the post. Interesting that he didn't mention it.

"Why? Everything was covered, and I looked good. Heather says they sold out of bustiers after that post."

He scoffs. "I'm sure they did. You will not post any more photographs wearing a bustier."

"How about a thong?" I say sarcastically.

A dark growl hums from his chest. Uh-oh. I've woken the beast. My stomach tumbles into knots. Dark Braden. The Braden who makes me want things I never considered before. Like right now, I'd like him to fuck me here, right on the sidewalk in front of Union Oyster House.

"Your body is for my eyes only." He glares at me.

I squeeze my thighs together to quell my desire. "I need the work."

He softens then, cupping my cheek and pushing my hair behind my ear. "I knew you'd look gorgeous in those rubies."

I sigh softly. I can't help it. I can be indignant one minute, and then, with one touch from him, I'm melting like drawn butter.

"How much are they offering you?"

"I don't know yet. You interrupted our conversation."

"Very well." He takes my hand. "Let's go back and see what Ms. Thomas has to offer."

Chapter Ten

Heather stands when we arrive at the table. "I took the liberty of having a place setting added for you, Mr. Black."

"Please call me Braden."

"Oh, fabulous. And I'm Heather."

Braden nods. "Please sit down."

Heather sits, and Braden pushes her chair in for her. He does the same for me. Always the gentleman—or the illusion of being a gentleman, anyway. It wasn't overly gentlemanly to drag me away from my business meeting.

"Our drinks will be here any minute," Heather says.

Thank God. But I don't say it.

"Heather," Braden says, "I understand you're interested in contracting Skye for some social media posts."

"Yes, definitely. We're very excited about getting Skye on board."

"Very good." He clears his throat. "What are you prepared to offer her?"

I open my mouth, but nothing comes out. Braden has

effectively taken over my negotiation, and I'm letting him. I don't want to let him, but I honestly don't know what to do. To argue with him in front of Heather will make me look unprofessional and childish. But to let him take control will make me look like I have no say over my own career.

Rock, meet hard place.

"We're not as big a company as Susanne Cosmetics," Heather says, "but I've been authorized to begin with a series of three posts for a payment of two thousand dollars."

"That's a good start," Braden says. "What products are you looking to promote?"

"I already told Skye that we're interested in having her model some of our garments as well as selected products from our intimate toy line."

"I see. So you're asking Skye to pose in her underwear wearing handcuffs?"

I can't help myself. I have to chime in here. "Braden!"

"We all know what kind of garments Crystal's sells," Braden says. "We also know what kind of toys they sell."

"Braden," Heather intervenes, "I assure you that everything will be done very tastefully."

"I'm sure it will, since Skye will be in charge of the photography."

"Actually...corporate would like us to bring in a professional photographer."

"Skye *is* a professional photographer."

"Yes, I'm sure she is, but you see, we're not looking for selfies so much as professional images."

"I'm an Instagram influencer," I say. "I take my own pictures. Photography is what got me into this business. I assure you I'm very capable of taking more than just selfies." Damn. Why hadn't I brought my portfolio?

"With all due respect, Skye," Heather says, "everyone

here at this table knows how you got into this business."

So Morticia has a non-hugging side after all. "What exactly are you implying?" I ask adamantly, though I already know exactly what she's implying.

"You're a beautiful woman, and you know the business because you worked for Addison Ames. Now you're dating Boston's most eligible bachelor. Do you think anyone would care what you have to say if you weren't Braden Black's girlfriend?"

Ten bricks in the gut this time. I'm shocked at her audacious words. If she's trying to get me to do business with her, this isn't the way to accomplish it.

So much for her "icing on the cake" comment. I knew it was bullshit.

I want to call her out. The only problem?

Her words ring true. Absolutely true. And I know it. The only reason *anyone* is interested in what I have to say is because of the man sitting at this table. I try to forget the fact, but it's always there, almost taunting me. *You're a fraud.*

"I assure you," Braden says, "Skye is an intelligent woman and knows what she's doing. She will be successful at any endeavor, with me or without me."

I'm not surprised that Braden leaped to my defense. He may even believe his words.

But Heather is right, ultimately.

We all know it.

"Honestly," Heather says, now smiling, "the why doesn't matter. We want to work with you, Skye."

"Then I take my own photographs."

"And she doesn't pose with any toys or in any undergarments," Braden adds, "including bustiers and corsets."

I'm not thrilled with Braden jumping in to my negotiation, but I say nothing because I agree with him. I'm not going to be an underwear model or a BDSM model. No fucking way.

"I can agree to the undergarment restriction," Heather says, "but corporate was very clear that they want the toys to be a part of the posts."

"Then I'm sorry," I say. "I agree with Braden. I'm happy to pose in your clothing line and post about it, but I can't post pictures of myself using your toys."

"Let me be clear," Heather says. "You don't need to be *using* the toys. I'm not asking you to do anything X-rated. Just holding up a toy and saying a few words about it."

"No," I say. "I'm sorry."

"I'll check with corporate, then, and I'll let them know your terms." She glances at her phone. "Goodness, I have to run. I'm so sorry to cut our meeting short. This should cover your dinner." She lays several fifty dollar bills on the table.

Braden picks them up and hands them back to her. "Please keep your money."

"I wouldn't think of it."

"I insist." Braden shoves the bills into her hand.

"All right, if you insist. Have a fabulous dinner." She rises hastily, her napkin drifting to the floor.

Fabulous dinner? We haven't even ordered yet.

Once Heather is out of earshot, I meet Braden's gaze. "We need to chat."

He peruses his menu. "About what?"

"About this. About you sticking your nose into my business."

"Skye, when it comes to you posing half-naked holding up leather whips, that is definitely my business. Besides, they weren't going to let you take your own pictures."

"And I was going to negotiate that."

"They're paying less than Susanne."

"They're a smaller company than Susanne. I'm new at

this. I need to take what I can get."

"She let her claws show, Skye."

I can't deny his words. When Heather felt forced in a corner, she made it known what she truly thought of me. Problem is, she's right. Both Braden and I know it. I just don't feel like rehashing it at the moment. The waiter comes and takes our order. Braden orders a dozen oysters on the half shell, and I can't help a smile.

"Any other news, Skye?"

"No. I'm pretty sure I just kissed the Crystal's Closet contract goodbye."

"You're better off not being associated with a company that sells sexy undergarments and bedroom toys." He clears his throat. "Are you sure there isn't any other news?"

"Yeah."

"No…impending *trips*, maybe?"

Shit. The New York trip early next week. How does he even know about that?

"You want to explain how you even know about that trip? Have you hacked into my emails or my phone?"

"Of course not. That would be a violation of the trust between us. Do you want to explain why you haven't told me about the trip?"

"Honestly? I forgot about it. I'm sitting here after you busted into the middle of my meeting with a potential source of income and blew the whole deal. New York next week isn't the first thing on my mind." I meet his gaze. "Now, can you explain to me how *you* know about New York?"

"Eugenie called me."

"What?" A spike of anger hits me.

"She called to let me know you're meeting with her early next week, and she wants to take us out to dinner and asked what restaurants I liked."

"What restaurants you like? Shouldn't she be more interested in the restaurants *I* like?"

Ten more bricks to my gut. I already know Braden's the only reason anyone's interested in me.

"Of course, but she knows you're not familiar with New York. I am."

Nice try. "And she just assumed you'd be coming with me?"

Braden sighs. "Skye, stop making this bigger than it is."

"Heather is completely right," I say. "No one gives a shit what I think. They give a shit what Braden's girlfriend thinks."

He nods. "That's a big part of it. You knew that from the beginning."

He isn't wrong. I *do* know that. When I was offered five thousand dollars to do a couple of Instagram posts, I kind of got over it.

Now? It's bugging me, like a gnat gnawing under my skin.

But a girl needs to make a living.

"I suppose you're going to tell me you'll be commandeering my meeting with Susanne."

"As a matter of fact, I won't be. I'll have meetings all day in the city as well for my own business. Remember my own business?"

Sucker punch to the stomach. In other words, my fledgling influencing business is nothing compared to Braden's billion-dollar corporation.

Again, he isn't wrong. But he's still being a dick.

I stand. "I'm suddenly not hungry."

"Sit down, Skye. Stop being petulant."

"Fine." I obey and sit. "Then you stop being patronizing."

That smile tugs at the corner of his mouth again, but he's nothing if not determined. "Deal."

As if on cue, our oysters arrive.

"It's time you learned how to slurp an oyster, Skye."

Chapter Eleven

By my sixth oyster, I have the slurping thing down. And I'm horny as hell.

Watching Braden suck an oyster off its half shell and onto his tongue is a sexy sight indeed. The man has a lethal mouth. I reach for my phone and snap a photo.

"You're not thinking about posting that," he says after swallowing.

"As a matter of fact, that's exactly what I'm thinking of doing." I giggle. "Influencing isn't just about sponsored posts."

"I'm happy to pose in a selfie with you," he says, "but oyster slurping? Not going to happen."

I huff softly. "Fine." I move to his side of the table, snap a quick selfie, and then sit back down in my chair.

Slurping oysters with @bradenblackinc! #unionoyster-house #oysterslurping #bostonsfinest

I click post. Then, watching him down another one, "Are you going to try one just with a twist of lemon?" I ask.

"Sorry. I like the cocktail sauce."

"You have a little smudge of it on the corner of your

mouth," I say.

The corners of his mouth tilt upward, and he pats his napkin to it, removing the sauce.

This man is so sexy.

"Braden…"

"Yes?"

"I wouldn't have taken the deal with Heather."

"I know."

"Then why did you interfere?"

"Because I know business. Crystal's Closet isn't the best-run corporation, and I don't particularly want you getting involved."

"You just said you knew I wasn't going to take the deal."

"I know you wouldn't have taken the deal as she first expressed it. The two of you may have come to terms."

I finish off my bourbon. "What's wrong with how they run their business?"

"They have some questionable investments."

"Like what?"

"Suffice it to say they keep a substantial amount of their assets in banks in the Cayman Islands, which is a huge red flag."

"Why?"

"Cayman banks are tax havens. That's certainly not a bad thing. I have investments there myself. But Cayman banks also take confidentiality very seriously. Hence, the red flag."

"Meaning?"

"Money laundering, Skye."

"That's a pretty significant accusation, Braden."

"I'm not making an accusation. I'm just telling you it's a red flag. If my girlfriend is going to model sexy clothes, I want to make sure the company she's doing it for is red-flag free."

I smile slyly. "So it's okay for me to model sexy clothes? Just not underwear and bustiers?"

"You really want to have this conversation in public?"

"Yes," I say adamantly. "Because it's my body, my choice. If I want to model sexy clothes, I'll model sexy clothes."

"Even if I'd rather you didn't?" He sears me with his blue gaze.

"Why not? That GQ spread showed you in skivvies, for God's sake."

That raucous laugh I hear so seldom flies out of his throat like holiday bells. "Skye, I've said it before. You *are* a challenge."

I smile. Yeah, I'm still only a budding influencer because of who my boyfriend is, but I feel better.

Braden considers *me* a challenge.

Me. Skye Manning, a Kansas farm girl.

He's the ultimate challenge, and I will figure him out. I *will*.

"Grasp the rungs of the headboard, Skye."

I'm already naked, of course. Braden made quick work of my clothes as soon as we got back to his place. I expect him to tie me to the rungs as he normally does, but instead, he returns from his dresser drawer with two different types of bindings. He secures them to each outside rung of the headboard.

"Give me your hand."

I reach toward him with my right hand. He secures it by buckling it into a leather cuff, which is attached to a thick leather cord and then to the outside rung. This is different. My arms will be spread out like a Y, but I have some movement. Interesting.

He secures my other wrist on the other side of the headboard.

"Let me know if you have any pain," Braden says. "This shouldn't be painful, although it is a stretch, and you will use some muscles you're not used to using."

"I will."

"This is one of my favorite positions, Skye. I've waited a long time to try it with you." He walks back toward the dresser but then turns to the antique wardrobe. He opens it.

I gasp.

The first time I saw this room, I wondered why a man with a giant walk-in closet needed a wardrobe.

Now I know.

The wardrobe is filled with…implements. Braden returns to the bed with what appears to be a step stool, only it's not high enough to help anyone but the tallest person reach something. The top is cushioned with black leather.

"Lift your hips," he commands.

I obey, and he slides the stool underneath me.

Then he gazes at me, subtly licking his lips. "Very nice."

I say nothing, just absently tug on the bindings holding me.

"Careful," he says. "Your instinct is to tug, but if you stretch your muscles too far, you'll be in pain tomorrow. Not terrible pain or anything, but you'll feel like you did some hard lifting."

"All right." I force my arms to relax.

"I have a marvelous view of your pussy from here," he says. "Already I see how wet you are for me."

My body quivers. Braden, of course, is still fully dressed, as usual. But he looks delectable. His lips full and firm, and his hands with those beautiful, thick fingers. I want them inside me.

He grabs one of my legs at the ankle. "I want to see how flexible you are. I'm going to bring your leg forward, and if it starts to pull too harshly, tell me to stop."

I'm not as flexible as Tessa—she out-yogas me every weekend—but still, I'm flexible enough. I keep my legs straight, and it isn't until my leg and my body form an acute angle that I tell him enough.

"Very nice." He repeats with the other leg. "Very nice indeed. I'll be able to bind your legs in many different positions."

I tingle. He's never bound my legs before, and while the idea intrigues me, with my arms bound, the only way I can touch him is with my legs. I can wrap them around his back, slide my calves over the globes of his butt, glide my feet down his hard thighs and calves.

"Not tonight," he says. "We need to ease into that. I want to see how you do with this new form of arm binding. Remember to relax."

I'm tugging again. I didn't even notice, but he's right. I consciously relax my arms once more, trying to think of them as rubber bands.

"I'm wondering… Should I blindfold you tonight?"

Is he asking for my opinion? I have no idea, so I say nothing.

"I think I'll let you keep your sense of sight tonight," he says. "I want you to see me fuck you. In fact…I want you to see *everything*."

Am I supposed to answer? He hasn't told me not to speak.

"Whatever you want," I say.

"Good answer." He smiles slightly as he loosens his tie.

"I'm going to undress for you now, Skye. Slowly. I want you to watch every deliberate movement I make, and I want you to tell me what you're feeling as you watch me."

"Okay. Right now I feel like I want you inside me."

"Easy. You know we always get to that. Focus on your sense of sight tonight, Skye. I told you I want you to *see* everything. Tell me what the sight of me does to you."

I nod, unconsciously moving my hips. Somehow, the slight elevation makes me move better.

Braden throws his tie over the back of the chair and unbuttons his shirt to reveal his white tank. He brushes the cotton dress shirt over his shoulders, bearing them.

I suck in a breath. "I love your shoulders. They're so tanned and broad."

He doesn't respond, simply pulls the tank over his head and tosses it.

My nipples are hard, and they're yearning for his fingers, his lips, his teeth.

"You're not telling me what the sight of me does to you, Skye."

"My nipples are so hard," I say. "I want you to touch them, to kiss them and suck them."

He unhooks his belt and kicks off his shoes. Then he unzips his pants, slides them over his hips, and steps out of them. He stands only in boxer briefs and socks. His bulge is huge.

"Braden, you're gorgeous. I want you so much right now." He removes his socks quickly, slides off his boxer briefs, and steps out of them.

His cock juts out long, hard, and thick.

"I'm so wet, Braden. So damned wet. I need you inside me. I need your lips on my nipples."

He approaches the bed and sits down. "Look at me."

I meet his fiery blue gaze.

"Do not take your eyes from mine," he commands. "Watch me. Watch my eyes as I fuck you. Tonight is about seeing, Skye. Do you understand?"

I nod.

"Tell me what you see."

"I see *you*, Braden. I see your beautiful blue eyes looking at me. I've never felt so beautiful as I feel when you're looking at me."

"You *are* beautiful. Very beautiful."

"And you're magnificent."

"I want you watching now. Not feeling, not hearing, not talking, not smelling or tasting. Simply seeing."

"Okay, Braden."

He brushes past me, completely ignoring my breasts.

"Braden…"

He swats me lightly on my thigh. "I said no talking."

I nod. Yeah, he did. I can handle no talking. How am I supposed to not hear or smell?

How in the world am I supposed to not *feel*?

He lightly trails his fingers over the tops of my thighs. I shudder. It feels as though butterfly wings are fluttering against me.

Except I'm not supposed to be feeling.

Concentrate on what you see, I tell myself.

His hands are large and manly. And they're touching me. His gorgeous hands are touching my thighs. It's a beautiful sight, and I begin to understand what he's asking of me.

He leans down and brushes his lips slightly over my navel. Now I realize why he's using such a light touch. He wants me to concentrate on what I see.

His lips pucker slightly each time he kisses me. Full and firm and dark pink. Then he positions himself between my legs and he closes his eyes. I take a second to appreciate his male beauty. He inhales, and a slight smile emerges. He likes the smell of me. I already know this, but watching it on his face makes it so much more profound.

Then he opens his eyes, and they're smoldering.

Just seeing the effect in his eyes awakens new needs in my body. I'm already wet, my nipples are already straining, but the vision of Braden wanting me forces every cell in my body to come to life.

I'm hot. My hips rise, almost of their own accord, as I search for him to fill me. All from seeing the effect I have on his eyes.

He spreads my legs farther apart and lowers his head. His eyes smolder, and a groan vibrates from him into me.

He inhales again, and my body responds, tingling and yearning.

Then—

My phone rings, a muffled tune coming from my purse on the nightstand.

Chapter Twelve

"Ignore it," he commands.

I obey, and oddly, though I wonder briefly who was calling me at this hour, I'm able to let it go.

That's so unlike me.

I can't take my gaze off Braden. The glory of seeing him, concentrating on the beauty of his movements, entrances me.

He lowers his lips and gives my clit a quick nip.

I jerk wildly. I'm not supposed to be feeling, but how can I not? Still, I try to focus on what I see. Braden's lips circled around my clit. He nips again and then once more. His tongue slides over my clit and downward until I can no longer see its movements.

What I *can* see? His eyes. His heavy-lidded, beautiful blue eyes, and they never leave mine.

He licks my folds, and still, I concentrate on his gaze. He's focused—*so* focused—on me. How have I never noticed that before? How much it pleases him to give me pleasure?

Is he going to let me come tonight? And what if I do? Will that mean I'm disobeying him? Because I can't come without feeling it. That's completely impossible.

Still, he looks at me, slides his tongue inside me, and then forces a finger inside my channel.

He stops licking me, leaving my clit alone. I continue to do as he asks.

I look.

I see.

My juices glisten on his chin and lips. The muscles in his forearm tense and contract as he fingers me. His dick is hard between his legs.

Should I tell him what I see?

No, he told me not to talk.

How have I never before understood how powerful the sense of sight is? When I separate it from the other senses, it takes over, and my body responds. I pull at the bindings absently and then quickly remember to ease the tension.

I expect him to speak, but he doesn't. Braden is normally very vocal during lovemaking, but then I realize what he's doing. He told me not to hear, just to see. He's helping me.

I smile, meeting his gaze. Though he doesn't return the smile, he does withdraw his finger and swiftly moves to thrust his dick inside me. He reaches upward, bracing his hands on the headboard. No kiss. As much as I love a kiss when he fucks me, I won't be getting one.

I can't see anything when he kisses me.

He positioned us perfectly so I can look directly into his eyes as he fucks me, but I can also lift my neck and watch him going in and out of me.

And my God, it's a beautiful sight.

His massive dick disappears fully inside my body, and though I feel so complete, I set that feeling aside and simply concentrate on the sight of him embedded inside me.

It's intoxicating. Truly intoxicating.

He pulls out then, and I marvel at the length and thickness of him, that I can take him inside my body so comfortably, indeed so erotically.

He's going slowly, which isn't the norm for him. He's doing it so I can watch. So I can see the beauty of our bodies coming together.

He doesn't tell me to watch.

He no longer has to, because I cannot look away.

He pushes back into me slowly, holds our bodies together for a few seconds as I gaze into his eyes, and then he pulls out, again so slowly. I imprint the visual in my mind, the head of his cock teasing my lips, but then—

"Fuck it," he grunts, and he thrusts into me hard.

Slowly is over, but still I watch as he pistons his hips and fucks me hard. One thrust, another, another, another, until—

He buries himself inside me so deeply, and though I'm not supposed to feel, I can't help it. He pulsates inside me. I regard his face, perspiration emerging on his brow line and moistening his black hair. His eyes are closed, and a subtle shudder racks his body.

This is what Braden looks like when he comes. I've always known it, but I've never taken the time to appreciate it. To *see* it.

Until now.

He finishes his climax and then rolls off me. He rests on his back and closes his eyes, breathing rapidly.

Am I allowed to speak now? I'm supposed to be seeing, even though I long to lean over to Braden and press my lips to his forehead.

I'm bound, though, so I have no use of my arms or hands. My hips are still elevated, and without my arms, I can't move the little stool.

So I watch him. I do as instructed. I *see* him.

His body shines with a subtle glimmer of perspiration, and his cock is still semi-hard. He keeps his eyes closed, and his breath comes in rapid puffs. Minute by minute, it slows down until he's breathing normally, his eyes still closed.

I realize how hard he worked to give me this. To arrange our positioning so that I could see every aspect of our lovemaking.

And I think I love him even more.

A soft snore drifts out of his mouth. Braden is asleep, but he didn't unbind me. He also didn't tell me I could speak. So now what? I can sleep like this, but eventually I'm going to need to get up to go to the bathroom.

Luckily, I'm flexible. I stretch my leg over and nudge Braden's calf with my toes. Nothing. I do it again, this time getting a response.

His eyes pop open. "Skye?"

I nod.

He smiles—that wide smile that is the sweetest reward because I see it so rarely. "You may speak now."

"That was amazing, Braden, but I don't think I can sleep tied up like this."

"I'd never expect you to." He sits up and deftly unhooks me.

I shake my arms out and rub my wrists.

"You aren't chafed, are you?"

"I don't think so. Just a little stiff."

"You did really well," he says. "Did you enjoy it?"

I nod. "I did. I really did."

"Does that surprise you?"

"A little. It was hard to turn off my other senses, especially the feeling part. But when I forced myself to, I was able to see the beauty that exists between us. And it *was* beautiful, Braden."

"Sex isn't all about orgasms, Skye."

How well I know. I never experienced an orgasm until Braden, and he isn't always generous about doling them out for me. Which, oddly enough, turns me on even more.

"Where did you learn all this?" I ask.

"What do you mean?"

"You know, the bondage. The sensory perception and deprivation. Everything you do. You've opened my eyes to so much."

"You're probably thinking I have some elaborate answer to that question," he says. "But I don't. I enjoy sex. I enjoy kink. I enjoy being dominant in the bedroom, and I enjoy showing my partner pleasure."

"But you've shown me things I've never imagined."

"That's because I see the big picture. There's more to sex than cock in pussy. A lot more. And Skye, we've only just begun."

Chapter Thirteen

"I'm having dinner with my family Saturday evening," Braden says at breakfast.

My fork of scrambled eggs stops midway from my plate to my mouth. He's not going to invite me to go along, is he? The thought scares me more than a little. But we *are* dating, and we do love each other. People who are serious about each other usually meet each other's parents. Which means a trip to Kansas might be in my future.

"Okay." I'm not sure what else to say.

"We have dinner together once a month. I'd like you to come along and bring Tessa."

"Tessa?"

"Yeah. My brother doesn't have the best taste in women. I think they might hit it off."

"Wait. Did you just insult my friend?"

He shakes his head. "Of course not. I like Tessa. I think Ben might like her. I know my father will."

"Wait another minute," I say. "Are you hoping she'll hit it off with Ben? Or with your father?"

Bobby Black is a widower. A billionaire widower thanks to his sons' holdings. And still a very handsome man.

"For God's sake, Skye, she could be his daughter. I'd like her to meet Ben."

"It was a valid question," I say. "Your father's very good-looking. I mean, you look exactly like him."

"Not exactly. My father and Ben both have brown eyes. I got the blue ones from my mom."

"All three of you are pretty rockin'," I say.

His lips curve slightly upward. "Rockin'?"

"Trust me, that's a compliment. And if you want to bring my best friend over to meet your brother, he needs to be fluent in Tessa."

"My brother doesn't have any problem with the ladies," Braden says. "He just seems to choose the wrong ones."

"He'll have some competition. Tessa's been seeing Garrett Ramirez since they hooked up at the MADD Gala."

Braden's eyes widen slightly. Only slightly, but I notice. "Are they serious?" he asks.

I roll my eyes. "Are you kidding? Tessa's never been serious in her life. But Garrett's a great catch."

Braden's jawline softens, as if he is relieved. "Not as great of a catch as my brother."

"Braden, your brother may be a great catch, but I have the distinct impression that he doesn't really want to be caught." Most would also have said that about Braden a few weeks ago.

But I caught him.

I can't help a sly smile.

"No, he doesn't. But as you say, Tessa isn't serious. I'd like to see my brother with a nice professional woman. Not the losers he brings home."

"Losers?" I shake my head. "Well, at least you didn't say

gold digger. Or sugar baby."

"I was trying to be a little more politically correct," he says, "but your words are just as apt."

"Surely you don't mean your brother pays for it."

Braden chuckles softly. "Sure he does. Maybe not by leaving bills on the bedside table, but he blows all kinds of money on the women he dates."

I pick up a piece of bacon. "Is that a bad thing? I seem to remember you having a little black dress professionally replicated for me."

"Because I ruined the dress, Skye. Besides that and a pair of earrings, which I saw and imagined on your beautiful ears, have I tried to buy you in any way?" He takes a sip of coffee.

"No, I've never felt that way, so I doubt that's what your brother's doing."

"My brother is extravagant," Braden says. "He likes lavishing the women in his life with expensive gifts."

I let out a giggle. "I can't see Tessa turning her nose up at expensive gifts."

"Does Tessa only date rich men?"

I swallow my bite of bacon. "Of course not."

"Then she's perfect for Ben. He attracts money grabbers because he throws his money around."

I pick up my coffee mug. "I suppose it all depends on whether Tessa is available. She may have plans with Garrett this weekend."

"Would it be better if I called her and invited her?"

"No, I'm happy to invite her." In fact, having Tessa there when I meet Braden's father and brother for the first time will help me be a lot less nervous. I don't say that to Braden, though. "How will Ben feel about all of this?"

"I don't care. I don't plan to tell him."

I drop my forkful of eggs onto my plate with a clatter.

"Wait a minute. You're bringing your new girlfriend home to meet your family for the first time, *and* you're bringing along a friend for your brother, without telling them first? As much as I'd love having Tessa with me, I'm not sure that's cool."

He pauses a moment, rubbing the stubble on his chin. "You may have a point."

"If you want to get them together and see if they hit it off, why don't the four of us go out sometime?"

"All right. You've convinced me. It'll just be the two of us at the family dinner."

A wide grin splits my face. Braden is not easily convinced by anyone. But plenty of men know nothing about matchmaking. Perhaps he's aware of his limitations.

"Do you still want me to come?" I ask, not sure which answer I'm hoping for.

"I do. I suppose if I'm going to have a girlfriend, my father should meet her."

I smile again. Good answer. Meeting the family is a good thing, right?

"What about your parents?" he asks.

"They live in Kansas."

"So we go to Kansas. Or we fly them here. Your choice."

"Hold your fire." I lift my hands in mock surrender. "Let's get your father and brother out of the way first, okay?"

"I can live with that." He bites a piece off a slice of bacon. "Wear something…refined."

Refined? Meaning…not sexy? My confusion must be apparent, because he laughs and says, "Not jeans. Dress slacks or a skirt and blouse. Either is fine."

"Okay. What will you be wearing?"

"Probably slacks and a jacket, no tie."

"All right. Then of course, don't forget I leave for New York Sunday evening."

He swallows a drink of coffee. "*We* leave for New York Sunday evening."

"Are you on the same flight?"

"I am, but you aren't. We're taking my jet."

"But Eugenie sent me a tick—"

"I took the liberty of canceling the ticket and refunding Eugenie."

Anger scrapes up my neck. Braden had no right to do that.

But it's classic Braden.

"You'll find the private jet much more comfortable," he says nonchalantly, as if it's the most normal thing in the world.

"It's a one-hour flight, and she sent me a first-class ticket."

"Trust me, the jet is still much more comfortable."

I twist my lips. "Braden, I never gave up my control outside the bedroom."

"I'm not interfering with your control."

I stand, the spark of anger flowing through me hotly. "You commandeered my meeting last night, and now you canceled my flight for my meeting next week. That is *definitely* interfering with my control."

"Do you want this new career move to be a success?" he asks.

"Of course I do."

"I'm about as savvy a businessman as you'll find. Most people would kill for my advice."

"I want your advice. I truly do. I appreciate how successful you are, and I admit you know a hell of a lot more about business than I ever will. But horning in on my business meeting is not offering advice. Neither is canceling a plane ticket."

He stands as well, towering over me. He seems taller

for some reason, and his eyes have darkened to that smoky blue I'm so familiar with. It's how he looks right before he kisses me.

And I want that kiss. He didn't kiss me last night.

I take a step backward.

He takes a step forward.

"What would it take, Skye, for you to give me control over everything in your life?"

A proposal of marriage and a big-ass engagement ring, for starters.

I don't say this, of course, because I don't actually mean it. I'll never give control to Braden over my *whole* life. I gave him control in the bedroom, and I don't regret it. He showed me some amazing and intense experiences. But my career is my own.

Which you wouldn't have if not for him.

I force the subconscious words out of my head, but they do make me wonder. Not whether they're true. I already know they are. But they make me wonder if Braden has been orchestrating this new career of mine from the very beginning.

He requested to follow me on Instagram, and I honored his request. He tagged me in a photo the first night we went out. Everything mushroomed from there.

Did he foresee all of it? His past with Addie probably gave him reason to know how she would react.

Of course, he also gave me some good advice when I was ambivalent about influencing. He told me I could use my platform to show people my photographs. To take pictures that moved them.

Was all of this in his plan the whole time?

I open my mouth to ask—

But he silences me with a kiss.

Chapter Fourteen

My lips are already parted, and he darts his tongue in. I respond. All thoughts of Braden exercising control over my budding new career fly away on a warm breeze.

Because this kiss… This is the kiss I yearned for last night but didn't get.

Already I'm getting wet for him, my nipples are hardening, and my body is awake with heat.

I clasp my arms around his neck, relishing his muscles. I let my fingers drift up to his face, scraping the tips of his stubble. He grabs my ass and pulls me to him so his hard bulge pushes against my lower belly.

He breaks the kiss with a loud smack. He speaks only with his eyes, gazing hard into mine. Then he turns me around, forcing me against the kitchen island, quickly pushes my sweats and underwear over my hips, and, in what seems like no time at all, shoves his cock into me.

I moan against the invasion, so tight with my legs together.

"I like control, Skye," he whispers in my ear as he pumps

into me harder and harder. "Haven't I given you pleasure in the bedroom?"

"Yes," I moan, my voice almost a sob.

"Would it be so bad to yield to me in other areas?" His breath is hot against my neck and ear.

He pumps into me, fucking me hard and fast. My clit is banging against the countertop, and I'm on my way to orgasm. Yes, on my way, climbing the mountain. I see the peak in the distance getting closer, closer, closer…

"Answer me, Skye," he says against my neck.

Answer me.

How easy to say yes, to let this amazing man control everything. He knows business, and he can easily take me to the top.

Yes. Yes. Yes.

But the words don't make it to my lips. Instead, I force my hips backward, letting out a wistful whimper as I lose the friction on my clit.

I give up an orgasm.

But it's a statement. An answer to his question.

I will *not* yield control of the rest of my life to anyone.

Not even Braden Black.

I'm not even sure if that's what he truly wants.

Later, at home, I sit down at my laptop to check on my posts. Braden didn't say much after I didn't answer his question vocally. He gave me a swift kiss on the cheek and told me he needed to get to a conference call in his home office, so Christopher drove me home. I know Braden, though. He will continue to push, so I need to be strong.

Will being strong cause me to lose him?

I'm hopelessly in love with him. No doubt about that.

I still don't know his deepest secrets. I don't know the full story of what went on between him and Addison. But I made a decision to trust him. Difficult as it may be, I have to give up this quest for knowledge about his past. First step is to see Betsy and thank her for what she tried to do and reassure her of my friendship. Plus, I can buy a treat for Penny. I head to the Bark Boutique.

Betsy's busy, probably because it's lunchtime. At least ten customers are browsing, which of course means I won't get a chance to talk to her anytime soon. I smile and wave to her and then browse the aisles, picking up a few things for Penny.

Customers leave as customers come in. By the time I have a chance to talk to Betsy, my shopping bag is full of treats for Penny and Sasha. Too many, in fact. I'll give some of them to Tessa's dog, Rita. Which reminds me that Tessa has called me three times and I haven't called her back. I file that in the back of my mind.

I finally make it up to the cash register.

"Nice to see you, Skye." Betsy doesn't meet my gaze.

"You too. Looks like a good business day."

"It never rains but it pours. I'm pretty close to getting my online ordering store up and running as well. After Tessa ran the numbers and they looked good, I hired a website-and-marketing consultant."

"That's great!"

And it gives me an idea. I never thought about hiring a marketing consultant for my own fledgling business. I don't actually have enough business yet to justify the expense, but I'll definitely keep it in the back of my mind.

"This is a pretty big purchase," she says, ringing me up.

"Nothing's too good for my new pup."

Finally she meets my gaze. "I can't tell you anything else."

"I'm not asking you to."

She looks down. "I just don't know anything else, Skye."

Classic tell. I'm not sure I believe her, but I didn't come here to pump her for more information. I trust Braden.

I smile. "It's okay, Bets. I understand. Are you free for dinner? My treat."

"Actually, I'm meeting Tessa for dinner. We're going to go over some more numbers and then hit a club she likes."

I resist an eye roll. Clubbing. Not my favorite thing.

"I'm sure you could join us," she says.

"Dinner sounds great. I'll probably pass on the clubbing."

Betsy smiles. "She told me how you feel about clubbing. We're actually meeting some guys there. Garrett, that guy she's been seeing off and on, and he's bringing a friend."

"Peter Reardon?"

"I think she said his name is Peter."

I nod. "I'll give Tessa a call and see if she minds if I crash your dinner date."

"She won't mind."

"Probably not, but I should check anyway."

Betsy hands me my receipt. "Okay, see you tonight, then. Tessa can tell you where."

"Thanks. See you."

I text Tessa quickly, asking if it's okay for me to join and apologizing for not calling her back before now.

No biggie on the calls. I was just checking in. Of course on dinner! I would've asked you myself but it's Friday night and I figured you'd be with Braden.

Oh yeah. Braden. I can easily take care of that. I text him.

I'm having dinner with Tessa tonight. Will I see you later?

No response. Well, he did say he'd be on calls all day.

I quickly text Tessa and tell her I'll meet her at the restaurant at six thirty.

I gave up an orgasm this morning to show Braden I won't let him control every aspect of my life.

We can start with Friday night dinners.

Chapter Fifteen

Betsy and I arrive at the restaurant at the same time. Tessa texts both of us that she's running about fifteen minutes late.

I can't help it. I'm secretly glad because it gives me some time to chat with Betsy alone.

Betsy doesn't look nearly as eager as I am.

"I talked to Braden," I say.

She lifts her eyebrows.

"Don't worry. I kept your name a secret, although I should tell you I did tell Tessa."

She smiles weakly. "That's okay. I figured you would. All I know is what Addie told me."

I nod. "I get that. You did what a friend would. You were trying to help me, to possibly keep me from getting hurt. I appreciate that more than you know."

"I'd never want to see you get hurt. Our friendship is new, but it means a lot to me."

I grab my napkin and place it across my lap. "It means a lot to me, too. I just want you to know that I've spoken to

Braden, and I feel good about our relationship. And also know that, other than to Tessa—and her word is as good as gold—I'll never say another thing about who told me."

"I wouldn't have told you otherwise."

"I know it was difficult for you to break Addie's confidence."

"I almost didn't," she says. "But on the off chance that it might be true, I didn't want you in harm's way."

"On the *off* chance?" I wrinkle my forehead. "So…does that mean part of you thinks Addie is isn't telling the whole truth?"

"I don't know." Betsy shakes her head. "Addie is a spoiled heiress. We both know that. She's not above lying to get what she wants."

I draw in a breath. "If Braden dumps me for whatever reason, I'll live. I'm not Addie." Though the thought of Braden leaving me makes me want to hurl. "I think Addie might have lied to you."

"Maybe, if she thinks he crossed her." Betsy sips her water. "As I told you, she was pretty obsessed with him."

"Did Addie go into any detail? You know, about what they were doing? What got her shaken up?"

"No. I can't even imagine what they were into."

I can. Sort of. Braden likes sex on the darker side. So do I, frankly. I never knew until I met Braden, but it's been eye-opening. Eye-opening and extremely gratifying.

But Braden is always very careful. He makes sure I give him a verbal consent, and he always asks if I'm comfortable when he binds me.

Of course, whatever happened between him and Addison occurred ten years ago.

Perhaps he wasn't as careful then.

"Whatever happened between them," I say, "Braden

didn't harm her."

"Well," Betsy says, "you know him better than I do."

I nod. She's right. I do.

The only problem is… I didn't know him ten years ago. But I promised to trust him.

Tessa arrives, the drinks Betsy and I ordered for the three of us follow, and I take a minute to check my phone. It's barely hanging onto a charge. Uh-oh. I should have plugged it in before I left. Not a great move for someone who hopes to make a living using social media. There's no indication that Braden saw my text from earlier, and then, as if in response, the phone goes dark and dies.

I half expect Braden to show up at the restaurant to commandeer this dinner as he has others.

He doesn't, though.

And that starts to bug me.

Will he punish me later? I have no idea, because I have no idea where he is or whether he plans to see me this evening. Since I haven't heard from him, I make a quick decision.

"I want to join you tonight."

Tessa swallows a drink of margarita. "At the club?"

"Sure. Why not?"

She laughs. "Because you *hate* clubbing, Skye."

"I do, but you've been trying for years to get me to go out more often. Why not tonight?"

Tessa smiles. "Why indeed not? We'll have a blast. Although…"

"What?"

"Betsy and I are meeting Garrett and his friend Peter."

"That's okay. I won't horn in."

No truer words. I have no desire to be with any man except Braden.

. Though I look down at my wardrobe. Skinny jeans, a silk blouse, and wedge sandals. Not really club fare. Tessa is wearing one of her little red numbers, and Betsy is wearing a denim miniskirt and a sequined blouse. A far cry from her normal boho look. Tessa must've taken her shopping.

"Never mind. I'm not really dressed for clubbing."

"Are you kidding? You look fab," Tessa says. "Besides, you're not looking to hook up. Just come along for the ride."

"Okay."

Why not? Braden doesn't control me, as much as he likes to think he does. Four hours have passed since I sent the text, and my phone's dead. Time to take a stand.

Besides, if I post on Instagram where I am, Braden may show up and take over the evening again, like he did at the MADD Gala.

Apprehension inches up my spine. Do I truly want to do this? I can easily borrow a charger to get me through the next few hours. My phone is my lifeline as a budding influencer. Also my line to Braden.

Take a stand, Skye.

No, Skye, don't. You know you want him to control you.

What the fuck? Ambivalence coils inside me, but I know what I need to do.

I shove the dead phone to the bottom of my purse just as our food arrives. "Ladies," I say, "I'm all yours tonight."

Chapter Sixteen

Once inside the glitz, I'm reminded why I hate clubbing. The noise. The crowds. The sloshing drinks. In addition, I'm constantly aware of my dead phone in the bottom of my purse. I haven't stopped thinking about it for a minute.

Damn. I know exactly what that means. Braden *is* controlling me.

Though Betsy and Tessa each had two margaritas with dinner, I only had one bourbon, knowing my presence at the club would require me to drink just to ease into it. Problem? I can't get near the bar.

Yeah, I *really* hate clubbing.

I follow Tessa and Betsy through the crowd to a table in the corner, away from the dance floor. How Garrett and Peter got a table, I'll never know. It's a table for four, and guess who's the odd person out?

Was this really my brilliant idea? I glance around. I'm underdressed, and although that doesn't bother me, it does make me stand out.

Tessa slides onto Garrett's lap, laughing and gesturing to

the empty seat. "See? There's plenty of room for you, Skye."

I reluctantly sit. The good thing about having a table is a server comes to take drink orders. Good. No more trying to elbow my way to the bar. I order a Wild Turkey, neat. Tessa and Betsy both order another margarita, and Garrett and Peter drink Guinness, same as they were drinking that night at the MADD Gala. And why I remember that, I have no idea.

My dead phone at the bottom of my purse seems to vibrate with a homing beacon.

I could leave. Go home and plug in the phone. Or simply ask if anyone at the table has a portable charger on them. Tessa might.

Damn it!

I will not give up control of my daily life. Not to anyone, not even Braden Black.

Betsy and Peter are chatting, despite the fact that it's too loud to hear anything, and Tessa is nuzzling with Garrett, still on top of him.

Just as well. I hate conversing in a loud atmosphere anyway.

Our drinks arrive, and I take a long, slow sip, letting the bourbon coat my throat with its spicy burn.

Something nuzzles my ear. "You seem kind of lonely over here."

I look up. A handsome man with sandy-blond hair crouches next to me.

"I'm fine."

"I'm sure you are, sweetheart, but it doesn't take a detective to see you're a third wheel." He chuckles. "Make that a fifth wheel."

"What do you know? Maybe I'm contemplating a three-some."

"If that's the case, sweetheart, I really *would* like to get to know you better. You want to dance?"

"That's kind of you, but no thanks."

"If threesomes are your jam, I know someone who'd be into it."

I can't help a roaring laugh. "I was kidding."

"Damn. Too bad. Though I wouldn't mind a twosome, either."

"Sorry. I'm involved with someone."

"Okay, I get it. You can still dance, can't you?"

I steal a quick glance at the two couples, one of them making out and the other having gotten closer within the last few minutes. "Thank you, but no."

The music grinds to a halt, and then a lively Latin number begins. Tessa pops her head up from her snogging session with Garrett. "Oh my God! I love this song. We've got to dance." She rises and pulls Garrett with her. "Come on, all of you!"

"See?" the guy says. "Let's go."

"I'm not sure—"

Before I can resist, though, Tessa and the others are dragging me to the dance floor. The blond man has somehow joined in our group dance.

"What's your name?" he asks.

"Skye," I nearly scream, to be heard above the noise. "What's yours?"

"Marty."

The music is fast, and within a few minutes of trying to follow Tessa's moves, I'm sweltering in my jeans. This is why women don't wear jeans to clubs. Men do, though. Don't men sweat more than women? Marty seems comfortable enough, and he's actually a really good dancer. Much better than I am. I try to take my mind off how hot I am and enjoy myself.

When the number ends and a slow song starts, I say, "Thanks. I think I'll sit this one out."

Marty pulls me into his body. "One more, okay? We both need to cool down a little bit."

Sweat coats my neck, and I really wish I had put my hair up. "Thanks, but no."

Marty doesn't appear to hear me, though. He starts moving slowly to the music. I pull away. "Sorry, I'm done for the night. It was great meeting you."

"Can I buy you a drink?" Marty asks.

"Thanks, but no. I'm pretty tired, and I think I'm just going to get out of here."

"You read my mind. I have my car. I'm happy to give you a ride home."

"Marty, I told you I'm seeing someone."

"I'm offering you a ride home. I'm not offering to take you to bed. Just trying to be nice here."

When we get back to the table, I turn to him. "Thanks for the offer, but I'll just get an Uber."

He gives me a mock bow. "At your service."

"What's that supposed to mean?"

"I'm an Uber driver. You'll see the sticker on my car."

"You can't possibly be on the clock right now. Haven't you been drinking?"

"Nope."

"But you offered to buy me a drink."

"Doesn't mean I was going to get one for myself. All it takes is a click on the phone. If you don't believe me, check me out on the app. I'm BostonMarty352. Four-point-nine rating."

My phone. Getting an Uber will require a phone that isn't dead. Oh, I'm tempted. I'm dying to see if Braden has texted me, and it certainly won't hurt to find out if

BostonMarty is on the up-and-up.

Marty pulls out his phone and smiles. "Just clicked on. I think I might be in your area."

Tessa and Garrett are still on the dance floor, and Betsy and Peter are nuzzling each other. That didn't take long.

Yeah, I really want to get out of here. An evening at home bingeing Netflix sounds great right about now. I'm a pretty good judge of character, and Marty seems okay. Plus, he's an Uber driver. Why he wants to leave the club right now, I have no idea. But going with him means I don't have to wait around for someone to pick me up.

I tap Betsy on her shoulder. She looks up and meets my gaze.

"May I borrow your phone to call an Uber?"

"You're leaving?"

"Yeah, but my phone died at dinner. Marty here says he's an Uber driver, but I want to make sure he's on the up-and-up."

Betsy pulls her phone out of her handbag. "Sure. Here you go."

I hastily pull up the Uber app, log out of Betsy's account and into mine. Sure enough, there's Marty. I type in my request for a ride, while Marty watches his phone.

"Got it," he says, showing me his phone.

Sure enough. BostonMarty352 in a black Honda Civic is only a minute away.

"Perfect," I say. "I'm ready for my Uber. I'll even add a generous tip, since I didn't have to wait."

"Good enough." He smiles, and we leave the club. He's parked about a block away in a city parking lot. Sure enough, the Uber sticker is on the back window of his car, a black Honda Civic. It's clean as a whistle inside, which also lends credence to his Uber story. So many guys' cars are pigsties inside.

He opens the door for me, and I climb into the passenger seat. Normally I sit in the back seat, but Marty seems cool.

He sets his phone on the little holder, and we get moving.

"Looks like I'll have you home in about twenty," he says, "unless you want to go somewhere else. Like…my place, maybe?"

Uh-oh. Time to plan my escape. Problem is, we're already moving. "I want you to take me home," I say adamantly.

"Okay, okay. Can't blame a guy for trying."

"Why don't you just pull over, and I'll order another Uber."

"Don't be like that," he says. "I said I'd take you home, and I'll take you home. I'm just teasing."

Marty *is* driving the route to my apartment. Unless, of course, he lives near me, and that's where we end up.

"Home, James," I say. "Or rather, home, Marty."

"You got it."

I spy a charging cord hanging between our two seats. I pick it up. "Do you mind?"

"Not at all. Go for it."

I pull my phone out of the bottom of my purse and hook it to Marty's charger.

Chapter Seventeen

My mouth drops into an O.

No text from Braden.

Not. A. One.

Marty's phone buzzes through his GPS app. "Sorry, I have to take this. Hey," he says into his Bluetooth.

I'm seething with rage. Not that I expect Braden to spend every Friday night with me, but he should've texted me back. Why the hell didn't he? If he's *that* into control, he should be texting me all the time.

Ten minutes later, Marty pulls up in front of my apartment building.

"Hold on a minute, Dave." Marty turns to me. "You want me to park and walk you up?"

"No, I'm fine. Thanks so much for the ride."

"No problem. Now you know I'm cool. I'm in this area a lot, so look for me next time you need an Uber."

"Will do. Thanks again." I do my best to sound cheery as I disconnect my phone and get out of the car.

But I'm not cheery.

I'm livid.

I seethe as I walk inside my building. I seethe as I call for the elevator. I seethe as I ride up to my floor, and I seethe as I stand in front of my door, searching for my key in my purse. It's buried, probably because it got tossed to the bottom when I had to dig out my damn phone. I sigh and lean against the doorway—

"Shit!" I scream out as the door opens against my weight and I tumble into my apartment, landing on my ass.

I left my door unlocked? No freaking way. I've never left my door unlocked in my life. But I must have, and apparently I also forgot to turn out the lights.

I stand, brush off my jeans, and—

"Hello, Skye."

I nearly lose my footing again. Braden sits on my love seat, his legs crossed.

"How did you get in here?" I demand.

"Your lock is a piece of shit," he says. "An amateur thief could get in here."

"Does that mean you're an amateur thief?"

"I've never stolen anything in my life. It means I grew up in South Boston and I know how to get inside a shitty lock."

"You're something," I say. "Why are you here?"

"Why do you think I'm here?"

"I honestly have no idea, Braden. I texted you and told you I was having dinner with Tessa and asked if I'd see you later."

"And I responded."

I grab my barely charged phone out of my purse and pull up the text string. "Uh…no, you didn't."

"I didn't respond by text," he says. "I sent you an email telling you I'd meet you at your place at nine."

I swallow. No, I didn't check my email. My phone is set

to notify me when I get a text or Instagram message, but not when I get an email. It blows up as it is. Besides, the thing was dead anyway.

It's nearly midnight. Has he been sitting here in my apartment since nine?

I bite my lip. *Damn it, Skye. No. You do* not *need to feel bad about this.*

"Why would you reply to a text via email?"

"Because your text came in on my computer, and I had my email open, so I replied that way."

I'm sorry. I truly want to say the words, but I can't.

"I find it hard to believe, Skye, that you didn't check your email. Email is part of your livelihood these days."

"Well, I didn't," I say flatly. "My phone was dead."

"And you couldn't find a charger somewhere?"

He isn't wrong. "I didn't think about it."

"I see." He nods, his lips trembling slightly, as if he's trying not to smile. "Where have you been?"

I cross my arms over my chest. "I told you. I had dinner with Tessa."

"For four and a half hours?"

"What if I did?"

"Then you'd be lying," he says, still not rising.

Even as he's seated on my couch, his presence fills the room. Though I'm looking down at him, I feel as though I'm tiny in comparison.

"If you insist on knowing my whereabouts, I was at a club."

"You hate clubs."

"Tessa talked me into it."

That gets a laugh out of him. A sarcastic, scoffing laugh. "If Tessa hasn't talked you into clubbing by now, she never will."

"Okay, I decided on my own."

"Why are you lying to me?" he asks.

"I'm not. I decided to go on my own."

"You know perfectly well what I'm talking about. You first said Tessa talked you into it, and you and I both know no one talks you into anything. Fuck it all, I should know."

He's right. I should not have lied. "I'm sorry."

"For what? Not checking your email or lying to me?"

"Both, I guess, but more for lying."

"What am I going to do with you?" he says, his voice dark.

I smile in an attempt to lighten the situation. "Whatever you want?"

"That is certainly tempting." He uncrosses his legs, letting his knees part.

His bulge is apparent. I'm not sure how he kept his legs crossed as long as he did. Must've been uncomfortable.

My body quivers. His presence—just his presence—sends me into a tailspin. Yeah, I'm angry. Angry that he didn't text me back. Do I have that right? He *did* respond, and if my phone had been on, I probably would've seen the email in enough time to come back here and meet him at nine.

This is my fault. No one's fault but my own. I resisted charging the phone to avoid temptation.

No, that's a lie.

I resisted charging my phone to avoid being controlled by Braden.

And I need to tell him that.

I clear my throat. "I didn't find a charger, Braden. On purpose. So I wouldn't get a text if you texted me back."

"I see. So if I had texted you instead of emailing you, we'd still be sitting here in the same situation."

I nod. "Yes, except that I would've seen your text when

I plugged my phone in during my Uber ride home."

His lips curl upward into that semi-smile that drives me into a frenzy. "So you charged your phone, and your first thought was that I hadn't responded to your text."

I nod again, this time numbly.

The smile stays on his face. He knows he got to me, and damned if he's not happy as a clam about it.

"You look very pleased with yourself," I can't help saying.

"I'm usually pleased with myself. Surely you know that by now."

Touché. I'm not sure what to say to that.

"Perhaps now you have an inkling of how you make me feel on the daily," he says.

"What's that supposed to mean?"

"You fight me at every turn," he says. "I almost wish I hadn't emailed you back at all. It would serve you right."

Tension coils through me. "What the hell is that supposed to mean?"

"It means you attempted to manipulate me, Skye, and you already know I don't take kindly to that."

"I did *not* try to manipulate you."

"Oh? And exactly what do you call deliberately not charging your phone so you wouldn't see whether I responded to you?"

"That's not manipulation, Braden. That's me controlling my own life."

"That's not control, Skye. If you don't want to respond to a text or an email, then don't respond to a text or an email. *That* is control. Keeping your phone dead to avoid responding to me? *That* is manipulation."

I open my mouth, but no words come out. What can I say? He's absolutely right. If I had any control where Braden is concerned, I wouldn't need to turn off my phone. And now he's got me right where he wants me.

I can't help a sarcastic laugh. "Funny. Okay, let's say you're right. Let's say I *did* manipulate you, or at least attempted to. What do you think you do to me every day? This almost sadistic need you have for control? I gave it to you. I gave it to you in the bedroom. But that isn't enough for you. You want it over every aspect of my life. If that's not manipulation, tell me what is."

He stands now, his bulge still apparent. He's turned on, and frankly, so am I. His very presence turns me on, his controlling nature turns me on, and the sight of his cock hard for me *really* turns me on.

"Manipulation, Skye, is skillfully controlling someone or something."

"I can't argue with your definition," I say. "And only one of us is a master of control here."

He laughs. Really laughs. "If I were the master of control you seem to think I am, we wouldn't be having this conversation."

"But you *are*, Braden. Why do you think I didn't find a charger?"

"I know exactly why," he says, grabbing my hair and forcing my head back. "Don't attempt to manipulate me again, Skye. You won't like the result."

His lips come down on mine.

Chapter Eighteen

I keep my lips glued together.

Why not? Braden will force them open, probe his tongue at the seam, and eventually I will succumb. I know this, and so does he.

Except he doesn't probe. He simply slides his lips over mine, and he doesn't attempt to coax them open.

Now who's manipulating whom?

I chuckle inside my mind at the inevitable answer to my own question.

By keeping my lips glued shut, I'm manipulating him. Because I want this kiss as much as he does. And I know he knows that.

My action is no different from denying myself an orgasm against his kitchen island or turning off my phone so I won't see his texts.

I'm manipulating him into thinking he doesn't control me.

Why not accept the kiss? Why not let it lead to the inevitable lovemaking we both desire?

We're here in my apartment. I don't have any leather bindings or floggers or butt plugs. Only vanilla sex here. Yet I'm resisting it.

You are a challenge, Skye.

I can almost hear the words coming from Braden, even though his lips are still pressed to mine, giving me short, sweet pecks that are setting my loins on fire.

He trails tiny kisses across my jawline into my ear. He nips at the lobe. "Stop it," he whispers harshly. "Stop denying yourself."

His words ring so very true. Just as I denied myself that orgasm, just as I denied myself an evening with Braden tonight, I'm now denying myself this kiss and where it may lead. Is my control worth giving up pleasures?

"Fuck it," I say out loud. I cup both his stubbled cheeks and lead his lips back to mine.

This time I open, and I take the lead. I slide my lips over his, swirl my tongue around his, savor the delicious taste of him.

Why deny myself?

No longer, at least for tonight. If I weren't so obsessed with my own control, we'd have already made love several times tonight, and I could've saved myself two agonizing hours at a club.

He breaks the kiss with a loud pop of suction and burns his gaze into mine. "I ought to smack your ass until it's cherry red."

Oh, hell no. Except… Oh, hell yes. Ambivalence whirls through me. I enjoyed that spanking he gave me. I didn't think I would, but God, I did. I long to experience the sensation again—his palm coming down on my ass, the pleasure-pain erupting in my body.

"Make no mistake, Skye," he continues, his voice a

husky timbre. "Pull a stunt like this again, and I'll leave your ass raw. You'll be wishing I only denied you an orgasm."

The thought both frightens and inebriates me. How far am I willing to go toward Braden's darker side?

What did he do to Addie that left her shaken? What did she refuse to do that led to their breakup?

I swiftly erase those thoughts from my mind. I'm ripe and wet and my entire body's an inferno. I want Braden. I'm ready for whatever he gives me.

"Get undressed," he commands. "Then wait for me on the bed with your legs spread."

I don't even consider disobeying. My blouse, jeans, and wedge sandals are off nearly instantly. Then my panties and bra. My breasts are already flushed a rosy pink, and my nipples are hard and tight. I walk to the bed, lie down, and spread my legs wide open.

Braden turns and stares at me. "You are lovely to look at. Honestly, Skye, sometimes just looking at you is enough for me."

His words arrow straight to my heart. This is why I love him. This is why I love Braden Black. Because of *these* moments, like the moment when I took my last photo for the Cherry Russet lip stain. I was wrapped in a sheet and standing at Braden's floor-to-ceiling window overlooking Boston Harbor. He took the photo and told me how beautiful I looked. Or when I woke up and found the earrings he left me, something he bought only because he knew I'd like them and that they'd look good on me.

Braden may be all about control, but he's also a romantic at heart.

And he loves me. Boston's richest and most eligible bachelor is in love with *me*.

He gazes at me for a few more timeless moments before he stalks toward the bed.

"You are delectable," he says. "I'd love to dive between your legs right now, eat you until you're begging me to stop. Or just stuff my cock inside your pussy and take you hard and fast. Or turn you over, lick your asshole, and then fuck you from behind. You'd enjoy all those things, wouldn't you, Skye?"

"God, yes."

"So would I. But you do have to be punished for attempting to manipulate me this evening. The problem is, I'm not in the mood to punish myself."

"Fuck my mouth," I say.

The left side of his lips quirks up into a half smile. "I've given that some thought, believe me."

"Why are you thinking when you could be doing?"

"Because I have something else in mind for tonight. Something new."

I'm awash in nerves. What new thing could he try in my apartment? I don't have any of his toys. I don't even have a blindfold, and he's not wearing a tie.

He undresses slowly. Slowly and deliberately. Too damned slowly. He folds each piece of clothing neatly and sets it on a chair. He's never done that before. He either throws it on a chair or lets it fall to the floor. Now, whatever he's doing, he's doing it very deliberately.

I salivate as inch by gorgeous inch of him becomes visible. When he finally stands before me, completely naked and beautiful, I'm so hot, I could incinerate.

He straddles me a moment, sliding his cock head through my slick folds.

"So wet, Skye," he says.

I close my eyes, taking fistfuls of my comforter and

waiting for him to thrust into me. I'm so empty. So needy and aching. *Take me, Braden. Please.*

But the thrust I expect doesn't come, and I open my eyes.

Instead of fucking me, Braden is masturbating. Fucking masturbating as he stares at me, his gaze locking with mine.

"Wouldn't you rather be doing that inside me?" I say.

"Of course I would," he says, "but I have a very vivid imagination."

I squeeze the covers in my fists again. This is my punishment. I have to watch him get off, while I get nothing. I'm here solely as a visual stimulation for him. He may as well be watching porn.

Fuck! My nipples are straining, and my clit is throbbing in time with Braden's jerks. My hips are moving of their own accord, and I force them to stop. I don't want to help him along any more than I already am just by being here naked.

"I can feel the inside of your pussy," he says. "So tight and warm."

Can he? Can he really? Because I can't feel anything inside me, and I desperately want to.

"You're so hot, Skye." He increases his tempo. "So hot, so sweet, so tight."

"Damn it, Braden!" I squeeze my eyes shut.

"Oh, no," he says. "You don't get off that easily. Open your fucking eyes."

Don't. Just don't do it.

But I do. Not only because it's in the bedroom and I gave him my control long ago, but also because I truly want to watch. I want to see him pleasure his beautiful body. I want to see the come spurt out of him. I want to see the look on his face as he cries my name.

Perspiration glistens on his forehead, groans emanate from his throat, and he bites on his lower lip.

"Fuck, Skye. Fuck." He's jerking rapidly now, and—

"Skye!" He releases, and his white fluid slides onto my abdomen.

He's panting now, finally closing his own eyes and letting go. Absently, I touch my abdomen and rub his come into my belly as if it's lotion.

Is this truly all I will get of him tonight? Or will he take pity on me?

No, he won't. Braden doesn't take pity on anyone. Least of all someone who spent the evening manipulating him.

This is my true punishment. I watched this beautiful man pleasure himself, and I got hotter than imaginable. And now?

Nothing.

"That's sexy," he says, still a bit out of breath. "The way you rub it on yourself."

I say nothing. Simply let my hand drift upward to my breast. My nipple aches for touch, so I give it a little pinch. I'm so needy that I let out a moan and lift my hips at that simple subtle contact.

"Nipples need some attention?" he asks.

"Yes. Please." I don't even care how desperate I sound. At the moment, I'll give my next breath of oxygen for Braden's lips around one nipple.

He lowers himself, his dark-pink lips coming closer, closer, closer...

Then he darts out his tongue and licks my right nipple.

I squirm beneath, arching my back, looking for more.

But Braden rolls over on my bed, his back to me.

"I never took you for a tease," I say.

"I'm not teasing you, and you know it."

Yes, I know it. This is punishment, pure and simple. Which I know I deserve.

I turn my head and regard his bare back, so tanned and strong, the muscles flexing lightly as he breathes.

And I wonder...

Can two play this game?

If so, do I even have what it takes?

Chapter Nineteen

Braden wakes before I do Saturday morning. The sound of the shower rouses me, and I rise and don my bathrobe. I washed up last night, but I'm tempted to join him in the shower. I resist. Instead, I pour a cup from the pot of coffee he made and take a sip.

Nicely done. He makes better coffee than I do, which is surprising given someone else makes his coffee at home. Why is he up so early, anyway? It's Saturday. Saturdays are supposed to be lazy. We should be in bed making slow, sweet love.

Is he still angry?

Why should he be? He already punished me. I had to fall asleep last night with the female equivalent of a hard-on. I considered masturbating, but I've never had any luck doing that, and besides, I kind of felt like it would be…disobeying him. Which shouldn't have bothered me, but it did.

I flash back to the evening a couple of weeks ago when I tried to re-create my first orgasm with Braden by using a vibrator. That vibrator still hid in my top dresser drawer, along with a couple of other toys.

Again, temptation. But Braden will be out of the shower soon. What will he think if he finds me lying naked on the bed masturbating?

Don't, Skye. You gave him control in the bedroom.

But I can't resist. I grab the vibrator out of the top dresser drawer and settle on my bed. I pinch my nipples lightly to start my body's motor. It doesn't take too long, especially since I was left wanting last night.

I moisten the tip of the vibrator in my mouth and then trail it over my abdomen and down to my pussy. It slips in easily even though I'm tight. How did I get wet so quickly?

It feels nice, but it's not Braden. I know already I won't be able to force an orgasm. For some reason, Braden's presence is required for that feat. I can put on an act, though. I can pretend I'm coming when he walks out of my bathroom.

I pull the vibrator out of my pussy and toss it on the other side of the bed.

He'll know. Braden will know if I'm faking. How he knows? I have no clue. But he will.

The door to my bathroom opens, and Braden steps out wearing nothing but one of my best towels around his waist. His hair is wet and slicked back, and he looks absolutely scrumptious.

He darts his gaze to the hot-pink toy on my bed. He cocks his head. "Having fun without me?"

"I gave it some thought," I say, "but it wasn't working for me."

He walks over and picks up the vibrator, brings it to his nose, and sniffs it. "This has been inside you."

"For a hot second, yeah."

"Why didn't you finish?"

Because I can't. I can't come without you, and you know

it. I gave you control over this part of me.

"Because…I guess I'm just not in the mood."

His gaze darkens. "You're lying naked on the bed, your nipples are erect, and your body is flushed warm pink."

I part my lips. He knows all my signals. I'm an open book to this man.

"Why would you lie to me?"

I'm not lying. But the words don't come, because they are a lie in themselves. I know it, and he knows it.

"I'm sorry," I say.

"Don't be sorry, Skye. Just don't lie to me. I can see right through you. I want your complete trust, and it goes both ways."

His blue gaze penetrates me then. And yes, in that moment I believe that he *can* see right through me. Into my mind. Into my heart. Into my soul.

"You look beautiful," he says.

"Ripe for the picking," I affirm.

"Unfortunately, I have a meeting."

"On a Saturday morning?"

"Racquetball. With my attorney."

"Oh." I try to hide my disappointment, but as usual, I know he sees right through me.

"I'll pick you up at six tonight."

"Okay. Where will we be going?"

"Dinner with my dad and brother, remember?"

Shit. That's right. I can't believe I forgot.

"Right, sorry."

He lets the towel drop, and I try not to gape at his firm ass and semi-hard cock. He dresses in the clothes he wore last night. Then he checks his phone. "Christopher's outside. I'll see you tonight." He stoops down and gives me a quick peck on the lips.

Please. Don't leave. Stay here and fuck me. I need you so badly.

But he's out the door, and I'm alone. Naked and alone and needy. I glance again at the pink vibrator. Then I pick it up, rise, and take it over to the sink to wash it. I put it away, buried in my top drawer once more with the others.

It's always been useless to me, and it still is.

Only one man can make me come.

Braden. Only Braden.

I walk back out to the kitchen for more coffee, and—

I zero in on a large gift bag sitting on top of my small table. How had I missed it before? Unless Braden somehow hid it and then brought it out before he left the apartment this morning. My heart races as I read the tag.

For my favorite photographer. Love, Braden.

I gulp as I remove the tissue paper surrounding the contents of the bag. Then I gasp.

It's a Canon EOS 5D Mark IV complete with lens kit—the camera of my dreams, which retails for about five thousand dollars.

My heart nearly stops.

He brought this last night—another gift he knew I'd love.

And I, because I insisted on taking control by refusing to find a phone charger, deprived him of his happiness in giving it to me.

"Oh, Braden," I say out loud. I open the box and stare lovingly at what's inside.

Man. I deserved that punishment.

• • •

"I just can't get over it," I say. "The camera…"

"You don't have to keep thanking me," Braden says during the ride to his father's home.

I called him, of course, as soon as I could wrap my head around the fact that I now owned the camera I'd always wanted. He was in the middle of racquetball, so I left another voicemail. When he returned my call, I thanked him, stumbling over words and nearly sobbing. Then I thanked him profusely again when he arrived at my apartment this evening.

"I do," I say. "You came to my apartment with a surprise for me, and I—"

"Stop, Skye. It's okay. You've already been punished for that. It's done."

"But—"

"I want you to have the camera. It's yours. You deserve it."

I have no words left. This man will be my undoing. He's stoic and controlling and a giant pain in my ass one minute. The next he's loving and generous and thoughtful and romantic the next. My eyes leak a few tears.

He brushes them away with his lips. "Easy, now. I don't want to introduce my girlfriend to my brother and father while she's crying."

I sniff back the tears and get hold of myself. "I love you, Braden."

"I love you too, Skye."

We arrive at a mansion in Swampscott. I try not to gape as Braden and I walk to the door.

"Your dad lives here?"

"Yep. This is where he hangs his hat."

"Wow."

"It's just a house, Skye."

"It's not like any house I've ever been in."

"You might want to save that judgment until you see the inside."

Okay, fine. My judgment still won't change.

A uniformed maid answers the door, her gray hair in a tight bun. "Good evening, Mr. Black."

"Hello, Sadie. This is Skye Manning."

"Ma'am," she says. "May I take your jacket?"

"Sure." I remove my cardigan, which isn't actually a jacket, and hand it to her. After two phone calls with Tessa and one with Betsy, I decided on black capri pants, black strappy sandals, and a gray silk camisole.

Braden hasn't said anything about my clothes, and because he was running late when he picked me up, I was already in the sweater and we didn't have a chance to talk at my place.

But here we are. A marble tiled foyer below me and a crystal chandelier hanging above me. A huge living area off to the right, where two gentlemen sit.

Braden takes my hand, and we walk over to them. They both stand.

"Hey, Bray," the younger man says.

"Ben, Dad, this is Skye."

They're both nearly as beautiful as Braden.

"Skye, this is my father, Bobby Black, and my brother, Ben."

I shake Bobby's hand first. He's actually slightly taller than both of his sons. His hair is completely gray, and he has some laugh lines around his dark-brown eyes, but talk about a silver fox.

"Pleased to meet you," he says.

"You too, Mr. Black."

"Call me Bobby."

"Okay, sure."

He releases my hand, and I turn to Braden's little brother. Although "little" is definitely not the word for Ben Black. He's every bit as big as Braden, and are my eyes deceiving me or is he slightly taller, too? How on earth is Braden the runt of this litter?

"Have a seat," Bobby says. "Ben's our bartender tonight."

"I'll get you a Wild Turkey," Ben says to Braden. Then to me, "What would you like, Skye?"

"Wild Turkey works for me. It's my favorite."

"Someone who shares your taste in booze?" Ben laughs. "She's a keeper, Bray."

Braden squeezes my hand. I warm. Does that mean what I think it means? That he agrees that I'm a keeper?

I sit next to Braden on the couch, across from where Bobby is sitting in a wingback chair. Ben brings our drinks, and I'm thankful to have something to do with my hands.

Ben chats about nothing in particular until the doorbell rings again.

"That will be Kathy," Bobby says.

"Who's Kathy?" Braden asks.

"Dad's date, apparently," Ben says.

Braden's eyebrows nearly fly off his forehead.

This is going to be an interesting evening.

Chapter Twenty

I keep my eyebrows firmly in place despite the fact that Kathy looks about my age. Seriously. *My* age. Either that or she has really good genes and a hell of a plastic surgeon.

"Braden, Ben, Skye," Bobby says, holding on to Kathy's arm, "this is Kathy Harmon."

"I'm so thrilled to finally meet you," Kathy gushes. She pulls Ben into a hug.

Another hugger. Braden is next, and he looks stiff as a board from where I'm sitting.

"And Skye," Kathy says, "you are adorable."

Adorable? Maybe I am, in my tight capri pants and camisole. Kathy is wearing a pink sundress and stiletto sandals. Her hair is long, straight, and blond and falls down her back in a thick waterfall. Am I supposed to stand? Ben and Braden, being gentlemen, stood when Kathy entered.

If I stand, she's going to grab me and hug me. Not looking forward to that, but I'm nothing if not polite.

I stand.

And she grabs me and hugs me.

Not just a run-of-the-mill I've-never-met-you-before hug. No, this is a squeeze. I can't help but inhale her floral perfume. Ugh. Headache city.

"Great to meet you," I say when she finally lets me go.

"Bobby," Kathy says, "I would love a scotch on the rocks."

"Ben, can you get that?" Bobby asks.

"I'm on it." Ben ambles over to the bar.

"So tell me everything about yourself, Braden," Kathy says.

"Not much to tell. You can google me."

In fact, I'm sure she's already googled all of them. She's probably googled me as well.

Ben brings her drink and she takes a sip. "Smoky and peaty. Just the way I like it." Then she sets the glass on a coaster.

"Kathy is a law student," Bobby says. "She's interning with us."

I do some quick math in my head. If she's interning, she's most likely a third year, and if she went straight from high school, to college, to law school, she can't be more than twenty-five years old.

Yep, I pegged it. My age. My age, and she's dating Braden's father.

Maybe I shouldn't have dismissed the Tessa thing so quickly. Having her here with me now would be a godsend. Funny how when Braden asked me to invite Tessa, I thought for a minute he wanted her for his father. Clearly Bobby likes them young, and Tessa has it all over this woman.

Makes me wonder what Braden's mother was like. He doesn't talk about her, says it's too hard.

"Dad," Braden says, "may I talk to you privately for a moment?"

No. *No, no, no. Do not leave me here with your brother*

and your father's girlfriend.

"What about?"

"An investment I've got my eye on. I wouldn't bother you during your dinner party, but it's kind of an urgent thing."

"Urgent" my behind. He's going to shred his father for inviting Little Miss Muffet along tonight. It's written all over his face.

"Sure." Bobby stands and leaves the room with Braden.

Not awkward at all.

"So, Skye," Kathy starts. "I hear you know Addison Ames."

And the name-dropping begins…

I try to smile. No reason to be impolite. Kathy has no way of knowing what a bitch Addie is. "I used to work for her. I don't anymore."

"I'd love to meet her sometime."

Oh, honey, you are so barking up the wrong tree. Addie would rather die than do me a favor. "Sure, I'll try to arrange it."

"Would you? I really want to get into the corporate hospitality and entertainment business after I graduate, and Ames Hotels would be a great place to start."

"Really?" I say. "Interesting. I suppose they need lawyers, too."

"Absolutely, they do."

And…we've effectively run out of things to talk about.

"If you're interested in corporate hospitality and entertainment," Ben says, "why are you interning with Black, Inc.?"

Nicely done, Ben. I smile his way. A darned good question, too.

"What can I say? Your father made me an offer I couldn't refuse."

Money. She's a money grabber, then. Not overly surprising, given she's dating a man twice her age.

"Where do you go to law school?" I ask.

"Harvard, of course."

Of course. Interesting. She must be intelligent if she got into Harvard. Either that, or her daddy bought her way in. I doubt that, though, or she wouldn't be gunning for Bobby Black.

Or would she? He's devastatingly handsome. Silver foxes don't come any hotter. *What's your angle, sis?*

"Are you in your third year, then?"

"I am. But as much as I enjoy learning, I really can't wait to get out into the real world. That's why I'm enjoying the internship with Black, Inc. so much."

"Where did you do your undergrad work?" I ask.

"Boston U."

"So did I." Which means, if she's a third-year law student, she and I were at BU at the same time.

"Really? That's amazing!"

I nod, although I don't see anything amazing about it.

"What did you study?" she continues.

"Photography."

"Interesting. Why were you working for Addison Ames, then?"

Good question. Kind of akin to the question Ben just asked her. Yeah, looks like Little Miss Muffet got into Harvard on her merits.

"Are you kidding?" I say, as though anyone with a brain would know exactly why I was working for Addie. "She's a mega influencer. It was a huge audience for my photography."

"But she posts selfies."

I can't help myself. "No, she doesn't. I took all her photos. I'm not sure who's taking them now."

"I see." She smiles. "Would you two excuse me for a minute? I need to use the powder room." She stands and walks directly out of the room without asking Ben where it is.

Bingo. Kathy has been here before.

Once she's gone, Ben smiles at me. "She's interesting," he says sarcastically.

How much am I allowed to say to Ben? Can I say what I'm truly thinking?

"Dad has a thing for younger women," he continues.

"Apparently." I smile.

"He's never serious." Then he lowers his voice. "I don't think he'll ever get married again."

"You better not tell Kathy that."

"Kathy doesn't want to marry him. She's like all the others. She's using him for his money and his contacts."

"And you're okay with her doing that to your dad?"

"Are you kidding? He knows it. He's using her, too."

Ben's outlook is interesting. Braden said he's attracted to the wrong kind of women and that he lavishes his money on them. Apparently his father does the same.

"Why don't you think he'll ever get married again?" I ask.

"Because he didn't do very well the first time. Don't get me wrong. He loved our mother, but they got married young when she got pregnant with Braden, and neither of them was ready for it. Dad did some things he shouldn't have done, and Mom paid the price."

"Braden doesn't talk about your mother," I say, trying to decipher Ben's enigmatic statement in my head.

Ben inhales and drops his gaze for a moment. "None of us does, really. Growing up in our house was...not optimal."

Not optimal? Boy, do I have questions. Does Braden's childhood explain the way he is? I already know they went hungry sometimes. But he seems to have some pleasant memories of his mother as well.

I could ask the same question about anyone. I grew up on a farm with parents who are still married. It wasn't perfect—my parents even separated for a few months once—but it was pretty harmless. Still, one freaky experience with a scarecrow in the cornfield and I became a mega control freak?

"I'm sorry to hear that."

"Yeah, well, Bray and I turned out okay. As for Dad, he's happy. I mean, who wouldn't be? His son made him a billionaire, and now he can have all the young pussy he wants."

I widen my eyes at his bluntness.

He chuckles. "Did I insult you?"

"Not at all. Just not normal dinner-party conversation."

"We Blacks aren't really the dinner-party type. We're blue collar all the way."

"I know how and where you grew up," I say, "but I wouldn't call your brother blue collar now."

"We have manners," Ben says. "We know how to act in pretty much every situation. Our business wouldn't be thriving if we didn't know how to do that."

"I wonder, though," I say, "if your brother would use the word 'pussy' in a conversation with *your* girlfriend."

"He wouldn't, but it's not because he's got an issue with the word. Braden's just not a big talker."

Ben apparently does know his brother after all.

"And you are?"

"Haven't you figured that out by now?" He smiles.

I look over my shoulder.

"You're wondering when Kathy will return," Ben says.

"Well…yeah."

"Not until after Bray and Dad return. She's eavesdropping."

I drop my mouth open. "How do you know that?" I whisper.

"I know her type. Besides, how long does it take to fix your lipstick and piss?"

I can't help it. I laugh aloud. Braden's brother seems like a lot of fun. I really should've brought Tessa. They would totally have hit it off.

"Doesn't it bother you? Kathy eavesdropping, I mean."

"Not really. If I know my brother, he knows she's there, and he's watching what he says. Besides, you and I both know Bray took Dad away to read him the riot act about inviting her to the dinner where we were both going to meet you for the first time. No chance of Kathy overhearing any business secrets."

I smile. "Yes, I can't deny that's exactly what went through my mind when Braden went to talk to your father alone."

"You know my brother well."

"In some ways," I say. "I'll be honest with you, though. He keeps a lot hidden."

"That's Braden," Ben says. "He's very careful. He's been burned, and he'll never let it happen again."

Chapter Twenty-One

B raden and his father return, and exactly sixty seconds later—seriously, I'm looking at my watch—Kathy comes back in. She dominates the conversation while I mull over Ben's words.

He's been burned, and he'll never let it happen again.

Does Ben know the whole story between Braden and Addie? If so, will he tell me? He's a talker for sure, but he and I just met. Plus, going behind Braden's back to get information out of his brother would earn me a dire punishment. I may never orgasm again.

But as much as I hate the thought of never climaxing again, that's not the main issue here.

I love Braden. I love him so damned much.

If I go behind his back and pump his brother for information, he may not forgive me.

And as much as I want to know, I won't abuse his trust again.

"What do you think, Skye?"

I suppress a jerk at my name from Braden's lips. I have

no idea what the rest of them have been talking about. Not cool.

"About what?" I say.

"About going downtown and listening to some jazz tonight," he says, a smile tugging at his lips.

Damn him. He knows I wasn't listening. "Sounds great."

"Wonderful," Kathy says. "I love jazz, don't you, Skye?"

"Sure." I'm so far from a music connoisseur. But hey, doesn't everyone love jazz?

The maid enters the living room and waits for a lull in the conversation before she says, "Mr. Black, dinner is served."

"Excellent, thank you, Sadie." Bobby stands. "Ladies first, of course."

Since I've never been here, I have no idea where the dining room is. I'm certain Kathy does, though, so I follow her. Sure enough, she leads me to the formal dining room. Bobby holds a chair out for her, and she sits.

Ben takes a seat next to her, while Bobby sits at the head of the table.

Braden holds out the other chair next to Bobby. "Skye," he says.

I sit down, and then Braden takes the empty seat next to me.

Kathy helps herself to a piece of bread and then hands the breadbasket to Bobby.

Yeah, she's definitely been here before. More than once, I'd say. I'm not sure I'll ever feel comfortable helping myself to anything on this table, no matter how often I end up eating here.

I admire her tactics, though. This is a woman who believes in going after what she wants. Part of that is making herself at home in any environment. I bet she'd never be embarrassed if a condom fell out of her purse in front of a devastatingly handsome man.

I don't have to worry about making conversation because Kathy takes over. Yes, she's very intelligent. More than that, though, she's also shrewd and cunning. She'll make a good lawyer. Why isn't Braden attracted to a woman like her?

Easy. *You are a challenge, Skye.* His words ring in my ears. Kathy is most definitely not a challenge. Intelligent, cunning, and shrewd, yes. But clearly she'll lie on her back to get what she wants. That's not a challenge for a man like Braden.

Dinner is delicious. Cream of tomato bisque with fresh basil and then prime rib of beef, garlic mashed potatoes, roasted Brussels sprouts, and au jus. Since I have virtually nothing to add to the conversation, I clean my plate before the others are done.

"Save room for dessert," Braden says to me.

"What's for dessert?" I ask.

"I don't know what they're serving here," he says, "but I know what *I'll* be having."

I squirm, trying to ease the pressure between my legs. Maybe tonight I'll finally get an orgasm.

"What did you think?" Braden asks after Christopher picks us up.

"I like your brother a lot."

"And my father?"

"He seems nice."

"But?"

"Braden, you know exactly what I'm thinking. What's he

doing with her? She's *my* age."

Braden chuckles. "She won't be around for too long. Once she gets what she wants, she'll be on her way."

"And you're okay with her using your dad like that?"

"My dad is a big boy. He can take care of himself."

"Your brother says he's using her as well."

"Of course he is. She's willing to spread her legs, and my father's willing to let her."

I groan.

"Do you find that distasteful?"

"Not in the way you're thinking. Your father is very attractive. It's just not...me."

"So you weren't working for Addie for the contacts?"

"I was working for Addie to make a living. The contacts were a nice fringe benefit. You'd better not be suggesting what I think you are. Besides, Addie is definitely not my type." I can't help a sarcastic chuckle.

"I'm not suggesting that at all. I know you wouldn't sleep your way to the top. But everyone takes advantage of opportunities."

"Are you actually defending what she's doing? I'm sorry, but in my mind, there's a difference between taking advantage of an opportunity and fucking someone to get somewhere."

"What's the difference? Aren't they both taking advantage of an opportunity?"

"One is good business, Braden, and the other is close to prostitution."

"And..."

"And...what?"

"Do you find prostitution distasteful?"

"I find prostitution illegal."

But he raises a good point. What Kathy's doing is

not illegal. She's taking advantage of an opportunity, and Bobby's letting her.

I sigh. "You're right. As long as she and your father are good with the situation, who am I to judge?"

He laughs and squeezes my hand. "You're exactly right."

His laughter thrills me, of course.

"You knew I'd agree, didn't you?"

"When you thought about it logically, yes, I knew you'd agree."

"Then why did you push me?"

"Because you're so adorably indignant."

"Since you're so fond of my indignation, why did you leave me alone with your brother and Kathy?"

"You held your own."

"Of course I held my own. Still, it was pretty uncool of you to leave me with two people I'd just met."

"I had something to discuss with my father that couldn't wait."

"Of course you did. You were giving him shit about bringing his current fuck to dinner."

"Actually, no, I wasn't. I was talking to him about an investment."

"And it couldn't wait?"

"No, it couldn't, because it was fake."

"Why would you drag your father away from his dinner party to—"

His lips curve upward slightly.

"You were baiting her."

"I knew you'd figure it out."

"Why? As you say, your father's a grown man, and he can take care of himself."

"I agree. If he wants to spend his money on some young woman who's only interested in one thing, that's his prerogative."

"Then why drop information?"

"Because this is *my* company, Skye. I love my father, and he does a good job, but sometimes he thinks with the wrong head."

"You don't really believe he'd give up trade secrets or anything, do you?"

"Not when he's in his right mind, no."

I giggle. "In other words, not when he's thinking with the *right* head."

"Bingo."

I smile and cover his hand with mine. "Tell me, Braden. Which head are you thinking with right now?"

He sears me with his gaze, saying nothing.

And I know.

Braden Black only thinks with one head, no matter what, and it's *always* the right one.

Chapter Twenty-Two

I'm in Braden's bedroom, naked and lying supine on his bed. I'm bound as I was last time, with leather restraints on my wrists, my arms in a Y above my head. He doesn't bind my ankles.

I'm both relieved and disappointed.

"Close your eyes," he says softly.

I obey, and the cool silk blindfold covers me.

"You won't be seeing things tonight, Skye."

I nod.

"Tonight I want you to concentrate on what you hear. Pay close attention to the sounds in the room."

"How?"

"The same way you paid attention to the sights last time."

"But there's so much to see," I say. "There's nothing to hear during sex."

"You're wrong," he says, "and tonight, I'll prove that to you."

"The feeling of what you do to me overshadows everything else. I could suppress it by watching the visual, but for sound? I don't know if I can."

"You can."

I open my mouth, but he places two fingers over my lips. "You're done talking. Don't speak unless I tell you to."

Again I open my mouth but shut it abruptly. He wants me to concentrate on what I hear, but I can't speak? What I say during lovemaking is a big part of the experience, isn't it?

I stifle a giggle. Maybe it used to be, but Braden so seldom lets me talk.

Maybe he'll play some music. I stifle another giggle. We were supposed to join the others for some jazz tonight, but Braden remembered he had an early meeting. I'm not sure the meeting exists, but I have no complaints.

I wait.

No music.

No kisses, no touch, no flicks of a flogger or anything else.

So I listen.

What I hear astounds me.

Braden's breath. It's rapid, and a low moan emanates from his throat. I've heard him moan many times before, but this is different. This is so low that I'm sure I've never heard it before.

"You're beautiful," he says. "So fucking beautiful, Skye."

More words I've heard before. But when I concentrate only on their sound, in the husky timbre of Braden's voice, they're so much more evocative.

My skin tingles, and energy arrows between my legs.

His lips press against mine, and though I'm tempted to open my mouth and let him in, he pulls back. Then he kisses me again. A short, sweet kiss to my lips. The sound is a soft smack, and it makes my nipples strain.

The sound of a kiss. I've never thought about it before. It's amazing, and electricity slides through me.

I let the sound travel through me as he kisses me again and again. He moves from my lips to my neck to my shoulders. Tiny smacking kisses, and each one leaves me scorched. He wanders over my chest to the tops of my breasts, where the kissing sound is joined by his low guttural moan.

"God, I love your tits."

They love you, too. I don't say it, of course. I shouldn't even be thinking it. I should be concentrating only on what I hear.

He kisses my nipple, and I suck in a breath. How do I escape from the feeling—the intense feeling of pleasure that surges through me every time he pays any attention to my nipples?

I don't want to. My nipples are so sensitive, and they love what he does to them. *I* love what he does to them. I don't want to ignore it.

"Concentrate, Skye," he says against my flesh.

Concentrate. The warm timbre of his voice. I let it rush over me and flow through me, and when he kisses my nipple again, the sound of the peck sends a thrill through me.

And I begin to understand.

The sound. His mouth touching my skin, and then the slight intake of air through his closed lips. The smack. The sweet smack.

It's the most provocative sound in the world.

"I'm going to suck on your nipples now, Skye," he says. "Listen. Listen to the sounds I make. Listen to the sounds *you* make."

The tug comes sharply. His lips are firm and tight over my nipple, and I moan. My moan is higher and louder than Braden's. Has it always been? Have I ever paid attention?

"Oh God," I say breathlessly.

Slap!

His hand comes down on my other breast.

"No talking," he commands.

The sound. The blow of his hand coming down on my flesh and striking me.

It excites me. It's dangerous. Dangerous and intriguing.

His lips clamp over my nipple once more. I gasp, suppressing the words that want to come spewing out of my mouth. Because God, it feels good. It feels so damned good.

How does he expect me not to *feel* any of this?

I remove the feeling from my mind as best I can. He's on my nipple, so I listen. I listen to the slurping of his lips. The low moan that comes constantly from his throat as he pleasures me.

The low moan that means he's receiving pleasure as well.

My nipples are so hard, so needy and aching.

And my pussy. God, my pussy…

He trails his fingers at my side and squeezes my other breast. Then he thumbs my other nipple. He gives me a pinch. A sharp pinch that makes no noise.

No, the noise is in the echo of his low groan and the gasp and moaning coming from my own throat. He continues sucking one nipple. The soft slips and smacks swirl in the air around me, making my body ache even more.

Braden finally lets my nipple go with a soft *pop*.

A waft of cool air flows over my nipple.

No, Skye. Don't feel. Just listen.

Braden spreads my legs. Tension whirls through me. I'm aching with need, and this waiting is driving me slowly out of my mind. *Lick my pussy, damn it!*

I say nothing, though. And again, I try to listen.

"You're beautiful," he says. "Pink and swollen and oh so wet."

Again the low moan. Braden's moan. The moan that says

he likes what he sees.

And what he sees is *me*.

That sound. I know that sound, and I love that sound. Yet only now do I realize its true significance.

"I'm going to eat your pussy," he says. "Listen to me eat your pussy."

Oh God. This will be one hell of a challenge. I'm supposed to listen and not feel? Is he going to let me come? Will I ever orgasm again? Braden has ensnared me with his control of my climax. I never know when or if I'll get one, and that intoxicates me all the more. He's a master.

But then I stop thinking. Because he's between my legs, his stubble abrading my thighs, his tongue sliding over my clit, and that low moan—always that low moan—vibrating against me and through me.

Like a warm waterfall. It comforts me. Both comforts me and makes me hot.

A smack as he kisses the inside of my thigh. A low hum as he slides his tongue along my slit. A brisk inhale when he clamps his lips over my clit.

All from him, while I do my best to keep quiet.

I embrace the music of his body as he licks me, let it flow around me like a melody written solely for us.

It's intoxicating.

Yes, I'm turned on. Yes, I'm floating toward the peak.

The climax is no longer my goal, though. Listening is. Hearing is. For I gain something nearly as beautiful as a climax itself.

The music. The beauty in sound.

When he moves his mouth away from me, I whimper at the loss. A soft whimper that comes from my body involuntarily. I listen. I appreciate the sounds I make.

A soft thud as one of Braden's garments hits the back of

a chair. A louder thump. A shoe. Then another.

Soft sounds of his clothes meeting the floor in a puddle of fabric.

My heart hammers. Each of these sounds means he's closer to being naked. Closer to his cock inside me.

I'm so ready for that.

The soft creak of the bed as he returns, and when his cock slides between my legs, a swift intake of breath.

His breath.

And also my own.

"I want to fuck you now. I can't wait to get inside you."

I gasp when he thrusts.

He groans. Much louder and longer this time.

He fills me, and the feeling—

But I'm not supposed to feel. Only to hear.

The suction of his cock sinking into me is subtle, but it's there. I listen, and I hear it.

His balls slap against me as he thrusts. I hear them.

The sounds of him fucking me. Of him making love to me. They're there, and I hear them.

The rhythm of his thrusts. The chorus of his moans and mine, his breaths and mine.

And the melody. The melody that is audible only to me. To Braden and me. A lovely tune that exists between us and around us and inside us.

And I understand. I understand.

"Fuck," he says. "I'm going to come, Skye."

He thrusts into me and stays there, moaning. I revel in the sound, in the music of his release.

And I don't miss my own release. I'm too busy listening to his.

The pure musical beauty of it.

A few moments later, he pulls out and rolls off me,

sighing. A soft yet masculine sigh. A sigh I've never bothered to listen to before now.

A moment later, he removes my blindfold.

"Well?" he asks.

I stay silent.

"You may speak now."

I smile. "It was amazing. I heard things I've never heard before."

"Good. That's the plan. You did well."

"But, Braden…"

"Yes?"

"Why?"

"You mean why all this? The concentration on only one sense?"

"Yeah."

He doesn't answer me for a minute. Instead, he moves downward and positions his head between my legs. My clit rushes to attention. I haven't climaxed, and I want to. I want to very badly.

He flicks his tongue over my clit.

I jolt, arching my back. God, I want that orgasm more than I want anything at the moment.

Is he going to answer my question?

"I will give you an answer," he says, "but first, I'm going to give you a climax."

Chapter Twenty-Three

Thank God. My whole body is aching for a climax. It's been so long.

Braden eyes me lasciviously. I warm all over, my nipples snapping back to attention and my pussy throbbing mercilessly.

Until his phone buzzes on the night table. He widens his eyes.

Ignore it. Please ignore it.

But he doesn't. Braden doesn't ignore his phone. It's nearly midnight on a Saturday night. Who's calling him? It can't be business, can it? At this hour on the weekend?

Except that Braden has deals and contracts all over the globe. Though his company started with construction equipment, which is still its backbone, Black, Inc. now invests in real estate, foreign currency, futures, and probably lots of stuff I don't know about.

Which is why he'll never ignore his phone, no matter the hour.

He moves from between my legs, and I hold back a

whimper at the loss.

"Black," he says into his phone.

Then he's all business. Even his erection falters as he stands there naked. My eyes have adjusted to the dark after he removed the blindfold, and I watch him.

His demeanor is pure professionalism, and if I couldn't see his majestic body, I'd swear he was standing in a three-piece suit, tie adjusted just so.

He may as well be.

And I know I can kiss my orgasm goodbye.

After what seems like hours, he ends the call.

"Is everything okay?" I ask.

"I have to go to New York," he says.

"We're leaving tomorrow," I reply.

He walks toward his closet. "No. We're leaving tonight."

I gasp. "Tonight? You mean right now?"

"Yes. Right now."

"I… I can't. What about…"

He turns and meets my gaze. "What about what, Skye? We were going to leave tomorrow afternoon anyway. Do you have some kind of plan for your Sunday morning that I don't know about?"

"The dogs. What about the dogs?"

"Who do you think takes care of the dogs all day when I'm not here?"

Laughable statement. What am I thinking?

I'm thinking I want that damned orgasm.

"What's wrong, Braden?"

"A key negotiation fell through."

"At midnight?"

"In China. I need to do damage control."

"Can't you do it from here?"

"If I could, do you think I'd be flying to New York in the

middle of the night?"

Good point. "What about Ben or your dad?"

"I run this company, Skye. You know that."

"Can't you delegate? Your father and Ben are perfectly capable of—"

"You've met my father and Ben once. You know nothing about them other than what you gleaned from one evening with them. Please don't presume to tell me how to run my company. You're a photographer, Skye. You don't know the first thing about my business."

My mouth drops open. *Maintain control, Skye.* But I can't. I begin to lose it. I feel the dreaded tears welling in the bottom of my eyes.

No. Just fucking no.

"Don't insult my intelligence," I say.

"I'm not insulting anything."

"The hell you're not."

He meets my gaze, his own cold. So cold. "This is business. *My* business. I'm not insulting you when I tell you that you don't know anything about it. I'm simply being truthful."

"But I don't understand—"

"That's right. You *don't* understand. This is something I need to take care of, and yes, I need to take care of it now. Now get out of bed and get dressed. We're leaving as soon as you're ready."

"If you'd just explain—"

"For God's sake, I don't have time to explain. You're not hearing me, Skye. You asked me earlier why I made you concentrate on one sense. For someone who just learned to hear this evening, you're not hearing me now."

My mouth drops open once more.

This is my life now? Braden tells me to do something, and I'm supposed to just do it? On blind faith?

"Your control over me in the bedroom doesn't extend to—"

"Damn it!" He scoops me off the bed and forces me to stand. "Hear me, Skye. We're leaving. We're leaving now."

And it dawns on me.

I don't have a choice. Braden canceled the plane ticket that Eugenie booked for me. My only way to get to New York to make my meeting on Monday is his private jet. Either that or fly standby, and I can't take the chance of not getting a flight. I could take a train, but I don't have a ticket. They might be sold out at this late date. Besides, I hate trains. I could drive, but I'd have to rent a car since I don't own one. This meeting is too important. His jet can't fly me to New York tomorrow if it's already in New York.

Checkmate. He wins.

I leave tonight.

I nod with resignation, pick up my clothes—luckily, he didn't destroy any of them tonight—and leave his bedroom silently. I walk naked to the stairway, not caring if Christopher or anyone else sees me, and head into my personal bedroom. I walk to the bathroom.

My reflection greets me in the mirror.

My makeup is smeared, and my hair is a tangled mess. Definitely a just-fucked look.

But something else catches my eye.

A look of defeat.

This is ridiculous, Skye. You're not defeated. It's business, and he can't help it. He needs to take care of business. You'd do the same. You haven't lost control. This is just business, and if you want to get to New York for your meeting, you have to go with him now.

All true. All very true.

Why is ceding control so difficult for me?

Is this another one of Braden's tests?

I shake my head at myself in the mirror. No. He's not that manipulative. Is he? Who in his right mind would stage a crisis where he had to leave for New York in the middle of the night?

No one.

Not even Braden Black.

Except I'm not sure. Braden gets what he wants, and what he wants is my control. Not just in the bedroom.

I can refuse to go, but that's cutting off my nose to spite my face. I need to get to New York, and this is the one sure way. Otherwise it's the bus or train because I can't depend on getting a flight on standby.

I sigh. Time to get ready. Because if I don't, I have no doubt Braden will come knocking on my door, making more demands of me.

I hastily cleanse my face of the smeared makeup, wash all other necessary parts, and dress in the clothes I wore to dinner earlier. I pull my hair into a high ponytail and then leave the room. My jacket and purse are still in Braden's bedroom.

I walk—not overly slowly but not overly quickly, either—down the stairs.

Braden stands by the elevator, holding my purse and jacket. He hands them to me. "Let's go. Christopher's waiting downstairs."

Chapter Twenty-Four

If I didn't know I was on a private jet, I'd be certain I was in a luxury apartment. Granted, a very narrow luxury apartment, but a luxury apartment nonetheless.

A bed. This jet has a bed. A flight to New York doesn't take long, so I doubt we'll use it, but there it sits. Perfectly made up, ready to be messed up. I chuckle to myself. Will Braden and I be joining the mile high club?

How many other women have joined the mile high club courtesy of this bed?

I erase that thought from my mind. This trip already makes me nervous. I don't need to think about all the other women Braden has bedded in this jet.

"Welcome aboard, Mr. Black." A blond flight attendant smiles. "And you too, Ms. Manning."

Braden nods. "Thank you, Robin."

I simply smile slightly and follow Braden on board. He leads me to two wide leather seats that make first class on any other airline look like steerage.

He gestures to me, and I take the seat closer to the

window. He sits next to me.

"I have a great crew," he says. "They see to every need."

"Is the pilot blond, too?" I can't help asking.

"The pilot is a fifty-five-year-old male veteran," he says matter-of-factly. "Do you want something to drink?"

"It's the middle of the night."

"It is. That doesn't mean you can't be thirsty."

He's right, of course. And I am a little thirsty. "Just some water."

He gestures to Robin, who stands next to another flight attendant, this one raven-haired with searing dark eyes. "Two bottles of water."

"Coming right up."

I roll my eyes.

"Something wrong?" Braden asks.

"How can they be so chipper at one in the morning?"

"They're paid very well to be on call at all hours."

I can imagine. I don't say it, though. Robin brings me a water, and I thank her and take a long sip.

"It's a short flight," Braden says, "but once we're at cruising altitude, you can lie down. Robin and Dani will see to your needs. Try to get some sleep."

"Maybe," I reply.

He takes my hand and rubs his thumb into my palm. "Skye, this isn't how I planned to spend this night, either."

"I understand."

My words aren't lies. I *do* understand. I even understand why I needed to come along.

"I didn't have time to pack anything," I say.

"You don't need to worry about that. I'll get you anything you need for your meeting on Monday."

"But the new camera. It's still at my place, and I wanted to bring it, to take photos of the city."

"This won't be our only trip to New York," he says.

I nod. He's right, and part of me jumps inside at the thought of many more trips with Braden. As far as my wardrobe goes? Surely I'll be dressed to the nines for my meeting. Better than I'd be if I wore my own wardrobe.

Another loss of control.

My control is rapidly becoming an illusion.

Like my reflection in the mirror, it's only a two-dimensional image of what I really am.

Perhaps it's time. Time to truly let go.

I scoff softly. I'm not thinking straight. It's the middle of the night, after all.

Still…I can't deny that the idea isn't quite as disturbing as it once was.

I've been obsessing about what I might lose, but what might I gain?

Braden sits next to me, his attention buried in his laptop. All business, Braden Black. And it dawns on me.

Braden runs his life like he runs his business. Everything under his control at all times.

Even *me*.

That's what he ultimately wants, and if I don't give it to him, he can easily find someone who will.

He's not his father. He won't settle for an opportunistic student who uses him as a ladder. No, Braden wants a challenge. He views his whole life as a challenge, and he thrives on it.

You are a challenge, Skye.

How many times has he said those words?

Braden is the kind of person who rises to every challenge and then defeats each one.

Is that how he sees me? As just another business deal? A challenging business deal, to be sure, but still just a business deal?

Does he simply enjoy the chase? If I give him all he asks for, will he grow bored? Find another challenge?

No. He thrives on winning. He thrives on overcoming every challenge and building his business. Can it even be called a business at this point? Or is it now an empire?

And if it's an empire, he's no longer a CEO. He's a fucking king.

Am I just one more business deal to negotiate until he gets what he wants? One more alliance to form?

Braden Black always gets what he wants.

Even in the middle of the fucking night, Braden gets what he wants. Even if it's just me on his private jet.

I turn to him. "Braden?"

He doesn't look away from his computer. "Yes?"

"Tell me what's going on with the deal."

"You wouldn't be interested."

"I wouldn't be asking if I weren't interested."

"You're an artist, Skye."

"Yes. I'm an artist—an artist who's trying to start her own business. Of course I'm interested in what you do."

"I don't have time."

"We have an hour in the air."

He sighs. "And you can see I'm online, dealing with this."

"You don't have two minutes to explain to me what's going on?"

"I couldn't even begin to explain this in two minutes. It's a complicated contract negotiation with three different distributors in China and Japan. If I can't work this out in the next twelve hours, I will probably be en route to China. I'd like to avoid that if possible."

"Why? Don't you want to see China?"

"Seeing China isn't the issue. I like to be on my home

turf. It's like having the home-field advantage."

The home-field advantage. Another means of control.

"That makes sense. I understand."

He looks at me then. Meets my gaze and truly looks at me. "Thank you, Skye."

"For what?"

"For hearing me. For finally *hearing* me."

And in that split second, I get him.

I *get* Braden Black.

He's a master of control in all aspects of his life. He's demanding and precise, but he's also loving and romantic. But beyond all that, he's a person just like I am—a person who wants to be heard.

He's Braden, and he loves me.

I want to please him.

And my fear of losing control lessens.

Chapter Twenty-Five

"Which hotel are we staying at?" I ask, too tired to appreciate the luxury of the limousine carrying us from the airport. Secretly, I hope it's not an Ames Hotel.

"We're staying in my Manhattan penthouse," Braden says.

"You have a Manhattan penthouse?"

"Does that surprise you?"

It does, though it shouldn't. The man has billions. He has a private jet with a pilot and crew on call, for God's sake. A Manhattan penthouse costs a heck of a lot less than that.

"Manhattan is my home away from home," he says. "There are things I do here that I don't do in Boston."

"What kind of business can't be done in Boston?"

"I'm not necessarily talking about business, Skye."

I suppress a jerk but cock my head. Do I want to know what he's talking about? I'm not sure.

Except I *am* sure. I want to know everything about Braden, and he's such a closed book on some things—not just the Addison Ames situation. Can I possibly uncover his secrets here in New York?

Finally, I speak. "What *are* you talking about, then?"

"I'm not sure you're ready," he says.

My skin tightens around me. "Ready for what?"

"The situation with this contract has…muddled things a bit for me personally."

"What the hell are you talking about, Braden?"

"There are things I do in New York that I don't do in Boston. Things I'd like to share with you. When you're ready."

"Maybe I'm ready."

He shakes his head. "You're not."

"How do you know if you don't tell me what you're talking about? And why do you only do these things in New York?"

"Boston is my home. Where I grew up. Where my father lives. I keep certain aspects of my lifestyle out of Boston."

"If this is about what you like in the bedroom, Braden, I already know all about that."

He shakes his head. "Oh, Skye… You don't even know what you don't know."

I glance through the tempered glass at the back of the chauffeur's head. Can he hear us? Probably not. I hope not.

"I know there's more. I remember that suspension thing hanging from your ceiling."

"I no longer indulge in that kind of play. I've told you."

"What if *I'm* interested in suspension?" I'm not, but what if?

"It's not a hard limit for me. If you're truly interested, we can look into it. But not without proper and well-built equipment."

"Hold on. What do you mean it's not a hard limit for you?"

"A hard limit is something I won't do, no matter what."

"Oh? What are your hard limits?"

"I only have one."

I lift my eyebrows. "What is it?"

"I don't talk about it."

"Don't you think I should know? So I don't bring it up?"

"Trust me, Skye. You will *never* bring it up."

Curiosity whirls through me. What is the one thing Braden won't do in the bedroom? I have to know. Just like I have to know what went on between him and Addie. Can the two possibly be related?

"Why haven't we talked about hard limits before now?" I ask.

"Because you weren't ready. But this contract…"

"Changes everything. So you've said. What I don't understand is why."

"I wasn't planning to bring you to my penthouse quite so soon."

"Then don't. Book us a suite somewhere. How about the Waldorf-Astoria?"

"I need to be in my penthouse. That's where I conduct my international business."

"Not in an office?"

"Black, Inc. has offices in Manhattan, but this negotiation is special."

"Too special to deal with in an office?"

"It's easier for me to get what I need to get done here in the middle of the night. I have even better security at this penthouse than I do at the office building."

"I see." Though I don't. Why would he need so much security? Unless… "Braden, are you doing anything illegal?"

He doesn't answer for a few seconds. Then, "No, Skye. I can't believe you would ask me that, but since our relationship is still new, I'll indulge you and say this one time and one time only. I do not engage in anything illegal in my business. You said you trust me."

"Braden, I—"

"The discussion is over. Either you trust me or you don't."

"I trust you."

It's the truth. The unadulterated truth. I trust this man. I've let him tie me up, bind me, blindfold me. I stayed with him after I found out he dumped Addie after she refused to do something in the bedroom, though I don't know what it was. Might it have something to do with the hard limit he won't talk about?

And I believe he conducts his business legally and ethically.

"Thank you," he says. "Breaking the law is a hard limit for me."

"For me, too," I say.

"Then we're on the same page."

"So what's your hard limit in the bedroom?" I asked.

"Nice try," he says. "I'm still not going there."

"Then…what kinds of things do you do in Manhattan that you don't do in Boston? In the bedroom, I mean."

And with whom? But I know better than to ask. We just had a conversation about trust, and anything he did before me isn't my business, no matter how curious I am. I already promised myself I'd let it go. Or try, anyway.

The limousine pulls up to a large building. In the darkness, it looks like any other skyscraper.

"I don't have to tell you," he says. "We're here. I can show you."

My heart pounds.

Am I ready for whatever awaits inside?

The chauffeur opens my door and helps me out of the car. Braden takes my hand, and together we walk toward the door of the building.

"Good morning, Mr. Black." A uniformed doorman tips his hat.

Braden nods as we enter, and he leads me through an ornate lobby of marble and crystal. I blink against the barrage of light. When we reach an elevator, Braden slides a card through the reader. So far, same as his penthouse in Boston.

We ride in the elevator, seemingly at the speed of light. My knees buckle at the upward thrust.

The elevator finally stops, and the doors open.

I blink.

Then I gasp.

Chapter Twenty-Six

Abustling office greets me.

Seriously. Men and women run back and forth from computers to copiers to phones.

This is Braden's home away from home?

"Mr. Black, welcome." A young man greets us. "We have the meeting set for an hour from now. Everything's ready in the conference room."

Conference room? This is a mistake. This isn't Braden's Manhattan penthouse. This is his office space. Has to be.

"I'll be with you in a few minutes." Braden turns to me. "Follow me, Skye."

He leads me through the front area to a door in the back. He slides a card through another reader, and we enter as he shuts the door behind us.

The office sounds disappear instantly.

This part of the penthouse is soundproof. Nice call.

Another large area greets us, this one more like what I was expecting. It's a living room decorated in a scant style. Seriously scant. Two wingback chairs, a sofa, and a coffee table.

Odd, since his Boston place is decorated so completely. To the left is a kitchen, much smaller than his kitchen in Boston.

"I know you must be tired," he says. "I'll help you get settled in the bedroom, and then I have work to do."

I nod. Tired is an understatement. I'm exhausted.

He leads me down a hallway and opens the door. I drop my mouth open. New York at night greets me, and it is splendid. Braden does like floor-to-ceiling windows. Just like his Boston penthouse, only instead of the harbor, the glitz of downtown greets me.

"Everything you need will be in the bathroom. Help yourself. If you're hungry or thirsty, the kitchen is stocked."

"But what about you?" I ask. "It's the middle of the night. You must be tired, too."

"Adrenaline," he says. "This is an important deal. I'll be fine."

I nod. I know better than to try to talk him into staying with me, maybe giving me that orgasm he promised. Not going to happen. Not tonight.

He kisses my forehead. "Get some sleep." Then he turns and walks out of the bedroom.

I sigh. This is life with Braden Black. Oddly, I'm okay with it. I love this man. I want to know this man. And coming here, to his Manhattan residence, will help me get to know him better—especially if this is where certain aspects of his "lifestyle" reside.

He said he'd show me. Apparently he meant later.

He's all business right now. An important contract. I have no idea why or how it's important, but I take him at his word. He'll see to business.

But what of the lifestyle he was talking about? The lifestyle he keeps in Manhattan, never bringing to Boston?

What does he mean?

I walk to the door of the bedroom and glance down the hallway. Several other closed doors line the wall. Extra bedrooms? The conference room the young man mentioned? I have no idea. Yes, I'm curious, but exhaustion takes over. Sleep first. Tomorrow, I'll look around.

Maybe I can uncover some of his secrets.

I open my eyes. Gray skies greet me. Ugh. For a moment, I think I'm in Boston at Braden's place. But I'm alone in the bed, and I remember.

I'm in Manhattan.

My phone sits on the night table where I plugged it in earlier. I grab it to check the time. Ten thirty a.m. Later than I normally sleep, but it was near four a.m. when I finally collapsed into bed.

Coffee. Must have coffee.

I rise, grab a robe from the bathroom, and pad out to the kitchen. At the Boston penthouse, Marilyn would already have the coffee ready. Here, apparently, it's up to me. No problem. If there's one thing I know how to do in a kitchen, it's how to brew coffee.

I get a pot going, and then I open the refrigerator. Braden was right. It's fully stocked. Bacon, eggs, cheese, deli meats, bread, juice, milk. Even a tube of chocolate chip cookie dough. I smile.

If Tessa were here, we'd have cookie dough for breakfast. Cookie dough and coffee, breakfast of champions. We ate that meal many times during our college years. I grab the cookie dough out of the fridge. Why not? It's Sunday morning, and I have a meeting of a lifetime tomorrow. Why not indulge a little?

I rummage through the drawers until I find a knife, slice off a nice hunk of the cookie dough, and pour myself a cup of fresh coffee. I take my gourmet breakfast into the living area and sit down on the couch, feet on the coffee table. I grab the remote control from the end table and click on the TV.

Where is Braden? He can't possibly still be in a meeting. He hasn't had any sleep.

Of course, nothing as mundane as a lack of sleep would keep Braden from taking care of business.

Nothing illegal, he told me. I believe him. Braden values trust, and he wouldn't lie to me.

I bite off a chunk of cookie dough and wash it down with a sip of coffee. Will Braden approve of my choice? I laugh out loud. Cookie dough for breakfast is probably a hard limit for Braden.

What is his hard limit in the bedroom?

And why won't he talk about it?

The other doors in the hallway edge into my mind. I polish off half the cookie dough, drain my coffee cup, and stand. No time like the present.

I rise and walk back toward the bedroom. Shower first and then be nosy?

No. My curiosity is killing me. I pad down the hallway clad only in the bathrobe and stop at the first closed door. I turn the knob.

Inside is another bedroom, smaller than the master and decorated in olive green and ivory. The bed appears to be a queen. I move through the room, opening the door to a walk-in closet and then another to a full bath. Okay. Guest room. Nothing to see here.

The next door offers a library with a desk and shelves covered in books. Everything from memoirs to science fiction. Does Braden read? He says he does, but when does he find the time? Or does he just like being around books? If that's the case, why no library in Boston?

Except there could be a library. He has another floor I haven't explored at all, other than the bedroom he created for me. I walk along the shelves, sliding my fingertips over the spines of the books. I love books. Always have, and this room is a booklover's paradise. The soothing aromas of leather bindings and paper waft toward me, and I inhale, closing my eyes.

A few minutes pass, and I open them, exploring the vast array of titles once more. He has the classics, and I pull out *Jane Eyre*, one of my favorites. Has Braden read this? I'll try to remember to ask him. I return the book to its place and walk to the next shelf, which seems to be mostly nonfiction. I scan the titles quickly, hoping to find a book about photography, but to no avail. He does have some *National Geographic* photograph volumes, and I move toward one when—

Oh. My. God.

The Art of Bondage.

I pull out the book. It's large—a coffee table book—and when I open it, I realize it's not an instruction manual but a book of photographs. It truly shows the *art* of bondage. I've opened the book to the middle, and splayed across one whole page in glorious black and white is a woman, naked and on her knees. She's bound with something that looks like regular off-white rope. Her ankles are tied together as well as her thighs, and her shoulders and arms are also bound, leading to her wrists, which are between her bound thighs and out of view.

The knots in the rope are art. They remind me of a macramé planter. There is beauty in their simplicity, but the real beauty is the woman bound by them.

She's looking up at someone.

The photographer, of course. As a photographer myself, I know this. But that's not what this photograph is supposed to show its observer. She's looking up to the person who bound her. Her lips are slightly parted, full, and painted dark. Dark red, I assume, though the photo is in black and white. That's the beauty of black and white. It forces the observer to imagine, to see in her mind's eye.

And what I see is a woman, bound and eager to please whoever bound her.

My nipples harden against the softness of the robe.

I'm not sure why. Sex is impossible in this position.

Except that it's not.

Her mouth is completely available to be fucked.

Absently, I trail one hand under the robe and cover my warm breast, flicking the nipple lightly.

Then, with my other hand, I turn the page.

Another naked woman, this time in color. She's on the floor—hardwood of some kind—and she lies in a mermaid position, her ass to the camera. She leans on one arm, and the other arm is bound tightly, upper arm to forearm, in an intricate knotted cuff. The cuff is attached to a braided rope that goes around her waist. Her calves are bound as well, also intricately, ending around the stiletto heels of her black pumps, which, other than the rope, are all she wears.

I give my nipple a quick pinch, and shivers rack through me, my skin tingling. I'm getting wet. I can feel it.

Has Braden ever bound a woman like this? Or does he just appreciate the art of the binding?

I turn the page once more.

Then—

"See anything you like?"

Chapter Twenty-Seven

Braden.

I close the book quickly, my cheeks and chest warming. "I wasn't…"

"Yes, you were. Don't lie to me, Skye."

I look down at the book lying on the floor. "Your library is beautiful."

"Thank you. I like it."

"So…I guess I should take a shower." I rise.

"I don't think so," he says. "I think I'd like to fuck you right here in my library, among all these books."

I part my lips, my body on high alert.

"God, you have the sexiest mouth I've ever seen."

The urge to smile overwhelms me, but I hold my lips in their parted position. For some reason, my lips drive Braden wild, and right now I want him madly wild and passionate.

He yanks the bathrobe off me, and in a second, it's a white puddle on top of the Turkish rug.

"I'll answer all your questions, Skye, but first I'm going to take what I need. Do you have any idea what it does to me to see you caressing your breasts while looking at that book?"

Am I supposed to answer? I already know. The book did the same to me. My nipples are erect and ready, yearning for attention.

"Yes," I say.

He grabs my hand and leads it to the bulge inside his trousers. "I haven't slept in twenty-four hours, and I'm exhausted. No other woman could get me hard under these circumstances. Do you know that?"

"No. I mean… Yes, I guess."

"You guess?" He pushes my hand farther into his crotch. "Do you seriously think I could be lying to you?"

"No. Of course not."

"On your knees," he says gruffly. "Take out my cock and suck it."

His command turns me on more than he even knows, given the first image I saw in the book. For an instant, I wish I were bound like that woman in black and white, so that all I can do is suck him. I drop to my knees quickly and unbuckle his belt. I slide his pants and boxer briefs over his hips, and his dick springs out. I lick the tip and savor the salty drop of liquid.

He groans, and I look up at him. His gaze is blue fire.

"Do you do those things, Braden?"

"Damn it, Skye. We'll talk later. Right now, I want my cock in your hot little mouth."

I don't question him. My body has already burst into flames, and I want this as much as he does. I take him into my mouth about three-quarters of the way before I pull back.

His groan fuels my desire, and when he grabs my hair and shows me the rhythm he prefers, I don't hesitate. This isn't a blow job. This is him fucking my mouth. I never realized there was a difference until now. With a blow job,

I'm in control. With a mouth fuck, he is.

The soft sucking and slapping sounds dance around me. I'm hyperaware of them after Braden's lesson in hearing. His cock head hits the back of my throat with about every other thrust, and I take it. I take it because it's what he wants. Because I want what he wants.

He thrusts and he thrusts, and soon I know he's close to release. He said he would fuck me in the library, and though this isn't what I expected when he said it, this is still a fuck.

"Damn it, Skye. Going to come. Going to come in your mouth. Fuck!" He rams into me and pulses as he releases.

I suppress the choke as best I can and take it. I take it all. All of him. All of Braden.

I ease my mouth away when he's done and inhale a much-needed breath. A few minutes later, he adjusts his underwear and pants. Then he pulls me to my feet.

"I needed that," he says. "I'm aware of your needs, too, Skye. We were interrupted last night. You'll get your reward. Anticipation makes it better."

I nod, my core throbbing as I force myself not to look down at the book still on the floor.

"I'm sorry for being nosy," I say.

"No apology necessary. If I wanted to keep you out of this room, I would've locked it."

"Okay. Good."

"So what do you think? Of the book."

"Honestly? It's amazing. The photography, I mean."

"I appreciate that, but I'm not asking you your opinion as a photographer. What do you think of the subject?"

I bite my lip. "I'm not sure."

"You're hedging."

"Braden, I'm not."

"You were playing with your nipple when I walked in

here, Skye. You were turned on."

"I admit that. That doesn't mean I'm sure about the subject matter."

"Fair enough," he says.

"Do you...do that?"

He lifts his eyebrows. "Practice bondage? You already know the answer to that question. I've bound you many times."

"Not like in the book."

"Of course not. The bondage in that book is not for beginners."

"I get that. I know I'm a beginner. But just how far advanced in this bondage have you gone?"

He gives me a half smile. "I can say this. I haven't tried *everything* in that book."

"The book is an inch thick, Braden. I'm not sure anyone has tried everything in there. You know what I'm asking."

"Do you want to tell me every detail about your previous dalliances?"

"There's not much to tell, but if you want to know, sure."

"I'll tell you this much, Skye. From the first time I saw you, embarrassed by a condom, your cheeks and chest red and your full lips parted in that way that drives me slowly to burning passion, I imagined you bound intricately for my pleasure."

I gulp. Loudly.

"Surely that doesn't surprise you."

Does it? I'm not sure.

"You like the idea. Your chest got noticeably pinker when I said the words."

He's not wrong. And I only saw two pictures. What other delicacies lie between the pages of that book?

"Is this what you meant when you talked about the part

of your lifestyle that stays here in Manhattan?"

"Partially."

"Why? Why only here?"

"I've told you. I'm too close to Boston. My father lives there. My mother…"

His mother. The mother he never talks about.

"What about your mother?"

"Nothing."

I don't push it. He's exhausted and needs to sleep. Not the time to get into a heavy discussion that he'll fight me on.

"Your private life is your private life, Braden. You should be able to enjoy it wherever you are."

"I do enjoy my private life in Boston. You of all people should know that."

"What do you do here, then? What does Manhattan have that Boston doesn't?"

"You'll see. Soon."

Chapter Twenty-Eight

While Braden got some much-deserved sleep—or so he said; I can't imagine him sleeping in the middle of the day—he sent me out in a limo with a personal shopper. A few hours later, without looking at a single price tag and posting on Instagram twice, I'm the proud owner of a beautiful wardrobe for my meeting with Susanne Cosmetics.

The price tag thing bugs me. Apparently, Manhattan's finest retailers don't believe in them, and when I attempted to ask, the personal shopper—a lovely older woman named Mandy—shushed me.

I eye the bags and boxes as the driver deposits them in the trunk of the limo. Exactly how much of Braden's money did I spend? At least a grand, and probably much more. The Chanel bag was probably a thousand dollars by itself.

I've never spent a hundred dollars on a bag, let alone a thousand.

I scramble into the back of the limo next to Mandy.

"Your new clothes are lovely," she says. "Mr. Black will be pleased."

"Isn't it more important that I'm pleased?" I can't help asking.

"Of course. That goes without saying. But you've already said you like the items."

I nod. I love the items, in fact. Everything we purchased is both professional and extremely flattering.

And ridiculously expensive.

I'll look better for this meeting with Eugenie than I ever imagined. Which reminds me. I forgot to call Tessa and tell her our shopping spree is off. It's nearly five p.m., and I haven't even checked my phone.

As I suspected, two texts and two phone calls from Tessa await me. I hastily call her back.

"Skye! Where are you? I've been worried sick."

"I'm so sorry. Braden had to fly to New York in the middle of the night last night, and I came with him so I'd be here for my meeting tomorrow. I've been exhausted, and I forgot we were supposed to go shopping today."

"You couldn't be bothered to send a text?"

"Seriously, it was the middle of the night, Tess. I just wasn't thinking, and I'm really sorry."

"Okay. I guess I understand," she says, her tone weakening.

But she doesn't. I hear it in her voice. It's not like me to blow her off, and she knows it. Consequently, I feel like complete shit, especially since I did two posts during the shopping spree that Tessa clearly hasn't seen yet.

"I'll make this up to you. The next time you ask me to go shopping, I won't whine." I force out a laugh.

"What are you going to wear tomorrow, then? In the middle of the night, you probably didn't even think about packing."

"Braden sent me out today with a personal shopper. I'm set."

"A personal shopper? I've been replaced?" She laughs, but like mine, I can tell it's forced.

She's feeling distant, and I can't blame her. I'm not sure what to say. My life has taken a drastic turn, but she's still my best friend and she always will be.

"Look, Tess—"

"It's okay. I get it."

"I had to go with Braden. He had already canceled my other flight, and I didn't want to take a train."

"You don't have to explain yourself, Skye. I said I get it. If my billionaire boyfriend wanted to whisk me away on a jet in the middle of the night, I'd go, too."

I believe she understands. I also believe she would have gone. Still, I feel like a shithead. A good friend would have called her and let her know.

"I know you understand, Tess. That's not the point. I'm not sorry I went. I'm sorry I didn't call you and let you know. That was shitty of me. Please accept my apology."

A few seconds pass before she says, "Of course I accept your apology. Did your personal shopper get you something nice to wear tomorrow?"

"Yes, but she's not as good as you are."

Tessa scoffs. "A professional personal shopper? I'm sure she's much better than I am."

"Are you kidding? You'd have had me looking like a million bucks for about a hundredth of the money she spent."

Finally, Tessa laughs. A real laugh. I think. "You got that right."

I sigh in relief. We seem to be friends again.

"Take a selfie," she says. "I want to see your new duds."

"I will. Tomorrow before my meeting."

"Is Braden going with you to Susanne headquarters?"

"Originally he planned to, but now, with this contract

emergency—that's the reason we had to fly here in the middle of the night—I'm not sure he'll be available."

I'll be on my own. The thought both exhilarates and petrifies me. I want to handle my career on my own, but to be honest, the thought of Braden being there gave me some strength. Now I'll have to find that strength on my own.

I'm a professional. I can handle a business meeting. Yes, I can handle a business meeting with a top cosmetics company in Manhattan. Why not?

"You got this, Skye," Tessa says, as if sensing my apprehension.

I clear my throat. "Yeah. I suppose so. Of course, whether I've got this or not really doesn't matter. I have a meeting tomorrow."

"You'll kill it. No doubt in my mind."

I smile into the phone. "Thanks, Tess. For always being in my corner."

"Besties forever," she says. "Call me after the meeting, okay?"

"I will. Thanks again for understanding."

"Always. Talk to you tomorrow."

I end the call.

And I still feel like a heel. My relationship with Braden can*not* interfere with my relationship with Tessa. I'll never leave her behind, and I already sense that's what she fears. Tessa is beautiful and outgoing and has a large circle of friends. Still, she and I have something special, something unique. A closeness that thrives despite our differences.

I can't—I won't—give that up.

Chapter Twenty-Nine

We arrive at Gabriel LeGrand, one of Manhattan's finest restaurants, and the maître d' leads us to an exclusive table. A votive candle flutters in the center.

Braden gestures to it. "Take that away."

"Of course, sir." The maître d' picks up the candle holder. "Seth will be with you shortly."

The chef himself has created a menu for us. I can't begin to imagine what it's costing Braden, but it's delicious so far, and I'm only on my salad. Our amuse-bouche—a pre-appetizer, who knew there was such a thing?—was a rye toast point with avocado and caviar. First time I've ever tried caviar, and it won't be the last. It was briny and delicious, better than the best oyster from the northeastern shores.

My first amuse-bouche! Rye toast point with avocado and caviar. Delish! #veryamusingtomybouche #caviarrocks #gabriellegrandmanhattan

Our appetizer was oysters Rockefeller with the chef's own twist. Instead of the usual parsley, the chef used lemongrass and cilantro, which gave the dish a delicious tanginess.

Now we're enjoying our salad of heirloom tomatoes, baby greens, slivered roasted almonds, and a house-made champagne vinaigrette.

"I have a surprise for you," Braden says.

I swallow my bite. "Oh?"

"Yes, but not tonight. I want you to get a good night's sleep for tomorrow's meeting."

"And this surprise necessitates that I *not* get a good night's sleep?"

"Oh, you'll sleep. But you may be a little…sore afterward. That's why it will wait until tomorrow evening."

I clear my throat, both fearing and anticipating what he might mean. "Sore?"

He raises an eyebrow. Just one. "Not anal sex, Skye. Not until you're ready."

I let out a breath I didn't realize I was holding. "Okay. Good. Why will I be sore, then?"

"You'll see."

"Braden…"

He lays his salad fork on his empty plate. "Nothing will happen without your express permission, Skye."

I push my salad plate forward, having only finished half. "I know, but about that… Maybe this isn't the best time to be introducing me to this other lifestyle of yours. I'm here on business, Braden."

"As am I."

True. That's why we left in the middle of the night. I'm interested in his business, so I need to make that clear. "Right. That reminds me. How's your contract going?"

"I don't have to fly to China, if that's what you're asking."

"Good. I mean, that's good, right?" I lift my eyebrows.

"Definitely good. I don't like being the visiting team."

I nod.

"You're changing the subject," he says.

I laugh nervously. "Guilty. But I am interested in what you do. I'd like to learn more about it eventually."

"You will."

"Are you planning to go to my meeting tomorrow?"

"Ah. And you were hoping my business would keep me busy."

I clear my throat. "I can't deny having you there would make me less nervous, but it's *my* meeting, Braden." True words. This is my budding career, and I need to find my own strength.

"I understand that. I've always understood that. I'm simply offering my business expertise. I've been in business a lot longer than you have."

"But they're expecting me. Not me and you. You'll intimidate them."

"And that's a bad thing?"

"Yeah, it is. I want to do this myself. I want them to want *me*, not Braden Black's girlfriend."

I nearly choke on the irony of the words. The only reason I'm a budding influencer is because of my connection to the man sitting across from me. I know that, and so does he.

"As you wish," he says. "I still have a lot of business I can attend to. A limo will pick you up outside the building at nine a.m. sharp. You'll have plenty of time to get to your ten thirty meeting."

"Thank you. I appreciate it."

"Not at all. I want your success, Skye. As much as you do."

Does he? I meet his gaze, and although Braden is usually unreadable, I read sincerity now. He *does* want my success. He's not intimidated by anyone's success, certainly not mine, which I haven't even achieved yet. No one intimidates Braden.

No one. Not even the richest person on earth.

I have a lot to learn from him. A *lot*.

I'll go into that meeting tomorrow armed with my own strength. Not Braden's or anyone else's.

I bite my lip.

I just hope I can do it.

Our server clears our salad plates and refills our wineglasses. "Your entrees will be out in a few minutes, Mr. Black."

"Thank you, Seth."

"Is there anything I can get you in the meantime?"

Braden glances at me. "Skye?"

"Nothing," I say. "Everything has been wonderful so far."

"I'll tell the chef you're pleased. Mr. Black?"

"Excellent, as always," Braden says. "We're looking forward to tonight's creation."

Seth smiles and leaves our table.

Braden takes a sip of red wine. "So…about tomorrow evening. I'm sure we'll be celebrating."

"Celebrating what?" I ask.

"Your new deal with Susanne, of course."

"Oh. Yeah." My cheeks warm.

"Dinner in, I think, and then…my surprise."

"O…kay."

"You'll enjoy it, Skye. I'm certain."

"How can you be certain if I don't have a clue what you're talking about?"

"Let's just say I know you."

"We haven't been together very long."

"True. But you've given me your control in the bedroom, so you must trust that I know how to please you."

He's been stingy with orgasms lately, but I can't deny he pleases me with or without release. I take a drink of wine, letting its tannins coat my throat. Smooth, dry, and delicious. A premier cru Bordeaux that Braden ordered. Supple and elegant. Already I've learned so much from this man. How to enjoy a fine wine, for instance.

How to let go in the bedroom.

Skye Manning, aged twenty-four. So young and innocent and naive.

No longer.

The innocent and naive part, anyway. I'm still pretty young.

"You said earlier that I wasn't ready for this part of your... lifestyle."

"I did. Then this morning happened."

I cock my head. "What happened this morning?"

His blue eyes smolder. "I saw you engrossed in a book in my library, touching yourself as you stared at the photographs."

My cheeks warm further. And not from the wine.

"You're a photographer, Skye, but let me ask you this. Do you like being the subject of photographs?"

"I don't mind if I look good. After all, this new career as an influencer means I need to take selfies."

"What about being photographed by someone else?"

"I'm okay with it. Like I said, if I look good."

"You have a beautiful body, Skye. May I take pictures of you?"

I raise my eyebrows and smile. "I had no idea you might like to take pictures."

"Photography is a hobby. I'm not remotely as good as you are."

A hobby? I should have guessed, given he knew exactly

what camera to buy for me. "I'm just beginning my career."

"But you studied the art. I haven't done that, other than read a few books."

"What exactly are you asking, Braden?"

He lowers his eyelids slightly. "I'm asking if I can take a photograph of you. A photograph of you nude. After I tie you up."

Chapter Thirty

I keep my expression as deliberate as I can, resisting the urge to drop my mouth open. I take another sip of wine, only to draw the time out a little bit.

Then, "I don't know."

"The photographs would only be for your eyes and mine."

I can't stop a nervous giggle. "I certainly won't be posting them on my account."

"It would be a sure guarantee to increase your following a hundred-fold."

Braden's voice is even-toned, as usual. I almost think he's serious.

"Is that the surprise? You're going to tie me up and take a picture?"

"I didn't say that."

"What, then? What's the surprise?" I smile, knowing full well he won't divulge the secret.

He chuckles. "If I tell you, it won't be a surprise. Nice try, though."

Seth returns with our entrees. "Filet mignon au poivre

with a hickory béarnaise sauce on the side. Zucchini blossoms a l'orange and gratiné of Yukon Gold potatoes and asiago cheese."

I inhale the savory aroma, but my hunger has dissipated. For food, at least.

All I can think of is Braden tying me up in one of those intricate ways and then taking my photo.

And after that?

Fucking me senseless.

Braden cuts a bite of his filet, brings it to his mouth, chews, and swallows. "Delicious. Aren't you going to try your dinner?"

I say nothing. Simply cut into my steak and bring a bite to my mouth. It's tender and flavorful, but I can't taste it. Not when I'm thinking about being bound in such an artistic and seductive way.

We don't talk much, and soon Braden has cleaned his plate. I've taken all of about five bites.

"You aren't enjoying your dinner?" he says.

"It's wonderful. I'm just..."

His lips edge upward. "Contemplating?"

I nod.

"Does the idea turn you on?"

I nod again.

"Eat, then. You'll need a lot of energy."

"But you said—"

"I know what I said. I won't be introducing you to anything new tonight, not when you have an important meeting first thing tomorrow. You'll still need energy for this evening, however."

I warm all over as tingles shoot through me.

Tonight.

I clean my plate.

Dessert turns out to be chocolate-orange mousse. By now I'm no longer hungry, and Braden asks Seth to wrap up our desserts for us.

"Please give Gabriel my compliments," Braden says as he signs the credit card statement and hands it to Seth. "Everything was spectacular."

"I'm delighted you enjoyed it, sir." Seth bows, taking the receipt, and leaves the table.

"Ready, Skye?" Braden asks.

I'm ready, all right.

Good and wet and ready.

Braden's bedroom in this Manhattan penthouse is different from his bedroom in Boston. It's more minimal. No wardrobe holding exquisite toys. No weird little notches on the headboard where he can hook ropes and cuffs. No spackle on the ceiling from a suspension device.

Indeed, it seems almost normal, which confuses me.

What kind of lifestyle does he practice here? In this vanilla bedroom?

I'm excited to find out.

Except he already told me that I won't find out tonight.

"Strip for me, Skye," he says, his eyes smoldering.

I nod and peel off my garments, one by one, slowly and seductively. I get wetter each time a piece of clothing hits the floor.

He is, of course, still dressed.

"I won't bind you to the headboard tonight," he says, "but I want you to grab two rungs and keep your hands there, as if you *are* bound. Can you do that?"

"Yes." I lie down and grab two rungs, my palms already perspiring.

"I haven't forgotten, Skye," he says.

"Forgotten what?"

His lips curve slyly upward. "That I've denied you orgasms the last few days."

My body throbs. Does this mean…?

"Lift your hips," he says.

I obey, and he shoves a pillow under my ass.

"Now spread your legs."

I obey once more.

"Mmm. Beautiful." He sucks in a breath. "Beautiful and always so ready."

"So ready," I echo.

"No more talking. Close your eyes and your ears. I want you to feel tonight, Skye. Feel everything I do to you."

I close my eyes and nod.

"I'm going to eat you, finger you, fuck you, make you come again and again until you think you can't come anymore. And then you're going to come again. I'm going to coax ten orgasms out of you tonight. Ten, maybe twelve, maybe fifteen. You're going to be fucking exhausted when I'm through."

I gasp at his words. I'm ready. So ready.

He sucks in another breath. "You have no idea what you do to me. No idea how just looking at you, bound only by the strength of my will, legs spread, ready for anything, makes me wild with desire for you. No woman has ever gotten under my skin the way you have."

I part my lips.

He sucks in a third breath. "Your mouth. Your lips. Fuck."

I'm desperate for a kiss, but he denies me. He's going straight in for the kill.

He caresses the lips of my pussy.

"So slick and wet already. I can't wait to taste you. To shove my tongue deep inside you."

God, please.

He continues with his fingers, sliding them over and around my labia and then down to my asshole.

I tense for a second.

"Easy, baby. Relax."

I attempt to obey him, and I find myself relaxing as he massages my anus.

"I can't wait to take you here," he says. "And tonight, we'll begin that journey."

I tense again.

"Relax," he soothes. "You'll be ready for what I do tonight. More than ready." He circles my asshole with one finger. Then he positions his head between my legs and kisses my inner thighs. "Such a good position. I can see everything from here. Every luscious part of your pussy and your ass."

He tongues my ass then, and I jerk at the attempted invasion.

"Easy. Let it go, Skye. Let your inhibitions go. You gave me control here. Remember?"

I remember.

I relax beneath him. He told me to feel, so I feel.

And it's amazing.

His tongue is soft as it massages me but then firm when he tenses it into a point and probes the tight hole.

Relax.

Feel.

Still holding onto the rungs, I force my nerves to settle.

Braden swipes his tongue over my pussy and up to my clit, where he tenses it again and pushes against the sensitive button. I'm ready. So ready.

He probes my clit a few more times and then relaxes his tongue and swirls the tip around me. I'm so sensitive. One little movement and—

One of his long, thick fingers eases into me. "Mmm. Tight," he says.

He moves the fingers slowly, touching every spot inside my pussy. It's a dreamy feeling. He's helping me relax.

"I'm going to put a finger in your ass," he says, his voice low and hypnotic. "Just relax."

His finger in my pussy is still moving in and out in a slow and deliberate pattern. His lips are around my clit, sucking gently, and I move my hips in circles, following his lips.

I'm relaxed.

And turned on.

And ready for anything—

"Ah!" I squeal.

Braden's finger is in my ass.

"Easy. Relax. You'll like this. I promise."

I already do. I like it because it's Braden inside me. Braden can do anything to me. I've given him my control, and I know he won't abuse it.

He adds another finger to my pussy and licks my clit.

Then…he begins to move the finger in my ass in and out slowly, in the opposite rhythm from the fingers in my pussy.

Pussy full and then ass full.

Clit licked and sucked.

And oh my God…

I need to come. I need to come so badly.

Do I wait for permission?

"Come, Skye," he says against my clit.

And I shatter. Everything. Everything and nothing all around me and all at once.

He probes my pussy and my ass, and with each probe, I soar higher and higher.

"That's right, baby. Come for me. Come all over my face."

He thrusts harder into my ass, and I find, to my amazement, that it's thrilling. Ecstatically thrilling.

I *feel.*

I feel so much.

"Come again," he orders.

I fly into another orgasm, a third and then a fourth. They roll through me, coiling into my belly and then bursting outward, sending sparks flying from my fingertips.

A fifth.

A sixth.

A... I lose count. They roll through me one after the other. One subsides and another begins. Up. Down. Up. Down.

"One more, Skye." He fingers me relentlessly, touching the spot that drives me insane.

I can't do it. Can't give him one more—

But I do. I explode again as shards of electricity blaze through me.

"Again," he commands.

I can't. I know I can't. I'm used up. Beautifully used up.

Then Braden growls. He truly growls.

And I give him one last orgasm.

It shoots through me like boiling honey in my veins. I cry out unintelligible words. I undulate violently. I grind against his face and mouth.

I soar and I soar and I soar, Braden still fingering me, still sucking me.

Until finally he releases me, moves backward slightly, and gently eases his fingers out of me.

I sink into the bed, still holding on to the rungs of the

headboard. I want to let go, but I can't. Braden's will over me is that strong.

That controlling.

Somewhere in a haze around me, I'm vaguely aware of Braden undressing. I don't see or hear him. I just know.

Then his cock is in my pussy, and he's thrusting, thrusting, thrusting…

Again and again and again, against my sensitive clit and plowing into my tight pussy.

I'm spent, completely spent.

Braden can do anything to me at this point. Anything, and I'll let him. If he wants my ass tonight, he can take it.

Any-fucking-thing.

Still he thrusts, and still I lie, open to him with my hands gripping the rungs.

"So hot," he says through gritted teeth. "Want you so much. Fuck!"

He rams into me, releasing.

So sensitive am I from all those orgasms, I feel every spurt of his cock inside me.

I feel.

I fucking *feel*.

Chapter Thirty-One

The next morning, I step out of the shower into the warm bath sheet Braden provides.

"Why didn't you join me?" I ask.

"Because we both have work to do today." He rubs the towel over my dripping body. "And if I had joined you, we'd be spending the morning in bed."

I smile. Sounds amazing, but he's right. My meeting with Susanne is important, and whatever he's working on is also important.

"I do have one surprise for you today, though," he says, his eyes afire.

My heart skips a beat. "What's that?"

He pulls a stainless steel object out of his pocket. "This."

My eyes widen. I know what it is. He used something similar to titillate my body a while ago. Only he didn't put it where it's meant to go.

"A butt plug," I say.

"That's right. You're going to wear this to your interview."

"The hell I am." I whip my hands to my hips, letting the

bath sheet fall to the tile floor.

"Oh, you are," he says. "You want to know why?"

"Please. Enlighten me."

"Because it will remind you of me. Every time you find yourself wondering what to say or how to act, this will remind you that I'm with you, and you'll know exactly what to do."

"It's not a *magic* butt plug, Braden."

His lips curve into that semi-smile I've grown so fond of. "It has its own kind of magic. It will remind you of my control over you, which in turn will remind you of your control over your career."

Is that really why he wants me to wear it? Or does he just want to think of me with a butt plug in my ass while I'm attending the most important meeting of my life?

Doesn't matter.

I already know I'll wear it, and so does he. I see it in his eyes.

He hands it to me. "Look at it. Feel its weight."

I examine the toy. It's the shape of a small light bulb with a pink jewel on the end—the part that will show from my ass. It's heavier than I expect, but not so heavy that it will hinder me.

It's pretty in a strange kind of way.

Braden pulls out a plastic bottle. "Water-based lubricant," he says, "to help it go in."

He stands over one of the sinks and squeezes a bit of lube onto the toy. He smooths it over the bulb with his fingers. "Ready?"

Am I?

It doesn't really matter.

"Bend over," he says. "Show me that gorgeous ass."

I obey, gripping the edge of the countertop.

He probes my ass with the slick tip of the plug.

"Relax."

I try.

"I'm going to slide the tip in. Breathe."

I wince slightly at the invasion, but once it's in and the thinner part between the bulb and the jewel rests against my rim, I relax.

It feels...interesting.

But not bad. Not bad at all.

"This will remind you who you are, Skye, as you embark on this new career. It will remind you that you're mine and that I believe in you."

"What will it remind *you* of?" I ask.

"It reminds me that I'm going to claim that ass soon." He gazes into my eyes. "*Very* soon."

I'm dressed to the nines in designer clothing. A Ralph Lauren double-breasted charcoal-gray suit and an Ann Taylor creamy silk blouse. My Chanel handbag and a pair of classic black leather Jimmy Choo pumps complete my ensemble. On my lips, of course, is Susanne Cherry Russet lip stain, perfect for any occasion—especially meeting with a Susanne executive.

After sending Tessa the promised selfie and doing a quick Instagram post, I take a moment to breathe deeply before I enter the gigantic skyscraper in Manhattan where Susanne Corporate is housed. I stop at security in the lobby.

"Good morning. I have an appointment with Eugenie Blake at Susanne Cosmetics."

"Name?"

"Skye Manning."

"All right. Sign in here, and I'll need to see your driver's license."

I pull my wallet out of my purse and remove my license. "Here you go."

"Thank you."

A moment later, I have a "visitor" name tag complete with my license photo, which of course sucks.

"Twenty-seventh floor," the receptionist says. "Elevators are down the hall to the right."

"Thank you."

I'm constantly aware of the butt plug, which makes me constantly aware of Braden.

And it helps to have him with me today.

It helps a lot.

I walk to the elevator, each step nudging the plug in my ass.

I smile as I push the up button.

I smile when I enter the elevator and push number twenty-seven.

I smile when I leave the elevator and walk toward the glass doors with the Susanne logo displayed prominently.

I can't stop fucking smiling!

All because of a butt plug.

Until—

My smile fades in a microsecond as I see who's chatting with the receptionist.

Addie.

Addison Ames is here.

And she's talking to the receptionist—the receptionist *I* have to check in with.

There's no avoiding her.

Fuck.

Chapter Thirty-Two

Braden's anal plug reminds me to walk tall. This is *my* meeting. Not Addie's or anyone else's.

I stride toward the reception desk, my head held high.

"Good morning," I say.

The receptionist turns away from Addie. "Yes, may I help you?"

"I'm Skye Manning. I'm here to see Eugenie."

"I guess that's my cue," Addie says, smiling. "See you soon, Lisa. Skye, nice to see you."

I meet her saccharine smile with what I hope looks like a genuine one. "Always a pleasure."

Addie wants to say something snide. It's killing her that she can't in front of Lisa.

I'm enjoying every minute of it.

Addie leaves through the transparent door and heads to the elevator.

"Do you know Addison?" Lisa asks.

"I used to work for her," I say.

"Lucky you! She's amazing, isn't she?"

She's a conniving bitch. "Oh, yes. Amazing. That's the word for her."

"Go ahead and have a seat. Eugenie is expecting you. I'll let her know you're here."

I nod and take a seat on one of the plush chairs in the large waiting area, ever aware of the invasion in my ass. I help myself to a small bottle of water. Won't hurt to ease the dryness in my throat. I feel like I swallowed a mouthful of sawdust.

My phone dings with a text.

Nice try. A Chanel handbag and Prada pumps don't make you me.

Addison.

Just when I wonder if it's possible to dislike her more than I already do, she always surprises me.

And my pumps are Jimmy Choo, not Prada. So much for her great influencing. Not that I can tell Prada from Jimmy, either, but then I wasn't born with a silver spoon up my ass.

I'm tempted to take a quick selfie and post about the fact that I'm sitting at Susanne Corporate, but I don't. That would be truly unprofessional. I'd only be doing it to show off, and that's not me.

God, Addie brings out the worst in me.

Ding!

Another text.

I roll my eyes and look at my screen.

That butt plug doesn't, either.

What the fuck?

First she knew about the nipple clamps at the gala and now this? Does she truly know Braden's MO that well? More than a decade has passed since they were together. What isn't Braden telling me?

Damn. I promised I'd leave this alone. So Addie knows

I'm wearing a butt plug. So what? Maybe I'm walking funny.

Except I'm not. At least I don't think I am.

If Braden is telling the truth, and they were over a long time ago, then she knows his MO for one of two reasons. He either did the same thing with her long ago, or she's still stalking him and knows his MO with women.

Which means he's doing the same thing with me as he's done with others.

It shouldn't bother me.

But it does.

Then I realize... This is exactly what Addie wants. She wants to knock me off my game. It's a mind fuck.

I'm not going to let her win.

"Skye."

I look up from my phone.

Eugenie stands in front of me, tall and graceful, her graying hair cut in a pixie Jamie Lee Curtis style. She's composed and elegant. The epitome of what an older executive woman should look like, at least in my mind.

Braden's plug reminds me why I'm here. I stand and meet her gaze. Sort of. She's taller than I am, so I have to look up.

Eugenie holds out her hand. "You're even prettier in person."

My cheeks warm, and I take her hand and shake it firmly. "As are you. So nice to finally meet you."

"Come on back. I have some of the marketing team ready in the conference room. We're all very excited to talk to you about what we have planned."

Are you still working with Addison?

I desperately want to ask, but I can't. It's childish and unprofessional. So what if they're working with her? What do I care, as long as they work with me? Addie still has a much greater following than I do.

We enter a conference room where three other people already sit. "Skye, I'd like you to meet Shaylie Morse, Brian Kent, and Louisa Maine. Shaylie and Brian are members of my social media marketing team, and Louisa is interning with us. She's a student at Columbia."

"Great to meet you all," I say, trying my hardest not to stammer.

"Come, sit." Eugenie gestures. "We have tons to talk about."

I sit down, resisting the urge to squirm against Braden's butt plug.

"Shaylie," Eugenie says, "why don't you outline our plan for Skye?"

Shaylie, a pretty redhead who wears heart-shaped glasses—yes, I'm serious—fires up her laptop, and an image appears from the projector onto the white dry-erase board. "Skye, we're excited to have you on board for several reasons. First, you know the business, having worked with Addison Ames. Second, your skill as a photographer is excellent, and your copy is always intriguing as well. And third—"

She doesn't have to say it. I know already.

"The fact that you're dating Braden Black has made you an instant celebrity."

Of course it has.

My skill as a photographer and copywriter means nothing next to my affiliation with Braden.

I smile, trying not to show my disappointment.

Why should I be disappointed, anyway? I already knew this.

"You have a natural beauty," Shaylie continues. "You're approachable."

In other words, I'm average.

I keep the smile pasted on my face.

"You have a lovely figure, as well. You're not supermodel thin—"

Gee. Thanks for pointing that out.

"But you'll look good in many different kinds of fashions."

I must seem confused, because she stops.

"Do you have a question, Skye?"

I clear my throat. "I do. You're a cosmetics company. Why would the way I look in clothing have anything to do with my posts? Aren't you concerned with what my makeup looks like?"

She laughs lightly. Is she laughing at me? I'm not sure.

"Fashion is related to all marketing," Shaylie says, her tone only slightly condescending. "The better you look in all areas, the more the masses will rely on you for advice."

Am I supposed to know that? I'm a photographer, not a marketing expert.

But I need to be. I need to be a marketing expert if I'm going to be an influencer. Influencing *is* marketing.

I almost hear those words in Braden's voice, as if he planted them in my head.

Again, I resist squirming against the jewel in my ass.

I worked with Addie for more than a year. She was always dressed to the nines. At the time, I figured she wore expensive clothing because she was rich and could afford it. That was probably part of the case, but perhaps she dressed fashionably for her business as well.

How many times have I posted while dressed in old jeans and a tank? Granted, I never posted if I looked like crap, but still…

Big problem, though. I can't afford the kinds of clothes Addie wears. Which is not apparent from the clothes I'm currently wearing.

Shaylie continues, "We're looking for a way to make our products more accessible to the common person."

Common person. Not a hotel heiress. A regular working girl.

Skye Manning, average working girl.

Great.

"We've devised a campaign for you to introduce and promote our new line of Susanne Cosmetics. It will be called Susie Girl by Susanne, and the products will be available in pharmacies and big-box stores like Walmart and Target."

"But—"

"This is a wonderful opportunity, Skye," Eugenie interrupts. "We're making our brand available to the masses, and we think you're just the face for this launch."

"I'm honored," I say, hoping I sound sincere, "but you said my posts for the Cherry Russet lip stain were successful."

"And they were. Very successful. We're happy to have you continue with them, but you stand to make a lot more money with this new opportunity. We have other ways to promote our luxury line."

Other ways. Addison Ames.

That's why she was here.

A lump fills my throat. What did I expect? I'm a nobody.

"This is something you can do that no one else can," Shaylie goes on. "You're a fresh face. And you're the girlfriend of our country's most famous blue-collar billionaire, a man who personifies the American dream. That's what this Instagram campaign is about. Anyone can find and afford Susanne Cosmetics."

Making the American dream all about cosmetics? That's a new one. What will Braden think?

"That's the general idea. I'll turn it over to Brian now, and he'll explain our compensation plan."

Brian, a young man with a receding blond hairline and dark-blue eyes, begins his presentation on the projector.

"The Susie line has been in the works for a couple of years," he begins. "Originally, we were planning a huge magazine ad and television ad launch with limited social media advertising"—he smiles—"and then you came along."

I widen my eyes.

"Does that surprise you?" he asks.

"Of course it does."

"We have a lot of confidence in you, Skye," Brian says. "You have the look of America's sweetheart."

He means Braden Black's sweetheart, but whatever.

"Surely you're not pinning this entire campaign on me," I say.

"Of course not. We're still doing the television and magazine marketing. But we've added a large social media component to our plan. For you."

"I'm…honored." I guess.

"Let me outline the compensation plan," Brian says. "I think you'll be very happy with it." A spreadsheet appears on the screen. "Susie Girl features a skin-care line as well as a cosmetics line. A hair-care line is in the works."

"Hair care?" I ask.

"Yes. It's a new venture for us, but if Susie is a success, we want to add premium salon-quality hair-care products at a bargain price."

"I see."

"We'll begin the launch with three posts per week featuring cosmetics and skin-care products. You'll be compensated at four thousand dollars per week while under contract, plus—and this is where you can make some real money—one cent per like on each post, an additional cent for each comment, and five cents for each sale we can trace back to your post."

"How can you possibly trace sales to my post?"

"It's a complicated algorithm. I can explain it if you'd like, but it's outlined in the prospectus." He nods toward the document sitting in front of me, which I only now notice.

I really wish Braden were here. He'd understand all of this.

"That's not necessary," I say. Braden can look at the prospectus and explain it to me later.

"When Shaylie talked about fashion," Brian continues, "she didn't mean you need to be wearing designer clothing. We're marketing to the masses. All we care about is that you wear something different each day and that you look fresh and polished. Jeans are fine as long as they're not ripped or too faded. We want to appeal to all walks of life. Some days you should wear business clothing, like what you have on today. Other days, go casual. Workout clothes are fine as well. If you're shooting at a beach, wear a swimsuit."

I nod.

"Don't hesitate to get personal," he says. "Your post wearing a sheet like a toga was wildly successful."

My cheeks warm. I posted that from Braden's bedroom in Boston. Did they know that? How could they not? The harbor was in the background.

"The reason Instagram influencing works," Brian says, "is because your followers feel like they're getting to know *you*. They talk to you via your account, and they get excited if you respond. They'll take advice from a friend more than a stranger on TV. You are the perfect friend, Skye."

I clear my throat. "How soon do I need to let you know?"

"About what?"

"About whether I want to do this?"

"Skye," Eugenie said, "this is a huge opportunity."

"I know it is, and I appreciate it, but I don't sign anything without having an attorney review it."

Eugenie smiles. She knows. She knows Braden will review it. "The launch is scheduled for next week," she says. "If you could let us know within twenty-four hours, we'd appreciate it."

I nod. "I can do that. Thank you."

"If you'll open your prospectus to page four," Brian says, "I'll take you through the proposed schedule."

Chapter Thirty-Three

"It's a good deal," Braden says, closing the prospectus. "You already get about ten thousand likes now, which will earn you a hundred per post. Three posts a week to start—that's three hundred plus the four grand they pay you per week under the contract. Add in the extra for comments and sales... Plus the number of likes and comments will go up as you gain more of a following."

"It's a drugstore line of cosmetics, Braden."

"So what?"

"They want people like Addie for their luxury line."

"Who cares why they want Addie? She's not your concern."

"It's like Addie's the Dom Pérignon and I'm the André Cold Duck."

He laughs. "Maybe a more apt metaphor would be that Addie's the Pappy Van Winkle's fifteen year and you're the Wild Turkey?"

I smile. "When you put it that way..."

"Skye, you're not average. You aren't now and you never

were. Do you really think I'd choose someone average to be my girlfriend?"

"That's not the point," I say.

"It's exactly the point. You're not Addison Ames, and from where I'm standing, that's a good thing. This is an incredible opportunity. They're unveiling a line of brand-new products, and they want you to help launch them."

"What if they flop?"

"What if they do? You're under contract, and the contract guarantees you your base pay of four thousand dollars per week for three months. That's roughly forty-eight grand. You'll still make more money than you ever have, gain more of a following, and come out smelling like a rose."

"Why didn't they just get Addie or someone else with a huge following?"

"Because they want you."

"Because of you. They tried to tell me I'm selling the American dream. Apparently, the American dream is cheap cosmetics and being Braden Black's girlfriend."

"Okay, their sales pitch may leave something to be desired. I'll grant you that. But they want you because you're *not* Addie. That's pretty clear."

I pause a moment. Then, "Addie was there. At Susanne Corporate."

"When?"

"This morning. She was leaving as I got there."

"So?"

"So…she knew about the butt plug, Braden." I squirm.

He wrinkles his forehead. Only slightly, but I notice.

"What do you mean?" he asks.

"She texted me." I quickly show him the texts. "She knew about the nipple clamps at the gala as well. How does she know all this? Did you use the same things on her?"

"What I did with her isn't up for discussion."

"But—"

"Damn it, Skye." He throws the prospectus down onto the table. "We've been through this. You have to let it go."

"It'd be a lot easier to let it go if she didn't know I was wearing a butt plug today."

"How could she have possibly known?"

"I don't know. You tell me."

He rakes his fingers through his hair. "Do you think *I* told her?"

"No. Of course not. I just don't—"

"I've already told you I won't discuss her with you. Why do you keep bringing it up? Is this what you want? To fight?"

"I don't want to fight. I just want to know how—"

"I don't know how she knows, Skye. Jesus Christ! Why do you even care? Block her fucking number on your phone, for God's sake!"

Huh. Good idea, and I'm not sure why I didn't think of it. Still—

"I see your mind working. Give this up. It doesn't matter. *She* doesn't matter."

I pull my phone out of my purse and let my finger hover over Addie's number, poised to block it. I should. No more snide texts from her. She could still email me. Still comment on my posts. So really, what would this accomplish, other than feeling like I did something, no matter how small?

"I'm thinking," Braden says, "that this trip isn't the best time to introduce you to the other facets of my lifestyle."

My heart drops to my stomach. "Why not?"

"I'm not certain I have your complete trust, Skye, and trust is paramount for what I'll be introducing you to."

"You mean the bondage stuff? Like in the book?"

"That…and other things."

My body heats. I've been apprehensive, yes, but I want to know all of Braden. "Please. Don't keep this part of your life from me."

"I fear you're not ready. The fact that you haven't yet gotten over my involvement with Addison—"

No. No, no, *no*. Addie will *not* ruin this for me. I put my phone away without blocking her number. "I *am* ready."

He meets my gaze, his own blazing. "It's not all pretty."

"That's okay."

And it is. In fact, *not pretty* appeals to me at this moment.

He regards me sternly and completely, studying me as though he's trying to read something secret in my mind.

Except I have no secrets from Braden. He knows all of me. I wish I could say the same.

"Please," I say again, softly.

"Are you going to sign this contract?" he asks.

I nod. "If you think it's a good idea."

"I see nothing wrong with it. You come out fine even if the products tank."

I grab the contract and scribble my signature.

"I'll have a courier deliver this to Eugenie in the morning," he says.

"And...?" I ask.

"And what?"

"And...what about tonight? About..."

"All right, Skye. I'll show you."

But his demeanor is dark and indecisive, as if he's afraid he's making a mistake.

Chapter Thirty-Four

Braden's and my celebratory dinner is put on hold when Eugenie texts me, inviting us both to join her and her team at one of Braden's favorite restaurants. We arrive, and the maître d' leads us to their table, where they're already seated.

"Mr. Black," Eugenie says, standing, "Eugenie Blake. So nice to finally meet you."

"And you. Please call me Braden."

"Of course, Braden." She introduces Shaylie, Brian, and Louisa. "We're so excited to bring Skye on board."

"Nice to see all of you again," I say. "I've been reviewing the contract."

"Oh, no business tonight," she says. "This is a dinner for all of us to get to know one another better."

I smile. Sounds good to me. I've already signed anyway, but she doesn't need to know that yet. Let her try to woo me, if that's indeed what she's trying to do. I'm not sure of anything at the moment.

Eugenie fires question after question at Braden, which

irks me a little but doesn't surprise me. We all know why
I'm here.

Because of Braden.

You're a fraud.

Stop it!

I peruse the menu and settle on grilled tilapia. Braden
explained earlier that I need to be comfortable and not
overly full for this evening.

Eugenie and Braden dominate the conversation while
I sip water and nibble on a salad.

They dominate the conversation while I pick at my fish,
leaving more than half.

They dominate the conversation during after-dinner
coffee and cognac as well.

I've become invisible.

B ack at the penthouse, Braden hands me a garment bag.
"Put these on."

I take the bag from him. "Okay." I lay it on the bed and
unzip the vinyl. Inside is a corset, garter belt, lace thong, and
fishnet stockings. My eyes widen.

"I'll help you with the corset," he says. "I want it nice
and tight."

"O...kay." I peel my designer business clothes from my
body as I throb all over.

Braden removed the anal plug before dinner, and I feel
oddly naked without it. Perhaps I'd have felt less invisible at
dinner if I were still wearing it. Will he put it back in after
I'm dressed in these gorgeously sexy things?

He watches, his eyes heavy-lidded, as I don the thong,

the stockings, and I fasten them to the garter belt. He stands, heads to his closet, brings out a shoebox, and hands it to me.

I'm topless, and I open the shoebox. I gasp. Inside, against black tissue paper, lies a pair of platform stiletto sandals.

"Braden, I'll trip and—"

"Put them on," he commands.

I sit down on the bed and slide the shoes onto my feet, buckling them into place.

He groans low in his throat. "Stand. I'll help you with the corset."

I obey and adjust the corset over my breasts and abdomen.

"Turn," he says.

I comply, my back now to him.

"A corset is an amazing piece of clothing," he says as he laces it up the back. "It's sexy as hell, of course, but it's also a method of control. I can control how you look, the size of your waist." He tightens it, and I inhale sharply. "It's a type of bondage."

His words turn me on more than they should. "Braden…"

"Don't worry. You'll be able to breathe fine. Trust me. Besides, you won't wear this all night."

"Are you going to tie me up tonight?" I ask, anxious but excited. "Like in the book?"

"Maybe," he says, his breath a hot whisper against my neck. "You'll have to wait and see."

I look around the room. "It's different here. So bare. Do you have another room? Like in *Fifty Shades of Grey*?"

He chuckles. "Never read it."

"Oh."

"I think what you're asking me is whether I have a dungeon in this penthouse. The answer is no."

"Oh. Then where—"

"Quiet," he says harshly. "Your questions will be answered, but they'll be answered on my time."

He moves to his briefcase sitting on one of the chairs in the bedroom. He opens it and pulls something out. Then he turns back to me, holding a black velvet case. He opens it.

I gasp.

It's a diamond choker. At least I assume they're diamonds.

"Kneel before me, Skye."

My eyes pop open into circles.

"Kneel before me," he says again. "I'm going to collar you."

"But I—"

"This is for your own protection."

"Braden, I—"

"I said kneel!"

I drop to my knees in front of him. "May I speak?"

"Yes."

"I don't understand," I say. "I don't know a lot about this lifestyle, but doesn't a collar mean that…?"

"That you're my property? Yes, it does."

"But we haven't discussed this."

"I know that. It's for tonight only. As I said, it's for your protection." He places the choker around my neck.

It's cool against my skin. Heavy, as well. I inhale sharply.

"This is temporary, Skye," he says. "You may rise."

I stand and meet his gaze. "Temporary?"

"You begged me to introduce you to my lifestyle, and I will, but I cannot do so without adequately protecting you. By wearing my collar, you are off-limits to anyone else. You belong to me, and no one else will touch you."

"No one else? What do you mean? Why would anyone else be in our bedroom?"

"Because we're not staying here, Skye. We're going to a club."

Fear surges through me. Or is it excitement? Since I met Braden, the two feelings are difficult for me to separate.

"I can't go out in public wearing this," I say.

He walks to the closet and pulls out a black trench coat. "This will adequately cover you. And don't worry. We aren't going far."

"What will *you* wear?"

He's still dressed in his suit.

"You'll see." He walks back into the closet, closing the door behind him this time.

I wait.

And I wait.

Finally Braden emerges, wearing another black trench coat that covers him from shoulders to knees. From his knees down, he's dressed in simple black pants and leather shoes.

What the...?

"Are you ready, Skye?" he asks, his voice low and dark.

I swallow. Then I nod.

"I need to hear you answer affirmatively."

"Yes, Braden," I say. "I'm ready."

I force myself not to stumble in the stilettos as we walk out of Braden's living quarters and through his makeshift office, which is now eerily empty—a massive change from the night we got here.

"Where is everyone?" I ask.

"I sent them all home," he says.

"Does that mean your business is concluded?"

"My business is never concluded. It simply means they're working elsewhere."

"But why—"

"Enough questions, Skye. I don't think anything I tell

you can adequately prepare you for what you'll experience tonight, so I've made the decision to take you in blind."

"Blind?"

"Not literally. I won't blindfold you. In fact, I want all your senses on alert tonight. I want you to take in everything. Only then will you be able to tell me truthfully what you think afterward." He slides a card through the device to call the elevator.

When the doors open, he gestures for me to step inside. He follows. Then he takes a second card out of his wallet and slides it through the device inside the elevator.

"Why do you need a card?" I ask. "Aren't we going to the lobby?"

"No."

"Then where are we going?"

"You'll see."

The elevator descends, and when the doors open, I gasp.

"Welcome," Braden says, "to Black Rose Underground."

Chapter Thirty-Five

We step straight from the elevator into what appears to be a luxury nightclub, with one blatant difference. Wardrobe.

Instead of skimpy club dresses, the women are dressed a lot like I am, some of them more scantily. Several of them are showing their nipples.

And the men? Some are dressed in suits, as if they just came from a workday. Others are dressed in leather, some bare chested. One man even has pierced nipples.

What would Braden look like with pierced nipples? The thought makes me tingle.

Jazz music wafts from the sound system, not too soft and not too loud. It's perfect. I can still hear Braden speak.

"What do you think?" he asks.

My heart is pounding. "Where exactly *are* we?"

"The bottom floor of the building. It's a private club."

"Who are all these people?" I move my gaze about the room rapidly. Everywhere I look, something—or someone—else stands out.

"Members, of course."

Braden walks me to a desk where a burly man sits. "Hey, Claude."

"Good evening, Mr. Black."

"This is Skye Manning, my guest."

Claude nods and pushes some papers toward me. "You'll need to sign these."

I lift my eyebrows at Braden.

"It's a nondisclosure agreement. Everyone who comes to the club must sign."

"You mean I can't tell anyone what I see here?"

"More than that," Braden says. "You can't even tell anyone you've *been* here."

"Not even Tessa?"

"Not even Tessa."

"But I tell Tessa everything."

"Not this." Braden hands me a pen. "Read through it if you'd like, or I can explain it to you."

"I'm capable of reading a legal document." I hastily glance over the papers. They're pretty straightforward. Then I scribble my signature. "Everyone here has signed this?"

"Yes," Braden says.

I look around. A dance floor lies to my left, but no one is dancing. Strange. Straight back is what appears to be a full bar. Two bartenders, one a topless female, mix drinks for guests. Several guests sit on black leather barstools. Others mingle, chatting, flirting. One man has his woman on a leash.

I hold back a gasp.

"We're all good, Mr. Black," Claude says. "Enjoy your evening."

"I plan to. Thanks, Claude." Braden turns to me. "Skye? Shall we?"

Heart still hammering, I bite my lower lip. "Sure. I guess."

"You guess?"

"Well…yeah."

"If you're not all in, Skye, we may as well leave now."

No. I don't want to leave. I *really* don't want to leave. "I'm in. I just don't understand. People are dressed like me, but nothing is happening here. I don't get it."

He curves his lips slightly upward. "This is only one part of the club. Would you like a drink?"

"God, yes." I never let alcohol affect me, other than to put me slightly more at ease. In that vein, a drink seems like a good idea at this moment.

"Only one," he says. "I want your mind clear for tonight."

I nod, and we head to the bar. The topless server jiggles toward us. "Nice to see you, Mr. Black."

"Good evening, Laney. Two Wild Turkeys, please. Neat."

"You got it."

The drinks appear in an instant. Braden pushes a fifty dollar bill toward the naked bartender.

I take a long sip of my bourbon, letting its spiciness coat my throat and give me courage. Then, "What is this place, Braden?"

"It's a leather club."

"Which is…"

"A place where people who enjoy the BDSM lifestyle can come and play together."

"Who knows about it?"

"Only the people here. It's very exclusive. Membership by invitation only."

"Oh? Who invited *you*?"

"No one."

"I don't understand."

"It's *my* club, Skye. I own it."

Chapter Thirty-Six

Red noise buzzes in my ears.

"You own it?"

"I own it," he repeats.

"So this is…"

"This is where I practice my lifestyle in New York."

"And you don't do this stuff in Boston."

"I do not."

"Why?"

"I've told you. Boston is my home. Where I grew up."

"So?"

He takes a sip of his drink. "I prefer to keep this side of me private."

"And you can't do that in Boston?"

"I could. I choose not to."

Why? I don't feel I've gotten an adequate answer, but I know Braden. This is all I'm going to get. "What do you do here?" I ask.

"Sometimes nothing," he says. "Sometimes I come alone and simply have a drink at the bar, as we're doing now.

Sometimes I help another member with a scene."

"A scene?"

"A scene is when members play together."

"And you…" I take a sip, gathering my courage. "You have sex with them?"

He shakes his head. "A scene doesn't always mean sex."

"So you don't have sex here?"

"I didn't say that."

"For God's sake, Braden, I'm ageing. What kind of play do you do here?" *And with whom?* I add in my head.

"First of all, you'll see all kinds of play here, and some includes sex. Some includes other types of intimacy, and some includes no intimacy at all. I'll tell you this. If I'm involved in a relationship, as I am with you, I will have sex only with you. In the past, when I haven't been involved with a woman and I've had sex here, I've always used protection and I've only had sex with women."

I'm awed by his candor. It's more than I get most of the time. "So some members…"

He nods. "Some members have sex with both men and women, yes. Some only with their own sex. Whatever their preference."

I nod. "What will you and I do here?"

"That's up to you."

I smile and swallow more Wild Turkey. "Really? I thought you had control in the bedroom."

"I do. But I've never done anything without your consent, have I?"

"No. Though sometimes it's implied."

"True. It won't be implied here. I'll get your express consent for everything I do to you."

My body is on fire. Seriously. I'm ready to burst into blue flames. What kind of stuff does he have in mind?

"You're flushing," he says.

"Am I?" I know damned well I am.

"This excites you." A statement.

I nod.

"And *that* excites me." He stands and removes his coat then, revealing his bare chest.

I suck in a breath.

He's magnificent, as always, but here, in the dim lighting, with others around so scantily clad, he's a fucking king.

"Stand up," he says to me.

I do, and he unties the sash of my coat and then unbuttons each button. He parts the fabric and takes the coat from my shoulders.

For a moment, I'm freaked. I've never been this exposed in a public place before.

But *is* this a public place?

Not really. *Members only*, he said.

I look around. Though the corset covers my breasts, my ass cheeks are completely hanging out. The fishnets and stilettos make my legs look longer and more slender than they are.

I look good. Damned good.

Yet no one even glances at me.

I'm not as gorgeous as Tessa, but usually I merit a look or two in a club. What gives?

I meet Braden's gaze. "No one is looking at us."

He smiles. Sort of. "You mean no one is looking at you."

"Well…yeah."

"You're wearing my collar."

"Oh. That's what you meant when you told me it was for my protection? So no one would look at me?"

He shakes his head. "No. If you weren't wearing a collar, others would feel free to approach you, ask you to join in their play."

"But I could always say no, right?"

"Yes. But if you're not collared, you're seen as available here." He lowers his eyelids. "And you're *not* available, Skye. You will play with no one but me."

That's fine with me. I'm not interested in anyone but Braden. Does he expect me to argue the point?

Braden finishes his bourbon. "Are you ready to see more?"

I glance down at my own glass. Only a tiny bit of amber left. I down it quickly. "Yes."

"Good." He hands our coats, along with another fifty, to an attendant who seemed to appear from nowhere. "I want to take you to the bondage room."

My heart races as I recall the photos in the book in his library. "Okay."

"I think you'll like it."

I have no idea what to expect as he leads me away from the bar, through a dark-red curtain, and into a hallway. Doors line both sides of the hallway. We walk about halfway down, and Braden stops at a door.

"Any member can enter this room," he says. "It's not private."

"Okay."

"You'll see bondage in here, but you may also see people engaging in intimate play. Are you ready for that?"

"I've seen porn, Braden."

"Live acts are a little different."

I'm oddly turned on. Maybe not so oddly. I'm fucking hot. I want to see what's behind this door more than I want anything else at this moment.

"Normal bodies aren't always as beautiful as porn-star bodies," he continues.

"I know that. Don't worry. I won't stare."

"Actually, stare all you want. Anyone engaging in intimate acts in a clubroom that's open to everyone is naturally an exhibitionist. They expect you to look."

I suck in a breath, remembering that first day in Braden's office when he fucked me up against his floor-to-ceiling window. I thought anyone could see us, and when he told me later that they were tinted and no one could see in, I was strangely disappointed.

Am I an exhibitionist? Will Braden and I play together in this room someday?

"All right," I finally say.

"You'll be tempted to look away," he says. "That's normal. These acts are private. But if you want to look, look."

I nod. "Do you like to look?" I ask shyly.

"I'm not a voyeur," he says, "but I enjoy the art of bondage. I come into this room to see the art more than the intimate acts."

"I see."

"Ready?" He clasps the doorknob.

"Ready."

He opens the door. An attendant sits right inside the door. "Mr. Black," he says simply.

"Good evening," Braden says. "My guest and I are here to observe this evening."

"Very good."

Braden takes my hand, and we step into the room.

And I nearly lose my footing.

The room is huge, the lighting is brighter, and the walls are white, which surprises me in an underground club. I was expecting dim light and black and red.

But I soon realize why the walls are white and the light not as dim as before.

Works of art are everywhere. Human works of art.

While the rope used in the photos I saw in Braden's library was all natural colored, the bindings in this room range from black to red to purple to green. Some multicolored.

Braden leads me around the room to observe. We stop first to watch a man whose arms and feet are bound with intricately knotted dark-blue rope. "This is an example of *shibari*," Braden says.

I lift my brows.

"It's a Japanese bondage form that uses simple but intricate patterns. Go ahead. Take a good look."

A woman wearing a corset similar to mine but no thong whips the man lightly with a flogger.

"Is this the kind of bondage you want to do to me?" I ask.

"No. What I do uses quite a bit more rope."

I nod. Like the photos I saw in his library.

"I'll go easy on you tonight," he says. "Baby steps."

Except, as I watch the show in front of me, I don't want baby steps. I want to go all in.

All fucking in.

We walk to the next scene. A woman is bound in natural-colored rope, the knots intricately wound all the way from her ankles to her thighs. Her wrists are bound together and hooked to what looks like a pommel horse. Her partner, another woman, is fucking her from behind using a strap-on. I hold back a gasp. I've never seen a strap-on before, though I know they exist. As the submissive's legs aren't spread, she must be tight, and the dildo the other woman wears is not small.

"That's right, you slut. I'm fucking you good, aren't I?"

The woman doesn't respond.

She's probably been told not to.

On to the next scene.

A curvy woman is bound with black rope and lying on her back on a leather table. A ball gag is in her mouth. Her wrists and ankles are bound together, and a well-endowed dark-haired man is fucking her boldly.

This room seems to go on forever. We watch several more scenes, and though Braden said not all of these scenes would include sex, most of them do.

I've soaked my thong already, and I want Braden badly.

Does he know what this is doing to me?

My clit is throbbing, and I yearn, more than anything, to touch myself. Even bound up in this corset, I want to swirl my fingers around my clit and force an orgasm.

I know it won't work. Only Braden can make me come.

I only *want* Braden to make me come.

I'm lost in a fantasy of being bound and fucked when we come to a scene that leaves me spellbound.

Chapter Thirty-Seven

My nipples strain against the corset, and I suck in a breath. Braden has left me plenty of room to breathe in the garment, but now it's too tight. I'm panting. I'm aching.

A beautiful dark-haired woman sits on her knees in front of a well-toned blond man. She's bound with dark-red rope that begins around her neck. From there, it loops over her shoulders and over her breasts, her nipples protruding through two tight knots.

The rope curves over her abdomen and around her hips, and then it coils over her thighs and calves, forcing her into the kneeling position.

The man pulls on the rope around her neck, and she gasps softly.

My whole body tingles with current. Sparks slide through me, and my already wet pussy gushes.

The man strips off his black pants, releasing a giant cock. He pulls the woman toward him and shoves it into her mouth.

What is different about this scene? They've all been

titillating, but this one…

This one makes me yearn.

For what? I'm not sure.

Something about her position, the ropes binding her.

"Skye." Braden breathes against my neck.

"Hmm?"

"Do you like what you see here?"

Does he mean the whole room? Or this scene? I'm not sure.

"Yes," I say, my breath catching.

"There's a lot more to see in this club, but for now, we're going to my private suite."

Private suite? Of course. He owns the club. "Does anyone…watch us there?"

"Do you want anyone to watch us?"

Do I? I'm not sure. Strike that. I'm sure, but not in the way he means. It's not that I want to be watched. More that I want to know anyone could see us at any time. There's a subtle difference that I'm not sure I can explain.

"I don't know."

"No one will watch us. I'm not an exhibitionist." He takes my hand and leads me out of the room and back into the hallway.

"What are all these other doors?" I ask.

"They're for another time." He cups my cheek. "I want you, Skye."

"I want you, too." If only he knew how much. I can smell the musk between my legs. Can he?

He leads me to a door at the end of the hallway. The sign on it reads simply PRIVATE. He keys in a code, shielding his fingers from view. From me? No one else is around.

"Are you ready?" His eyes burn into mine.

I nod.

"I need an answer."

"I'm ready," I say, willing myself not to stammer.

He turns the knob and opens the door. "After you."

I hold my head high and walk in.

And I gasp.

It's not a dungeon—at least not what I ever thought a dungeon might look like.

At first glance, it's a beautifully decorated bedroom. A king-size bed is the centerpiece. The head- and footboards are lovely black lacquer, and the bed is covered in mahogany silk. For a moment, I imagine we're at Braden's penthouse in Boston, except there are no windows in this room. No Boston Harbor. No Manhattan skyline.

We're truly underground.

Though the bed draws my gaze, when I allow my eyes to wander, I realize this isn't a bedroom at all.

In one corner is a leather table with straps and stirrups. In the other corner is what looks like a stockade, but it can't be. Can it? Hanging on the wall are floggers and handcuffs and whips, oh my.

Against one wall stands a chest. What's inside I can only guess.

Braden walks toward the chest and opens the top drawer.

Rope. All different colors and textures of rope.

"I can't tell you how pleased I was when I found you masturbating to the bondage photos," he says. "I enjoy many aspects of this lifestyle, but bondage is my favorite."

My flesh tingles. Is he going to tie me up? Artfully, like in the book? Like in the scenes we just witnessed? And then…what will he do to me?

Anticipation courses through me. My pussy aches with need.

"What are you going to do to me?" I ask.

"What would you like me to do?"

Bind me. Fuck me. "Whatever you want."

"Good answer." He fingers the diamond choker at my neck. "You're wearing my collar tonight, but as I said before, that's only for your protection. We're alone here, and you may remove it before we play if you'd like."

His use of the word "play" takes me aback. I don't consider what I do with Braden playing. We make love.

I bring my hand to his fingers at my neck. "I'd like to wear it. For tonight, anyway."

"As you wish."

Is he happy at my decision? I honestly can't tell. His demeanor is stoic.

"Braden?"

"Yes?"

I clear my throat. "How many other women have been in this room with you?"

"Skye..."

"I'm not asking for names or anything. I just... I'm not naive. I know I'm not the first."

"What if I told you that you *were* the first?"

"I'd say you were lying."

He resists breaking into a grin, keeping his stoic demeanor. "You'd be correct. You're not the first. Perhaps, though, you'll be the last."

I widen my eyes. "You mean that?"

"I never say anything I don't mean, Skye. You should know that by now."

"You want me to be the last?"

"I said *perhaps*, Skye. I'm not clairvoyant. I can't predict the future."

"But you want—"

"I love you, Skye. I've never said those words to any

woman before you. I make no promises about anything other than this moment, but at this moment, I love you."

I warm all over. "I love you, too, Braden."

"What we've done in my bedroom in Boston only scratches the surface of what I can show you. Of what I *want* to show you."

"Is this the kind of stuff you like to do all the time?" I ask.

"Yes, this is a lifestyle choice. I don't indulge in club scenes regularly, as I'm not always here. I still live in Boston."

"Why not?"

"I've already explained part of that, but also, by only indulging in my darkest side on occasion, it's more special. Like anything, if you do it constantly, you become used to it. The thrill lessens."

"I see." And I do. I truly see, as if Braden has ordered me only to see.

"Are you ready, Skye?"

"For...all of this?"

"To follow me under. To the darkest side of my fantasies."

I swallow, my heart stampeding. "Yes, Braden. I'm ready."

Chapter Thirty-Eight

Braden loosens the ties on my corset and helps me step out of it. Then he removes my stilettos, my garter belt and stockings, and my thong.

"Put the shoes back on," he says, his voice a low rasp.

I obey.

I'm naked except for the black platform stilettos.

He sucks in a breath. "Fuck, you're sexy. Take a seat on the table." He gestures to the leather-covered table in one corner of the room.

I walk to the table and comply.

Braden bends over the chest of rope, pulls out some dark-red pieces, and returns to me. "We'll start slowly. You're not ready to be completely bound."

The image of the woman tied from neck to toes forms in my mind. *I am ready. Please. Bind my neck. Make me yours.*

I say nothing, though he hasn't ordered me not to speak.

"Lie facedown," he says, "with your arms behind your back."

I obey, placing my face in the cradle.

Though I can only see the floor in front of me, I feel the texture of the rope as he pulls my wrists together and binds them. It's soft, which surprises me. But of course. This is meant to be pleasurable for both of us. Scratchy twine wouldn't be pleasurable.

He pulls my arms and binds my forearms together, stretching me. "Okay?" he asks. "Any discomfort?"

"Just a stretch."

"Good. That's good."

Is this it? Just my arms?

"I'm going to remove the bottom half of the table now," he says. "Drop your feet to the floor with your legs spread."

The table releases, and my feet end up on the floor. Braden adjusts the height so my legs are spread the way he wants them.

"Keep your face down," he says.

A few seconds pass, and then I feel the head of his cock nudging at my ass.

"So tempting," he says. "But not tonight." Then he pushes his cock into my pussy.

I tense at the sweet invasion, and the ropes binding me pull, adding more tension. It's not comfortable, but it's not uncomfortable, either.

"Feel it all, Skye," he says. "Not just me fucking you but how the binding enhances it." He pushes into me again and then again. "God, you're so wet. So wet and still so tight. The perfect pussy for me."

His words spur me on, and with each subsequent thrust, he pushes my clit against the leather table, the friction delicious.

I'm ready. So ready. I'm climbing, running toward the peak…but I don't get there.

Don't get there.

Until he says, "Come, Skye."

I shatter, pulling at my bindings, trying to reach to touch him.

But I can't. Can't touch him. I'm bound. At his mercy as I break into a million shards.

And it's fucking thrilling.

"That's it," he says, his voice so low, it's almost a growl. "You're so hot, Skye." He pumps again and again, until he locks himself inside me, releasing.

As I come down from my own climax, I feel every contraction of his.

Every single one.

We're joined as bodies. As hearts. As souls.

And this is only the beginning.

Minutes later, he pulls out. My face is still buried in the table. I can't see, but I feel. He's touching me. His fingers trail lightly over my warm flesh—over the cheeks of my ass, over my back and shoulders. Then over my upper arms. He helps me roll to my side, and then he pushes my legs upward so I'm in a makeshift fetal position. I close my eyes, letting the nirvana from my recent orgasm wash over me. A few seconds—or minutes, I'm not sure which—later, Braden rolls me faceup so my arms are now underneath me, forcing my back to arch.

I'm awash in a dreamy haze. Are my eyes open or closed? Braden is a blur moving above me. What's he doing? I'm not sure. All I know is the utter peace I'm feeling.

Finally, he pulls me into a sitting position, loosens the rope, and removes it slowly.

Then he massages my forearms. "Okay?" he asks.

"Yes."

"Was the stretch too much?"

"No."

"Good. You'll be able to take more next time."

"Are there other places like this?" I ask. "I mean, I know there are, but…"

"This is tame compared to most," he says. "I couldn't find a place that suited me perfectly, so I built this one."

"When did you…you know?"

"Get interested in bondage?"

"Yeah. Bondage, and the rest of it."

"I've always been interested in it. It's part of who I am."

His need to be in charge. I get it.

What I don't get is why I'm so interested in the other side of it, given my own need for control.

And I *am* interested.

The image of the woman bound at her neck still titillates me.

Why? I don't know.

But it does.

"Braden?"

"Yes?"

"This is all…normal, right?"

"Normal? Depends, I guess. If normal is what the majority of people like, then no, this probably isn't normal. But if normal is whatever consenting adults choose to do without harming anyone or breaking any laws, then yes, this is perfectly normal."

"Do you always look at both sides of everything?" I ask.

"Always. And you should, too. It's how you make a success in business."

I regard him. His bare chest, muscled arms, bronze shoulders, perfectly sculpted abs. There is so much more to Braden Black than meets the eye, and even though he's let me get closer than anyone, I've only just begun to scratch the surface.

He's a good man. An excellent businessman. A philanthropist. A dominant.

A generous man and a generous partner.

So much to love.

And I do love him. I love him so damned much.

But there will always be a part of Braden I can't touch.

Always.

And I have to accept that.

Chapter Thirty-Nine

My phone rings, waking me from a sound sleep. I jerk upward. Where am I? Still at Braden's penthouse in Manhattan. I look toward the other side of the bed. No Braden.

Shit! My phone's still ringing.

"Hello."

"Skye, it's Eugenie Blake."

"Oh." I clear my throat. "Good morning, Eugenie."

"Good morning?" She laughs.

I eye the clock on the night table. Noon? My God. No wonder Braden's gone. He's probably already put in five hours this morning.

"Sorry. Afternoon," I say. "What can I do for you, Eugenie?"

"I'm just calling to see if you've made a decision on the contract yet."

"Oh. Yes. I'd be delighted to sign with you. I can bring it by your office today."

"That would be great. It will be wonderful to see you

again. How does two p.m. sound?"

"I can do that. See you then."

Now, where did I put the contract? First things first. I need a cup of coffee and a shower. I rise and stretch—

Ouch! My arms and shoulders are sore.

I don't mind, though. It's a reminder of how Braden bound me last night, just the beginning of what he has in store for me.

Excitement courses through me. I don a robe quickly and walk to the kitchen to get some coffee. I have to start a pot. No Marilyn here to make me coffee no matter when I rise. Odd that Braden doesn't keep a staff here.

I laugh out loud. Since when is not having a full-time staff odd? God, I sound like Addie.

Time to come back down to earth, thank you very much.

Once the coffee is brewed, I pour myself a cup and head back to the bedroom. I shower quickly and dress in another one of the outfits chosen for me by Mandy, the personal shopper Braden hired. Now, to find the contract. I'm due at Susanne Corporate in an hour, so time is of the essence.

I text Braden, but he doesn't reply. Probably in a meeting.

Crap! We were reading it in the kitchen before we met Eugenie and the team for dinner. I head back to the kitchen. No contract. The dining table. Nope. It isn't in the bedroom, so where is it?

Okay. Not a huge deal. I can ask Eugenie for another copy and sign it at our meeting at two. But that won't make me look very responsible.

Where *is* the fucking thing?

Shit! Why did I offer to bring it by? Why didn't I just say I'd have it messengered over?

I sigh. If I were a signed Susanne Cosmetics contract, where would I be?

Does Braden have an office here? Other than the big one in the front of the penthouse?

Who knows?

Ding!

I jerk. A text from Braden. Thank God.

I had it messengered over to Eugenie this morning.

Fuck. That's right. He said yesterday he'd do that. How could I have forgotten? Now I look disorganized. I have a meeting with Eugenie to deliver the contract, which she'll already have in her possession by then.

I text him back.

Okay. Thanks. I'm on my way to see Eugenie.

Then I race toward the elevator, using the card Braden supplied me with. Time to hail a cab.

I walk into the building that houses Susanne Corporate, check in with security, and make my way to the elevator.

Only to see—

"Skye. Back again?"

Addison Ames. Seriously?

"Yes," I say simply.

An elevator opens.

And it's fucking empty.

Which means I get to ride up to floor twenty-seven with Addie.

Only Addie.

I hold my head high and enter the elevator ahead of her. I push twenty-seven. "Floor?" I ask her.

"Same," she says.

Which I already knew anyway, but I was hoping she was

going somewhere else.

"You'll make a wonderful discount-cosmetics influencer," she says snidely.

God, she's such a bitch!

"Nice outfit," she continues.

I say nothing.

"Cat got your tongue today, Skye? Or has Braden forbidden you to speak?"

Nice touch. Not only does she diss my new contract, she brings Braden into the mix, and she seems to know he likes to keep me from speaking during sex. Not surprising, since she also knows about his penchant for nipple clamps and butt plugs.

I say nothing.

But only for a couple of seconds.

Before I can stop myself, I turn to Addie, my temper on fire. "You want to have it out? Take your best shot."

She gazes down at her hand, looking at her perfectly manicured fingernails. "Please. Your immaturity is showing, Skye."

I resist the urge to whip my hands to my hips. And the urge to bitch-slap her. "*My* immaturity? I'm not the one sending snide texts and making rude remarks."

She meets my gaze. "Don't pin this on me. I told you Braden Black was trouble. I told you to stay away from him."

This time my hands hit my hips. "Why? Because you want him for yourself?"

"Because I care about you," she says, though her tone negates her words, "or did you forget that conversation we had at the office?"

"Before or after you fired me?"

She shakes her head. "You're so young."

"I'm older than you were when you were involved with

him, Addie." I smirk.

She opens her mouth but says nothing.

Ha! Point, Manning.

"You're nothing but a spoiled brat," I say. "You're obsessed with Braden and you can't have him. Now, because I have what you want, you're trying to break me. Like I said, give it your best shot, Addie, because I'm a hell of a lot stronger than you seem to think."

"Please." She scoffs. "We both know how you got this job. I can bury you in a minute."

Can she? Probably. Her platform is much larger than mine. But how will that make *her* look? Of course I know how I got that job. I've been ruminating on it all week, but right now my anger takes charge over my feelings of fraud. For the third time, I say, now through clenched teeth, "Give it your best shot."

She huffs. "You're hardly worth it."

"If that's true, why the snide texts and comments?"

She huffs again without replying.

"I can't believe it," I say as I finally understand her. "You're insecure. The great Addison Ames is a scared little girl."

"You don't know what you're talking about!"

Another point, Manning. I can't help a self-satisfied smile. I've hit a nerve, and damn, it feels good. After all her bitchy comments that undermine my confidence, I'm freakishly glad I'm getting to her. "Don't I? I guess we'll see."

As if on cue that our conversation is over, the door finally opens on the twenty-seventh floor. I walk out ahead of her, enter through the transparent doors, and approach the receptionist. "Hi, Lisa," I say. "Skye Manning for Eugenie."

"I don't see you on her schedule."

"She's expecting me."

Eugenie comes walking out to the reception area. "Skye," she says, "I tried calling you. I got the signed contract by messenger. You didn't have to come over today after all."

"Good," I say, warmth creeping up my cheeks. "I just wanted to make sure it arrived."

"It did. Thank you." She looks beyond me. "Addie, come on back."

Please, *please*, let a giant hole open up and swallow me. I may have given Addie a taste of her own medicine in the elevator, but at the moment, I look like a complete airhead.

Addison's face splits into a giant grin as she smirks at me and then follows Eugenie.

"Don't let her get to you," Lisa says.

"Who?" I ask, feigning innocence.

A young man approaches. "Ready for your break, Lisa?"

Lisa grabs a purse. "Yeah. Thanks, Brody."

"How long do you get for your break?" I ask.

"Fifteen minutes."

That's enough time to find out more about Addie. "Can I buy you a coffee?"

"Coffee's free in the breakroom," she says.

"Of course." I smile. "It was nice to see you again."

Lisa comes out from behind her desk. "Walk with me for a minute."

"All right."

We leave the reception area, walk outside the transparent door to the ladies' room, and enter.

Lisa looks under the stalls. We're alone.

"I just want to tell you that Eugenie talks about you all the time," she says. "We all know how Addison is. She makes the company a lot of money, but no one likes working with her."

"You told me yesterday that she was great."

"I did. I wouldn't dare say anything other than that in the office."

"Are you sure you should be telling me this?" I ask.

"I'm sure I shouldn't be, but I see the way she treats you. She treats me the same way. She thinks everyone is beneath her. I've even seen her treat Eugenie badly."

"Then why—"

"Money," Lisa says. "It's all about money."

"I see."

"In a perfect world, only good people would get ahead. Unfortunately, we don't live in a perfect world."

I chuckle with sarcasm. "True enough. Thanks, Lisa."

"Don't mention it. You just seem like a person I can trust."

"Absolutely."

She checks her lipstick and then washes her hands. "I've got to get back. I'm sure we'll see each other again."

"I'm sure we will." I smile as she leaves the restroom.

Lisa means well, and I appreciate her candor.

She knows all about Addie, just like I do.

So why do I feel like such a fake?

A fraud?

A piece of shit?

The answer comes to me, only it doesn't. It's been there from the beginning of this new venture.

Deep down, I know the truth.

No one cares what Skye Manning thinks.

People only care what Braden Black's girlfriend thinks.

I'm losing myself.

I'm selling my soul for an influencing career.

Yes, it's a wonderful opportunity.

Yes, it's a way to showcase my photography.

And yes, it's an income stream I need, since I'm unemployed.

So yes, I'm in.
I'm *all* in.
The only problem?
I'm not sure who *I* am anymore.

Chapter Forty

I feel a strange sense of loss when Braden and I leave New York. We leave behind the lifestyle he introduced me to, though I'm not ready to.

I want more of the bondage. I feel whole when I'm tied up, though that makes no sense at all, given what I know about myself.

"You don't seem like yourself," Tessa says to me at lunch later in the week.

I can't fault her observation. "I'm okay."

"You should be freaking ecstatic. This new contract is amazeballs."

Again, I can't fault her observation.

"I'm grateful," I say.

"Don't take this the wrong way, Skye, but you seem about as grateful as a pig going to slaughter."

I smile. Sort of. Tessa always has a way of putting things into perspective.

"Come on," she says. "Dish. What else went on in New York?"

If only I could tell her! That damned NDA I signed is eating at me. I understand. I truly do. Braden isn't the only high-profile person at the club. The clientele need to be assured their confidentiality will be respected.

But I tell Tessa everything.

And I can't tell her this.

I can't tell her that I, Skye Manning, Kansas farm girl, went to a leather club in Manhattan.

I'd never tell her what Braden and I did there, but how I wish I could describe the ambiance to her.

"Hello?" she says.

I swallow my bite of sandwich. "Yeah?"

"You going to answer my question?"

What was her question again? "Not much else went on. Braden was in meetings most of the time, though we did have some amazing meals."

She nods. "I'm not buying."

"You're not buying what?"

"You're keeping something from me."

I stiffen.

"Either that," she continues, "or something else is bothering you."

Something is, but I can't talk about it to her or anyone. It's so innately personal.

How do you tell your best friend of the last six years that you're losing something you can't even put into words?

I'm supposed to sell a new cosmetics line.

Me.

Skye Manning.

Except I'm no longer Skye Manning.

I'm Braden Black's arm candy.

"Skye…" Tessa urges.

"I'm fine," I say, a little more harshly than I mean to.

"Can you come to my place? I'm expecting a package from Eugenie. Samples of the cosmetics. They launch next week, and I start my posts tomorrow."

"Uh…no, I can't."

"Why not?"

"Skye…I'm on my lunch hour. Work. Remember?"

Shit. I feel like a bitch. "I'm sorry. I don't know what I was thinking. Tomorrow, then? It's Saturday."

"Sure. After yoga. You still do yoga, don't you?"

Indeed, I've been picking up extra classes without Tessa since I no longer have a day job, but I missed the last Saturday with her.

"Of course. I'll see you there. Tomorrow morning."

Tessa excuses herself a few minutes later. "I'm meeting Betsy for drinks tonight. Want to come along?"

As much as I love them both, I'm not in the mood for hearing all about their antics with Garrett and Peter when I can't tell them anything about mine. "No, thanks," I say. "Maybe next time."

"Sure. Next time." Tessa leaves without meeting my gaze.

And I have a really bad feeling.

Lip gloss. Blush. Foundation. Eye shadow. Mascara. Nail polish. Daily moisturizer. Tinted moisturizer. Night cream. Toner. Finishing spritz with SPF fifteen.

These and myriad other Susie Girl products lie on my floor after I opened the package from Eugenie.

Tomorrow, I post for the first time under my new contract…and I don't have a clue what I'm doing.

I have a lot of leeway. I post what I want, as long as I

mention a product. I can be out and about—doing yoga, having coffee, eating brunch, taking a walk...whatever. I have a few guidelines, but for the most part, I'm on my own.

They're putting a lot of stock in me.

Rather, they're putting a lot of stock in Braden's arm candy.

I sigh. Time to get hold of myself. Whether they want me or someone else, I've got the contract. I signed on the dotted line.

I must do the work.

I decide to begin with the cosmetics line. I want to use the skin-care line for a week or so before I post about it.

I find a good spot in my apartment, adjust the lighting, and take a selfie. This is my "before" shot. After I've used the skin care for a week, I'll take another selfie, and I hope I see a huge difference.

My skin has never been a big problem. I had a few bouts of adolescent acne, but in the last five years, my complexion has been clear as a bell. My skin does tend to be a little dry, though, so maybe I'll see a difference. Even if I don't, I must post about the products. I'm under contract.

I check out the colors Eugenie sent me. I have to hand it to her. She's good. Each color she chose will work for me.

Those first three posts, though... How am I going to top them? Especially the last one, where I stood in front of Braden's window wearing a sheet, a black mask, and Cherry Russet lip stain?

I *have* to top them. I have no choice.

I'm an artist. A photographer. This is what I do.

So why do I feel so inadequate?

Easy.

I know the answer, and I don't feel like dwelling on it.

Braden and I didn't make plans for dinner this evening. Maybe I should have accepted Tessa's invitation to have drinks with her and Betsy. I could use some time with friends—with people who know me and accept me for being simply Skye. So what if I can't dish about my boyfriend?

Too late now.

I jerk when my phone buzzes. Hmm. Not a number I recognize, but I don't hesitate to answer. It might be opportunity knocking.

"Hello."

"Hi, is this Skye?"

"It is."

"Great. This is Kathy Harmon. We met at Bobby Black's. Remember?"

"Oh, sure. How are you, Kathy?" *And why are you calling me?*

"I'm fine, thank you. This may sound a little out of the blue, but I was wondering if you were free for dinner tonight. My treat."

If only Braden and I had made plans…

Now what?

"Sure. What did you have in mind?"

"I just want to bend your ear a little. About influencing."

"I'm pretty new at it," I say.

"Oh, I know, but you certainly know more about it than I do. How about Ma Maison at seven? I'm in the mood for some escargots."

"Sure. Sounds good. I'll see you there."

"Looking forward to it. Ta!"

I text Braden quickly.

Your father's girlfriend, Kathy, invited me to dinner tonight at seven. Will I see you later?

The three dots move.

Be at my place by ten. Don't be late.

Okay, I text back.

Three hours for dinner with Kathy will be more than enough. Especially once she finds out I don't know shit about influencing.

Chapter Forty-One

The escargots at Ma Maison are scrumptious. I take a selfie. Maybe the restaurant will appreciate a freebie. Their food is delicious.

Snails, anyone? The escargots at @mamaisonboston are fabulous! #yesieatsnails #escargots #frenchcuisine

"I find what you do fascinating," Kathy says. "It's so amazing that people are interested in what you're eating."

"I won't lie," I say. "It's pretty surreal."

"Like I said. Fascinating. Do you mind taking a selfie of us together?"

Publicity. That's what she's after. She's not interested in influencing at all. But what will it hurt? The more I post, the more I seem like a normal person to the people I'm trying to influence. Why not post that I'm having dinner with a new friend?

"Not at all. Come around to this side of the table."

She nearly jumps out of her seat, her head bobbing. "Do I look okay?"

"You look great. But don't even worry about that. I edit

all my photos. You'll look great no matter what."

"Perfect."

I click a few photos of the two of us and show them to Kathy.

"Use that one." She points.

I shake my head. "There's a glare in the background. The third one's the best."

"But I don't look as good."

In reality, she looks identical in each one. "Don't worry. You'll look amazing when I'm done."

"Oh, perfect! Don't forget to tag me!" She smiles wide.

"What's your Insta handle?"

Her cheeks flush.

I raise my eyebrows, waiting for her response.

"It's at Harvard law hottie," she finally says. "Underscore between each word."

I hold back a chuckle. "Got it." I quickly make the post.

"So how are things with you and Braden?" she asks.

"Fine."

"He's an amazing catch," she says.

I'm not sure what to say to that, so I simply nod.

"His father's a tiger," she offers.

Yeah. TMI. I smile and pop another escargot into my mouth.

"When he first asked me out," she continues, "I almost said no. I mean, you know. The age difference and all. But he's so handsome."

Am I supposed to comment? "Yes, he is."

"My father about had a nervous breakdown when I told him, but my mother's thrilled."

"Oh?"

"Well, of course. Isn't yours?"

"I haven't really talked to her about my relationship with

Braden." Try not at all.

"You haven't?"

"No. My parents live in Kansas."

"So? You haven't told them *anything*?"

I take a sip of water. "I've told them I'm seeing someone."

Her eyes are round as dinner plates. "Someone? You're not seeing *someone*, Skye. You're seeing Braden Black."

Kathy makes a point. Why haven't I told my parents more about Braden? Or that I lost my job with Addie and am now influencing on my own? We have a perfectly fine relationship. I speak to them once every two weeks or so, but that's it. They're not really into email or social media, and neither of them has an Instagram account, so they know nothing about my recent posts.

It's just that... It's all so new. So...different. Especially the relationship with Braden. Not that my parents need to know the kind of sex we have. It's not like I ever described my sex life with any other boyfriend.

"Our relationship is still pretty new," I say.

"He brought you to Bobby's for dinner. According to Bobby, Braden almost never brings a woman home."

I resist the urge to lift my eyebrows, but I can't deny her words make me a little giddy. "Oh?"

"Yeah, that's what Bobby says. I believe his exact words were, 'He seems serious about this one.'"

"Like I said, our relationship is still pretty new."

"I'd grab on to him and never let go if I were you." She smiles coyly. "I'm just sorry you saw him first."

"Don't you work at his office?"

She nods. "It's been a fabulous opportunity."

"Then you probably saw him first," I can't help saying.

"A few times," she admits, "but we never formally met, and he never gave me the time of day. Bobby says he doesn't get involved with people at the office."

"But Bobby does, apparently."

"Apparently." She takes a sip of her water. "Where is the waiter with our wine?"

"Tell me about you and Bobby," I say.

She smiles. "Like I said. He's a tiger. In the boardroom and in the bedroom. You wouldn't believe what he's into."

Yeah? Try me. I don't say it, though. No way am I going to talk about what Braden and I do in the bedroom with a virtual stranger, NDA or not.

"He has the stamina of a guy half his age," she continues. "And his body… Dreamy. The best body I've ever been with, and most of my dates have been with significantly younger men."

Most? Interesting, but not surprising, given what Ben seemed to think of Kathy. "Yeah, he seems to stay in shape."

"A lot of it's in his DNA," Kathy says. "I mean, look at his two sons. But he works out almost every morning."

Does Braden work out? Funny that I don't know the answer to that question. Other than his racquetball date, he's never mentioned exercise. He must, to maintain that perfect physique. I've let this man tie me up and take control of me, yet I have no idea if he works out.

"Skye?"

"Yeah?"

"You seemed to zone out there for a minute. Oh! Good. Here comes our wine."

Our server sets the two glasses of Bordeaux in front of us. "Your entrees will be out in a few minutes."

"Thank you," Kathy says. She picks up her glass. "To us."

"To us?"

"Yeah. A new friendship."

I pick up my glass and clink it to hers. This is a new

friendship? She's not just here because she wanted the selfie? Perhaps I misjudged Kathy. Maybe she truly has feelings for Braden's father.

If that's the case, should I tell her that he's just using her? At least according to Ben?

I hold back a sigh. This is all so none of my business.

I smile. "To a new friendship."

My smile wavers and my stomach drops.

A maître d' leads two women through the restaurant, and my gaze meets one of theirs.

It's Tessa.

Chapter Forty-Two

Tessa raises an eyebrow at me.

I smile weakly.

Tessa and Betsy sit down at a table behind me, thank God, so I don't have to see them.

I'm the shittiest BFF ever. I turned down Tessa's invite, and here I am sitting with a woman she doesn't recognize. It could be business, of course. That's what I'll tell Tessa if she asks.

But that's a lie.

The truth is that I just didn't want to talk to Tessa and Betsy, and not because I can't tell them about my trip to New York.

That bad feeling I had after I turned Tessa down at lunch?

It's back with a vengeance.

"Something wrong?" Kathy asks.

I smile at her. Again, weakly. "No. Why do you ask?"

"You got a weird look on your face."

"I'm fine."

Except I'm not. I look at my phone, which I've silenced to avoid the tons of notifications from my Instagram posts. Kathy and I are front and center. Tessa would have seen the post anyway.

Should I go over and explain this to her?

If I do, what do I say?

Who the hell am I?

Kathy chatters the rest of the way through dinner.

I can't tell you a word of what she says.

At five minutes until ten, I text Braden.
I'm in the lobby of your building.

A few minutes later, the doors to his private elevator glide open, and Christopher emerges.

I walk toward him, but he gestures for me to stay put. I widen my eyes.

"Mr. Black asked me to take you somewhere," he says.

"Where?"

"I can't tell you that."

"Christopher, I can't just go somewhere without knowing where I'm going."

Christopher chuckles. "He expected you to say something like that."

I roll my eyes. Perfect. Braden knows me better than I know myself, which ironically isn't that surprising.

I look down at my dressy jeans and blouse. "What if I'm not dressed appropriately?"

"You're dressed fine. Come with me."

I relent and let Christopher lead me to the Mercedes in the garage. Before we leave, he hands me a piece of black silk. "Put this around your eyes."

"Seriously?"

"Have you ever known Mr. Black to *not* be serious?"

He's got me there. "I suppose you won't take me if I don't put it on."

"Right."

"Well, that's fine—"

He interrupts me with a burst of laughter. "He said you'd say that as well."

I huff and tie the blindfold around my eyes. "Satisfied?"

"Doesn't matter to me," he says, "but Mr. Black will be satisfied."

Which is all that matters, of course.

My flesh tingles. Is he taking me to a…

No. Braden was clear. He only engages in the leather lifestyle in New York. So where are we going?

About twenty minutes later—I'm guessing, as I can't see my watch or my phone—the car stops.

"We're here," Christopher says.

"May I take off the blindfold?"

"Not yet. Mr. Black will come get you, and then he'll tell you what you need to do."

A few minutes later, the car door opens. "Skye."

Braden's voice. It's low and sexy.

"Hi, Braden."

His fingers touch my arm. I shudder.

"Come with me."

He helps me out of the car and then places his arm around my waist. "Don't be afraid."

I clear my throat. "I'm not."

"You are. I can feel the tension in your body. There's no reason to be afraid."

"I know that."

"Good. You'll enjoy tonight. I promise."

A few moments later, we're inside a building. The scent of cigar smoke wafts toward us. Where are we? Smoking is illegal in public places in Boston except for cigar bars. Braden didn't bring me to a cigar bar, did he?

Jazz music plays softly.

"Where are we?" I ask.

He gently pulls off my blindfold. "Look around. See for yourself."

My eyes adjust to the darkness. The atmosphere is smoky and hazy, and I don't have a clue what's going on.

"This is another place I own. An investment. It's a cigar bar and jazz club, but tonight, it's all ours."

"What?"

"I closed it to the public tonight. Just you and me, Skye. We're going to listen to some incredible music."

"Oh." I sigh softly. "It sounds wonderful."

"Not only that," he continues, "but we're going to make love here, Skye."

"But what about the band?" I ask, looking around.

The stage is empty.

"The music is on the sound system," Braden says. "I had them record a set, and then I gave everyone the night off with double pay."

I warm all over. He closed up a jazz bar for me. The scent of cigar smoke doesn't bother me. In fact, it seems normal for this place, adds to the ambiance. The leather chairs are worn, the lighting dim. I feel like I've walked into an old speakeasy during Prohibition. Any minute, I expect Al Capone to appear with a flapper on each arm.

"Why, Braden?"

"Because it's different. It's exciting."

Different, yes. Exciting? Had I not experienced the

leather club in Manhattan, I'd be very excited right now. But since the Black Rose Underground, everything else seems so…tame.

Braden's blue eyes smolder.

And I know he has something in mind.

Something that will excite me.

I look around. A wooden bar stands along one side of the large room. Tables with worn leather chairs are scattered throughout. A small area by the stage provides a makeshift dance floor.

Everything in here exudes character.

"What's the name of this place?" I ask.

"It doesn't have a name," he says.

I lift my eyebrows.

"It's a secret club," he says.

"So I was right!"

"About what?"

"It feels like an old speakeasy."

He lifts the corners of his lips. "That's the idea. Except nothing is illegal about this place."

"I didn't know there were places like this in Boston."

"Every major city has places like this. They're iconic."

"And you…"

He chuckles. "Of course I had to have one."

I nod. It makes an odd sort of sense. Braden is secretive about so much of his life. Of course he wants to own a secret bar. Hell, he owns a leather club in New York.

I uncovered another layer of Braden Black tonight.

I smile to myself.

"The bar," Braden says, "is antique wood from the roaring twenties. I like to think it might have sat in a real speakeasy once."

I nod.

"Undress, Skye."

I widen my eyes.

"Do it."

I timidly look around. No one is here but us, of course. He said he'd closed the place. Still, we're in a public place…

Which is kind of exciting. I almost wish someone could walk in at any moment.

"Do I need to repeat myself?"

I peel off my blouse and my bra. Then my shoes and jeans, until I stand only in my lacy panties.

"Keep going."

I nervously glance around, still expecting—hoping for?— someone to walk in.

"No one else is here, Skye."

I shimmy out of my panties and hold them out to Braden. He takes them and stares at them for a few seconds. I half expect him to sniff them, but he doesn't.

"Now, get on the bar."

I walk toward the bar and hoist myself onto it. The wood is cool against my bare skin.

"Spread your legs."

I obey. I'm wet and ready, but something is missing. I can't say what. I look around at the dusky ambiance, listen to the jazz filtering through the sound system.

A week ago, this atmosphere, Braden ready to do whatever he wants to me, would have me already clawing for an orgasm.

So what's missing?

Braden is as handsome and magnificent as ever. He loosens his tie and removes it. He discards his suit coat and unbuttons the top two buttons of his white shirt. His black chest hair peeks out.

Yes, he's majestic as ever, and the thought of him sliding

his cock into me makes me shiver.

I'm always ready for Braden.

But tonight…I want more.

What? I can't say.

Braden pulls up a barstool and sits down in front of my bare pussy. He inhales. "Mmm. I love your scent, Skye. I love that you're always ready for me."

I am.

I'm soaking. I want him. I always want him. But what—

"Oh!"

He jams two fingers inside me, and I jerk. The feeling is wonderful…and unexpected. Usually he licks me first.

Still, I'm ready. Wet. And as he slides his fingers in and out and around, I undulate on the bar, my hips circling.

"Touch yourself," he says. "Play with your nipples."

They're already hard and straining, and I finger them lightly, my own touch sending me into shudders and moans.

"You're so beautiful," he says. "So hot."

I close my eyes, chasing an invisible rabbit down a hole. He eludes me, though, even as I grind against Braden's hand.

The zing of his zipper.

Then he's inside me, pumping. How he reaches me at the height of the bar, I have no idea. I don't care. The friction of his pubic hair against my clit sends me reeling, and I'm almost there… Almost there…

But the climax is quicker than I am. I can't catch it despite the glorious friction against my clit.

Something's missing.

Something I reach for… Reach for…

"Come, Skye."

Finally, I grip the pleasure that was eluding me. My climax rolls through me and around me. "Braden!" I cry out. "More! I need more!"

"Keep going," he says through gritted teeth. "Keep going, Skye."

His words. All I need are his words.

Usually.

But tonight…they don't work.

Chapter Forty-Three

"That's it, baby." He rams into me harder, harder, harder... until— "God, yes. So tight. So sweet."

His release is long and sustained. He pushes into me, perspiration dripping from his brow, his eyes squeezed shut.

I watch him. Watch every microsecond of his orgasm. He's beautiful. Big and strong and beautiful when he comes.

And I realize...

I'm no longer coming.

My orgasm has subsided.

In this forbidden place. This beautiful forbidden place with the man I love and adore. I should be coming and coming and coming, but once I came down from the first orgasm, I was done.

Odd.

Odd and unsettling.

Braden finally withdraws. "Skye?"

"Yes?"

He frowns slightly. "I thought you'd enjoy this. Coming here."

"I did. I do. This is a beautiful place. Dreamy, even. Reminiscent of another time."

"Yes, it is."

"I'd love to do a photo shoot here sometime. Maybe for one of my posts."

"Of course. Anytime. But there's something you're not telling me."

I stay silent.

"What's wrong?"

How does he know? "Nothing. Why?"

He trails a finger over my jawline. "You seem…elsewhere tonight."

I force a smile. "You're imagining things."

He cocks his head. "Don't lie to me, Skye."

I sigh.

"Out with it," he says.

"It's silly, really."

"Nothing is silly. Let me help you."

"I'm feeling… This is difficult for me to say."

"Just say it."

"I'm not sure. Inadequate, I guess."

"Why?"

"A lot of reasons. I'm not being a good friend to Tessa. I'm letting Addie get to me. I feel like I'm not…"

And I've given up control to Braden in the bedroom, though in all honestly, that makes me feel more like me than I've ever felt.

It's the rest of the stuff, mostly, but I can't deny Braden is a part of it.

"Not what?"

"Like I'm not *me* anymore."

I expect him to frown. To tell me I'm being ridiculous. To...do just about anything other than what he ultimately does.

He cups my cheek, runs his thumb over my lower lip. "Look at me."

I meet his blue gaze.

"Tell me, Skye. Since we met, when have you felt the most like you?"

"It's little things, Braden. It's not—"

He touches his fingers to my lips. "Just answer me, Skye."

I close my eyes, let out a soft sigh.

Apprehension knifes through me.

Not because I'm afraid to answer him.

But because I know the answer, and that's what surprises— and frightens—me.

Chapter Forty-Four

"Skye..." he urges.

I open my eyes, turn my head, and kiss the palm of his hand.

"In New York," I say. "At your club."

He smiles. "That pleases me."

"Why?"

"Because at the club is when I feel the most like me," he says.

"Then why do you indulge only in New York?"

"I've already answered that question."

"But—"

"There are certain things I keep out of my Boston life. Aren't there certain things you keep out of your Kansas life?"

The fact that I haven't told my parents about Braden spears into my head. Why haven't I? They'll be thrilled that I'm happy, not to mention that I'm dating a billionaire. What parents wouldn't be?

"I suppose so," I say.

"Speaking of Kansas..."

God. He's going to say he wants to meet my parents. After all, I met his father and brother.

"I've never been there."

"Oh?"

"Does that surprise you?"

"A little. You've been everywhere."

"Not everywhere, but a good many places both here in the U.S. and outside."

I can't help a smile. "Kansas never made your list, huh?"

He smiles back, which makes me smile wider. Every time I see his real smile, I get warm inside. He's usually so stoic.

"Not yet. But it will. You and I will go there."

"When?"

"When would you like to?"

"I don't know. I start my contract with Susanne tomorrow. I'm not sure Eugenie wants her posts taken from a Kansas cornfield."

He kisses my forehead. "Probably not."

"But New York, Braden. I could do my posts in New York."

That delicious smile spreads across his face once more. "You want to go back to New York?"

I close my eyes. "More than anything."

"I have meetings all next week here in Boston," he says. "But we can go next weekend."

"I'd love that."

He kisses me again, my lips this time. Just a soft brush against them, but I tingle all over.

"So would I."

. . .

I leave Braden's the next morning at ten to meet Tessa for yoga. She's already at the studio warming up.

"Hey, Tess," I say.

"I wasn't sure you'd make it," she says.

"Why wouldn't I? We had plans."

"Right," she says, not meeting my gaze. "Plans."

She's thinking about last night, how I turned down her invitation for drinks, which apparently turned into dinner at Ma Maison, with Betsy.

"Tess…"

"Don't worry about it," she says.

"I just feel a little uncomfortable around Betsy," I say. "I'll get over it." It's not a lie, but it's not completely honest, either.

"She feels terrible," Tessa says.

"About what?"

"About spilling the beans about Braden and Addison."

"There's no reason for her to feel bad. She was being a friend. Looking out for me."

"So you're okay with everything?"

I shrug. "Why wouldn't I be? It was ten years ago. So he dumped her. Whatever."

"But something happened that left her freaked out."

I sigh. "If she was so freaked out, why was she upset that he ended things? She could by lying for all we know."

Tessa says nothing, just moves into a downward dog to stretch her hamstrings and calves.

I hate the damned downward dog. Hate it with a passion.

We don't talk for the remainder of the hour.

• • •

"Coffee?" I ask, wiping my neck with a towel after class. "I'm not sure I'm up for it," Tessa says.

"We always have coffee after yoga."

"And we always keep our shopping dates," she counters.

Is that what she's upset about? That I forgot to cancel our shopping date because Braden and I went to New York early? She didn't say anything about it when we talked on the phone earlier. Of course, that was before she caught me at Ma Maison with Kathy.

I thought we were past it, but I've still been neglecting her.

"Coffee," I say. "We need to talk."

She holds my gaze for seconds before she nods. "Okay."

Once we're settled at Bean There Done That, I take the lead. "I'm sorry."

"It's okay."

"It's not, or you wouldn't still be upset. I should have texted you and canceled our shopping. And I should have been honest with you about drinks last night."

"I just miss you is all," she says.

"I miss you, too."

She stares down at her latte. "I feel like you're leaving me behind. You've got this new influencing venture. You've got a billionaire boyfriend. You're finding new friends. Like that Kathy you had dinner with last night. Who is she, anyway?"

"How did you know her name?"

"You tagged her in your post, genius." Tessa chuckles nervously.

"Oh. Right." I resist rolling my eyes at myself. "She's a law student at Harvard. She's interning at Black Inc., and get this. She's dating Braden's father."

Tessa's dark eyes widen.

"She invited me to dinner last night after I told you no.

Braden and I hadn't made plans, so I went. Turns out, she's just using me."

Tessa wrinkles her forehead. "Why do you say that?"

"She said she wanted to talk to me about influencing, but we talked very little about it. Instead, she jumped at the chance to take a selfie with me and get her name in front of my followers."

The lie tastes bitter in my mouth. It's not all fabricated. Kathy is definitely interested in publicity, but she's also nice in her way. We toasted to our friendship last night.

Why am I being untruthful with Tessa? She's my best friend. She's not going to judge me.

Who the hell am I?

"I can't blame her," Tessa says. "I've gotten a ton more followers since you posted with me."

"I suppose." I take a sip of coffee. "How's Betsy doing? Business-wise, I mean."

"She's about ready to launch her online store. I've been helping her with the accounting end of it."

"I'm glad to hear that. And how's Rita?"

That gets a real smile out of Tessa. "An adorable ball of fluff! How's Penny?"

"I swear, she grows more each day. I have no idea how big she's going to be. I can't wait until I get a new place and can bring her home."

"Why don't you just move in with Braden?"

Her question jars me. First, he hasn't asked me. Second, I haven't thought about it.

Third, because I know I'd do it in a minute if he asked, and that's a little freaky.

"We're not there yet," I say. It's not a lie, but it doesn't feel like the truth, either.

"Oh."

"How are you and Garrett doing?"

"Good. I like him a lot. He's no Braden Black, of course." She takes a drink and then wipes her mouth with a napkin.

I'm not sure how to respond to that, so I take another sip of coffee and let the warmth sit on my tongue for a moment before I swallow.

Finally, I say, "Tessa, what's going on?"

"Nothing."

"I've apologized. I fucked up, and I'm sorry. Are we ever going to be normal again?"

She looks down, swirls her latte in her paper cup. "I don't know, Skye."

"Look at me, Tess."

She meets my gaze.

"What do you mean you don't know? I'm still me."

"Yeah, but you're *not* you, too. You're Braden Black's girlfriend. You're a rising star on Instagram. You're the new face of Susie Girl cosmetics. Next thing you know, you'll have galleries fighting over who gets to display your work. You're moving up, Skye, and I feel like you're leaving me behind."

I touch her forearm. "I'll never leave you behind. We've been besties for six years."

"Yeah, and during those six years, we were always equals."

"We're *still* equals."

She shakes her head. "It doesn't feel that way."

I flash back to freshman year at BU. Tessa and I weren't roommates, but we lived on the same corridor in the same dorm. Though we both got on fine with our respective roomies, neither of us made a huge connection with them. In fact, we laughed at my roommate, Mary Ellen, who once told us that girlfriends sometimes had to break up as if they were a couple.

"Are you breaking up with me?" I ask, trying to sound jovial.

I expect her to break into giggles at the memory of Mary Ellen's statement that we thought was hilarious at the time.

She doesn't. Instead, "I don't know. Maybe we need to take a break."

"Like Ross and Rachel?" I can't help asking, even though I know now isn't the time for my silly attempts at humor.

"Well…Ross and Rachel did eventually get back together," she says. "I'm not saying it's forever, Skye."

"Seven years later," I say.

She stays silent.

"Fuck," I say. "You're serious."

"Things are easier with Betsy," she says. "We're on the same level."

"What level is that?" I ask sarcastically.

She shakes her head slowly. "Don't act like you don't know what I'm talking about. You're different. The old Skye never would have forgotten to cancel a shopping trip."

My heart beats rapidly. This isn't happening. "It was a mistake. For God's sake, Tess, Braden and I flew to New York in the middle of the night. That whole weekend was out of whack."

"I know. I actually do understand, and I accept your apology. But then you were supposed to call me after your meeting in New York, and you didn't."

My heart drops to my stomach. She's right. "God, Tess, I'm so sorry."

"It is what it is," she says. "Things aren't the same."

"We're no longer college students, if that's what you mean. But I'm still the same. I'm still Skye."

Even as I say the words, though, they don't ring true.

Who is Skye Manning, anyway?

The answer is...

I don't know.

The Skye Manning who's the most at home at Braden's underground leather club isn't the Skye Manning who is Tessa Logan's best friend.

Is she?

What about the Skye Manning who's taking Instagram by storm?

The Skye Manning who Addison Ames hates?

Which one am I?

Am I all of them? Or none of them?

I swallow the last of my coffee and rise. "I have to go. Call me if you change your mind."

"Skye..."

Tessa keeps talking, but I'm out the door.

She wants to trash a six-year friendship?

Fine.

I text Braden.

I want to go to New York. Tonight.

Chapter Forty-Five

We're not going to New York tonight.

Braden's text is short and succinct and reiterates that he has work to do here in Boston.

I'm sitting on my couch having a pity party when I remember—

I have to do my first post for the Susie Girl line today!

Fuck. I'm about ready to destroy everything for this pity party. Of course, I literally just lost my best friend. We're "on a break." How cliché.

Still, I signed a contract. I have a job to do.

The cosmetics and skin-care products are still spread out on my table where I left them yesterday after opening the package. My new camera from Braden sits next to them. I haven't yet tried the camera. Today's the day. But first the Susanne post.

I choose a lip gloss and apply it. I'm still in my yoga clothes, and I wish I were still at the studio. The photo would be better there.

What the heck?

New camera in tow, I head back to the studio. If only I'd thought of this earlier…but I was in the middle of best-friend drama.

It's getting to be late afternoon, but two classes are still in session. One is hot yoga, which I hate. Sweating my ass off won't make for a good Instagram post.

The other is prenatal yoga, also not a good look on me.

Instead, I walk into the locker room and do the post there.

Sheer lip gloss in Honey Glaze by @susiegirlcosmetics is perfect after a yoga class! #sponsored #yoga #lipgloss #susiegirl

Not the most exciting copy I've ever written, but I want to be done. I edit the photo quickly and post.

Okay, that's done. Braden and I don't have dinner plans.

I sigh.

I miss Tessa. I mean *really* miss her, as if I've lost a limb. We hardly ever go a week without seeing each other, and we usually talk daily.

It's only been a few hours, and I feel the loss acutely.

Still in my yoga clothes, I grab my purse and the new camera. I walk along the street, shooting candids, which always puts me in a good mood.

It doesn't today, though. Shooting photos with my dream camera isn't helping my state of mind.

But I know what might.

Thirty minutes later, I'm outside Braden's building. It's Saturday, nearly dinnertime, and I have no idea if my boyfriend is even home. I inhale deeply, smile at the doorman, and walk into the building. I head straight for Braden's private elevator and press the button.

"Yes?" Christopher's voice over the intercom.

Good. If Christopher is home, Braden probably is as well.

"Hi, Christopher. It's Skye."

"Is Mr. Black expecting you?"

"Probably not. Is he there?"

"Yes. He's on a call in his office."

"May I come up?"

"Let me check with him."

I look at my watch. It's a little after four. On a Saturday. But Braden's business doesn't have regular hours, as I learned last weekend.

I wait.

And I wait.

Ten minutes later, the elevator doors open, and Christopher stands before me. "Come on up, Ms. Manning."

I step into the elevator, my nerves on edge. "It's Skye, Christopher. Skye."

"Skye." He clears his throat. "Of course."

We ride up to the penthouse without saying anything more until we arrive. Penny and Sasha run to greet me, and I kneel down and accept their happy puppy kisses.

"What good girls!" I pet them both and then pull Penny into my arms. She's a bit heavier. Soon she'll be as big as Sasha. "Have you been good for Christopher?" I kiss her soft head.

"She's a good pup," he says. "Accidents here and there, though."

"She's just a baby. She'll learn."

Penny squirms out of my arms to roughhouse with Sasha.

"Mr. Black is still on his call," Christopher says. "You may wait wherever you like."

"Do you know how long he'll be?" I ask.

"I don't. Make yourself at home."

Okay, then. I walk into the kitchen. "Hi, Marilyn."

"Ms. Manning."

"Please. Skye."

She nods. "I'm getting ready to prepare Mr. Black's evening meal. Will you be joining him?"

Will I?

"Sure," I say. "Why not?" Then an idea pops into my head. "In fact, I'd like to cook for him tonight. Why don't you take the night off?"

Her eyebrows rise.

"I *can* cook, you know."

"I'm sure you can, but Mr. Black asked for his dinner at six p.m. tonight. Sharp."

"That gives me almost two hours. I think I can scare up something by then." I whisk past her and open the freezer. I pull out a bag. "Shrimp. Perfect. I make a mean étouffée."

"Skye—"

"Please. I want to do this for him." I open the refrigerator. Onion, check. Garlic, check. Celery, check. No green pepper, though. "I need to run to the store," I tell Marilyn.

"What do you need? I'll have Christopher pick it up."

Even better. I make a quick list on my phone. "I can text him the list. What's his number?"

I enter the digits as she gives them to me, and then I press send.

He texts back. I'm on it.

I text a thumbs-up and thank you and get back to my kitchen.

Except it isn't my kitchen.

But tonight it will be.

Tonight, I'll prepare dinner for my boyfriend. I'm no gourmet, but I have a decent repertoire. All he's had so far is my leftover beef stew. We're in a relationship. I should be able to cook for him.

Plus, it gives me something to do to get my mind off Tessa.

And to get my mind off my post from earlier. I'm not satisfied with it. It was quick, and I gave it almost no thought whatsoever.

I need to up my game.

Yeah, I'm under contract and will get paid for three months no matter what, but I've never half-assed anything in my life.

And I half-assed that post.

That *first* post.

I wish I could delete it and begin again, but I already have over five thousand likes, which has earned me another fifty bucks. I'm up to nearly fifty thousand followers, and they're responding.

Still, I feel like I did a half-assed job.

No longer.

Tomorrow's post will be perfect. Three posts per week. I'll do Wednesday, Saturday, and Sunday. People are more active on social media on the weekends.

Plus, I need to do regular posts as well. The public needs to see me as a real person, not just as the face of Susie Girl.

What better way to do that than to show them as I cook a meal?

Addison is right. I'm the face of discount cosmetics. Oh well. I can at least be a normal person, right? Maybe that's the key. If a nobody like me can win the heart of Braden Black, anyone can.

Ugh. Not a good thought. I erase it from my mind.

Now, on to dinner.

Problem number one—I have no idea where anything is in Braden's kitchen.

I open my mouth to call for Marilyn but then decide against it. I'll find everything myself. Sure, it'll take me longer, but what the heck? I open and close cupboards until I find what I'm looking for.

The food processer.

Of course Braden has a top-of-the-line Cuisinart.

I plug in the appliance and mince my celery and onion. Into a cast-iron skillet they go, along with a stick of butter.

Yeah, shrimp étouffée isn't exactly good for the cholesterol, but it's delicious. A recipe I learned from my mother, who loves Cajun cooking. She's a wonderful cook and baker.

God, my mother.

I really do have to tell her and my father what's going on in my life.

Tomorrow. Tomorrow is Sunday. I'll give them a call.

For now, I'll concentrate on this amazing meal I'm making for Braden.

I snap a photo of the celery and onion simmering in the cast-iron pan. I'll document the process in pictures, right up to the finished product. At least my followers will have something interesting to see tonight, since my Susie Girl post is bound to flop.

I can't begin the étouffée until Christopher returns with the peppers, so I get out the eggs and cream for the chocolate mousse I plan for dessert. In the corner is a KitchenAid stand mixer. Now, where is the whip? I open drawer after drawer until I find it. Then I separate the eggs and whip the whites. I snap another photo.

Christopher returns with my groceries, and I melt the semisweet chocolate in a double boiler over low heat. Once it's cooled, I add the cream, a touch of vanilla, and then fold it into the egg whites.

I smile. My mousse turns out perfectly fluffy…and delicious after a taste test. I gently spoon it into parfait glasses, snap a quick pic, and set them back in the refrigerator.

Back to my étouffée. I rinse, cut, and process the peppers, and then add them to the skillet. Time to turn on the heat. While my étouffée sauce is cooking and reducing, I snap a photo. Then I open the door to the walk-in pantry and find a bag of long-grain rice.

Mmm. The aroma of my étouffée makes my mouth water.

I'm pleased with myself.

And that's a welcome feeling after most of today.

Marilyn pops her head into the kitchen. "Smells amazing! Is there anything I can help you with?"

"Thanks, but no." I want this to be *my* gift to Braden this evening.

Now, for a wine with dinner…

Braden has a refrigerated wine cabinet in the kitchen and a wine rack in the dining room. Maybe I need Marilyn's help after all. I'm not sure how to choose a wine. I tend to drink red with everything, but Braden did order a white with our oysters and seafood the first time we dined together. Perhaps he'd prefer white with shrimp.

I run my fingertips over the green bottles in the wine rack. Syrah. Too dark for shrimp. Beaujolais. That's a light red that's drunk young. Could work, but I'm not sure.

Light bulb moment.

I'll ask Braden to choose the wine.

Perfect.

But we'll start with Wild Turkey neat, of course.

Crap! That means I should have an appetizer with the bourbon.

Back to the kitchen, where I rummage through the pantry while my étouffée simmers. What will go nicely with my spicy entree? It's not like I have the ingredients to make alligator bites or boudin balls, and I don't even like the latter.

A bag of raw almonds catches my eye. Perfect. I'll pan

roast them with some Cajun seasoning, and they'll be delicious with our Wild Turkey.

I find another pan, begin the process, and then check the étouffée. It's ready for the shrimp. I add it, give everything a quick stir, and let it continue to simmer. Time to begin the rice, as well. I snap two more photos.

Ten minutes later, dinner is nearly complete.

Braden has yet to make an appearance. I check my watch. Ten until six. Marilyn said he wanted his dinner at six, so he should be coming out of his office shortly.

My heart skips.

Will he be pleased with the meal? With me?

He loves me, but he's so hard to read sometimes.

Correction—*all* the time. Except in the bedroom.

The bedroom, where I've given him my control.

And even then, I never quite know for sure.

I sigh.

Nothing more to do. Dinner is warming on the stove and is ready to be served. One more photo of the étouffé when I plate it, and then I'll post the series.

I look down at myself.

I'm still in my yoga outfit, and because I neglected to find an apron, I have spatters down the front of me.

Great.

I regard my watch again.

Five minutes until six.

Time to race up to my room on the second floor and hope I find something I can change into.

Chapter Forty-Six

At six o'clock p.m. sharp, I descend the staircase wearing a green sundress I found in my closet. It fits me like a glove, and I added brown leather sandals. I didn't have a chance to do any more than pull my hair out of its ponytail and run my fingers through it. I painted on some of the Honey Glaze lip gloss and that's it.

This is me as I am.

Braden still hasn't come out of his office, and I sigh in relief.

Now what?

I haven't set the table, so I find dishes in the cupboards and take care of that. Then I pour two Wild Turkeys.

And I wait.

And wait.

And wait some more.

The clock ticks.

I return to the kitchen, turn off the stove, and cover the étouffée to keep it warm. I return to the dining room and eat a couple of my Cajun almonds. Yum.

Finally Braden emerges.

My breath catches.

He's in jeans and a T-shirt, and he's fucking luscious.

Have I ever seen him dressed so casually? Other than the black pants and no shirt at the club in New York, and that didn't strike me as casual at all. He was dressed for the club.

"Skye," he says. Then he inhales. "Something smells amazing. What did Marilyn prepare for us?"

"Nothing," I say, smiling like a giddy schoolgirl.

"Nothing?"

"Marilyn didn't make dinner tonight. I did." I hand him his glass of bourbon and then hold up the bowl of freshly pan-roasted almonds. "Cajun almonds. Try one and then take a sip of Wild Turkey."

"Skye…"

I lift my eyebrows. "Yes?"

"We didn't have plans tonight."

"I know, but I wanted to see you." I stride toward him, hoping I look more seductive than I feel. "Is that wrong?"

"It's…" He rakes his fingers through his hair. "It's not wrong."

"Then what's the matter? Do you have someone else coming over here?"

"Of course not!"

"Then why can't I come over and surprise my boyfriend with dinner?" I close the distance between us to the point that I'm nearly touching him.

"God, your mouth," he rasps.

I smile. "I wanted to cook for you. I hope you like Cajun food."

"I love it."

"Good. I made shrimp étouffée. Why don't you pick out a wine for us? You know so much more about that stuff than I do."

He sighs. "Skye…"

I step back, getting irritated. "What? What is it, Braden?"

"I didn't give you permission for this."

I roll my eyes. "Are we really going to go there, Braden? I've had a shit day. I wanted to do something that made me feel good. It made me feel good to come over here and cook for you. Do I need permission to do something nice for the man I love?"

He doesn't answer.

Which gives me my answer.

Finally, "I'm sorry you had a bad day," he says.

I set down my drink and fall into his arms. "That is just what I needed to hear."

He kisses the top of my head. "Can I help?"

I pull back and meet his gaze. "You can help by picking out a bottle of wine and then eating the dinner I made for you."

"All right." He walks toward the wine rack, pulls out a bottle, and returns. "This Beaujolais-Villages will be perfect. It's light in body, and its acidity will complement the food."

I take the bottle from him, secretly pleased. It was one I considered. "Sounds perfect." I set it on the table.

He nods, still stoic.

"Something's bothering you still."

"It's not what you think it is."

"So you're not bothered that I showed up and commandeered your kitchen?"

"No, Skye. I'm not."

"Then what is it?"

He touches my cheek. "I'm bothered that I'm *not* bothered that you showed up and commandeered my kitchen."

My mouth drops open.

"Don't look so surprised."

"Why should you *want* to be bothered by this? We're in a relationship, Braden."

"Skye, you know I made a lot of concessions for you."

"Yeah, yeah, yeah. I know. You didn't want a relationship. But *you* changed your mind. I didn't *make* you change your mind."

"I know that."

"Don't tell me," I say. "It *bothers* you that you changed your mind."

"A little."

My heart drops. He loves me. He changed his mind on relationships for me.

But it's bothering him.

Still so much I don't know.

He avoids relationships for a reason—a reason I need to uncover if I'm ever going to truly know him.

Uncovering it will be a huge task—one I'm not sure I'll ever be able to complete.

One thing's for sure. This has made me forget, if only for a few minutes, about the shitty day I had.

I sigh. "I made this meal. Will you please sit down and eat it with me?"

He trails his index finger over my lower lip. "Of course."

I hold back another sigh. "Have a seat, then, and open the wine, okay? I'll serve the dinner." I walk back to the kitchen.

I spoon rice onto plates and then take the lid off the étouffée.

And my heart sinks.

I meant to turn off the burner. I was sure I had, but in a kitchen I'm not used to, I turned the knob the wrong way.

My étouffée has cooked down to nothing except some rubbery shrimp and a sauce the consistency of wallpaper paste.

Ruined.

Completely ruined.

I choke back a sob.

I've never cried in front of Braden, but I fear I won't be able to stop myself now.

I lost Tessa today.

I did a half-assed Instagram post.

I'm losing myself.

And now this.

My dinner—my beautiful dinner that I prepared for the man I love—is ruined.

I can't serve Braden a plate of plain rice.

I slide to the floor, my dress riding up. My head falls into my hands as I work hard to hold back the sobs that really want to come pouring out of me.

How much time passes, I have no idea.

But eventually, Braden's jeans-clad legs appear in front of me. "Skye?"

Then the tears come.

I can't stop them.

I try. Truly I do. I heave and gasp and try to swallow them into nothingness.

None of it works.

He drops down next to me and touches my cheek. "What's the matter?"

"It's ruined. Dinner is ruined."

"What happened?"

"Instead of turning the burner off, I turned it to high. Much longer and it would have scorched the bottom, and your whole penthouse would smell like burned étouffée."

"It's okay."

"It's not okay. Not even slightly. It was delicious, Braden. The best étouffée I ever made, and I ruined it."

"I'll take you out. Wherever you want to go."

"Nowhere. I don't want to go anywhere. This day can just go to hell."

"Surely you can't be this upset over a burned dish."

"I am."

"Skye… Don't lie to me."

I erupt then, like Mount St. Helens. I pour out everything that happened today. How I lost my best friend. How I nearly forgot to do my first post under my new contract and how I feel it's half-assed. How I snapped a bunch of photos while I was cooking dinner, and how I can't post any of them because said dinner is ruined. How he's bothered by the fact that he's *not* bothered that I'm here.

All of it.

Fucking all of it.

Tears roll down my cheeks. I sniff back the snot that wants to pour from my nose. I know I look atrocious—face red, eyes swollen—but I can't stop.

I can't fucking stop.

Then something happens. Something I don't expect.

Braden sits down next to me, pulls me into his arms so I'm sobbing into his shoulder, kisses the top of my head, and says, "It's okay, baby. Everything's going to be okay."

Time passes in some kind of a warp. I have no idea how long we sit there, but eventually my sobs soften, I'm breathing more regularly, and I feel…comforted.

Truly comforted.

I don't recall feeling like this since I was a small child sitting on my father's lap after that horrible day in the cornfield.

And I love Braden all the more.

He holds me, never letting go, until finally I pull back slightly.

"I have to blow my nose."

He pulls a handkerchief out from his pocket and hands it to me. I blow unceremoniously into it, nearly filling it, and then I crumple it in my fist. I meet his gaze. His blue eyes are kind. Full of love. A look I've never seen on his face before.

"I'm sorry," I choke out. "I wanted to make you a wonderful dinner."

"You did."

"It doesn't count if you don't get to eat it."

He smiles. That smile I see so seldom and love so much.

"What can I do for you? How can I make this day better for you?"

I sniffle and meet his loving gaze.

I know just what to ask for, what will help me put this day of misery behind me.

"You can take me to New York."

Chapter Forty-Seven

He kisses me tenderly on the lips. "Okay, Skye. You win. We'll go to New York."

The anvil rises from my shoulders. New York. Braden's club. I'll find peace there.

"When?" I ask.

"Tomorrow. I'll call and have the jet ready to leave in the morning."

I smile through the mess that is my face. "Thank you. Thank you, Braden."

"But Skye…"

"What?"

He brushes a tear from my cheek. "New York isn't an escape. The club isn't an escape."

"I know that."

"Do you?"

"Of course." I sniffle. "I just feel like… I don't know. I feel like everything will be okay there, you know?"

"I do know, probably more than you even comprehend, but I don't labor under any delusion that real life ceases to exist in the club."

I do know.

He understands. The club is something he needs, too.

But he keeps it in New York for a reason—a reason other than what he says—and I'm beginning to understand.

Why, though? If it gives him pleasure—gives him an escape from real life, if only for a few hours—why limit himself?

I don't ask, for I know he won't answer.

I just revel in the knowledge that we're going back to New York tomorrow. I'll do an amazing post for Susie Girl in downtown Manhattan. I'll write copy that makes cosmetics fly off the shelves, not something mundane about lip gloss after yoga.

I'll restore the faith Eugenie has in me.

"Oh!" I jerk upward into a stand.

Braden rises as well. "What?"

"Chocolate mousse! I made dessert, and it turned out perfectly. I can't offer you shrimp étouffée, but I can offer you rich and delicious dessert."

"We haven't had dinner yet, Skye."

"So? What's wrong with dessert first? We can order something to be delivered and have our dessert while we wait."

Braden opens the refrigerator and pulls out the two parfait glasses of chocolate mousse. "Fine. I'll have Christopher order something for us, and we'll eat this first, with only one condition."

"What's that?"

His gaze darkens. "We eat it in the bedroom."

My skin warms. The bedroom. He has plans for my chocolate mousse, plans I know I'll love.

But my face. I'm red and swollen and tear-stained. "Braden..."

"Follow me," he says, his voice low and dark.

Apparently he doesn't care about my face, which should please me but doesn't. Because I care what I look like for him. I want to be beautiful—or at least not repugnant.

We enter his bedroom, and he closes the door. Then he does something he almost never does. He sets the two parfait glasses on the night table and strips off all his clothes without having me do so first. I catch my breath at the beautiful sight of him, his masculine perfection.

He turns to me. "Take off your clothes."

I'm only wearing a dress, shoes, and panties, and I discard them hastily.

He approaches me, his cock huge and erect. I expect him to grab me and kiss me or to order me onto the bed. Instead, he cups my cheek.

"Something broke in me today, Skye."

I part my lips and widen my eyes.

"When I saw you so distraught, so sad, so upset, something squeezed my heart. I knew I had to act, had to do whatever necessary to make you smile again."

I curve my lips upward. "I'm smiling now, Braden."

He trails his finger over my lower lip. "You have such a sexy mouth. Do you have any idea how you affect me?"

"I'm beginning to."

"I'm not just talking physically. When you part your lips in that seductive way, I want to plunder them. But mentally, Skye. Emotionally. When you were sobbing, I was sobbing, too."

I cock my head.

"Not physically but emotionally. I hurt when you hurt." He shakes his head. "That's never happened to me before, at least not to this extent."

I part my lips farther, resisting the urge to drop them into an O.

"You've gotten inside me somehow. Yes, I've fallen in love with you, but it's more than that. It's... Fuck. I don't have the words. I'm not sure they exist."

"Braden, I—"

Then his lips are on mine, his tongue inside my mouth, his hand on my bare breast, squeezing, thumbing the nipple. Another hand between my legs, parting the slick folds of my pussy. I wrap my arms around his neck and melt into him, our bodies touching everywhere. His cock pushes into my belly. I grind into him, thrusting my clit against his hardness.

I love you, Braden. I love you, Braden. I love you, Braden.

The emotion swirls around me, coils through me—all the love I never knew I could feel, I feel now. In this moment. For this man.

He rips his mouth from mine and gasps in a breath. Then he clamps his lips onto the top of one of my breasts and bites me.

Hard.

Fucking hard.

I cry out at the pleasure-pain. "Marking you." He pants against my flesh. "You're mine."

My hand trails to my bare neck. He removed the diamond choker after our first time at the club. "The collar..." I say.

"Not enough. Not enough to make you mine." He lifts me then, right over his shoulder as if I'm a sack of potatoes. He nearly throws me on the bed. "The feelings I have for you are strong. So strong."

"I have strong feelings for you too, Braden."

He shakes his head, threads his fingers through his

disheveled hair. "No. You don't understand. They're…
disturbing."

He's used that word before. I don't want to disturb him.
"Braden…"

"No! Don't talk. Don't tell me what I'm feeling is normal,
that it's okay. Fuck!"

Then a sound comes from his throat. It's not a groan or
a growl. No. It's more like… More like…

A *roar*.

He picks up one of the parfait glasses filled with
chocolate mousse. "I'll take you to New York, Skye. I'll
take you back to the club, because the truth is, I want it, too.
I want it more than you can possibly imagine. The timing
sucks. I'll have to rearrange some things. But I'll do it. I'll do
it because I'll do fucking anything to make sure you never
cry like that again."

"I can't promise that—"

"Quiet! I told you not to talk!"

I press my lips together.

He sticks one finger into the chocolate and then holds
it to my lips. "Taste."

I lick the rich sweetness from him and savor its
creaminess.

Then he kisses me—an openmouthed kiss where he
swirls his tongue over my teeth and gums and then releases
me.

"Delicious," he says. "Rich, creamy, dark. But not nearly
as delicious as you are."

My body throbs.

"I'm going to paint you with mousse and then lick it off
you."

"The bedding. It will—"

"No talking! Do you think I care about the bedding? It

can be cleaned. It can be replaced. Right now, I need *you*, Skye. I want to eat your chocolate mousse off your beautiful body, and I mean to do it."

I lie flat and close my eyes.

"Oh, no," he says. "You keep your eyes open. You're going to watch everything I do to you." He scoops out more mousse with his fingers and paints it over each of my nipples.

They were already hard, but the coolness of the mousse combined with the heat of Braden's fingers makes them strain farther. Braden hovers over me, his lips close to my nipple. I arch my back, trying to make the chocolate-laden nipple reach his lips.

Still, he teases me. Makes me want him even more.

And of course, that's what he's trying to do.

"You're fucking beautiful," he says. "Love your tits." Finally, he licks the mousse off one nipple.

"Oh God…"

"No talking," he growls against my flesh.

I strain forward, undulating my hips, trying to reach his tongue again.

He nibbles on the other nipple, licking away the chocolate and then sucking my nipple between his lips. I moan, my pussy aching. Friction. I need friction on my clit, but I can't find it. His dick is hard, but it's between my thighs as he sucks my nipples.

And oh, he's a god at sucking my nipples.

My whole body is blazing, aching, yearning for more, more, more…

He scoops out more dessert, this time onto my abdomen, and then he licks it off, each stroke of his tongue sending me further into a heated frenzy.

He's so close… So close to my clit.

Finally, he covers my pussy in mousse, the heat of my

body melting it onto the covers. But if he doesn't care, why should I?

"I can't imagine anything making you taste better than you already do, but let's see."

He dives in, sucking the chocolate off me, pulling at my folds with his lips and teeth, shoving his tongue deep inside me. Then licking down farther still, where the mousse has trickled over my asshole.

I shiver.

Is tonight the night?

"No," he says against my flesh, as if reading my mind. "We'll save that for New York."

I'm both relieved and disappointed, but those emotions flee as he eats me, swirling his tongue around my clit and then shoving it inside my heat.

He plunders me, devours me, all the while I chase the peak that eludes me. I reach upward to grasp the rungs of the headboard.

Even unbound, I want to be bound. Want to be laid out for Braden's pleasure.

Not want. *Need*.

"God, delicious," he murmurs against my flesh. "I could eat you forever."

My fists clench around the wood, and when he nips my clit, I let go and fly, tingles shooting in toward my core and then outward, through my fingertips, taking me on the wild ride I've become accustomed to—the climax only Braden can give me.

I moan. I shout. Not in words but in pure emotion.

Vaguely, I'm aware of Braden crawling upward, kissing my nipples, my chest, my neck.

Then his cock is inside me, and he's thrusting, pumping, making glorious love to me as my climax continues.

Still I grasp the headboard, my bindings only Braden's will or my own. I don't know which, because they're bound together. His will and mine.

He meets my gaze, our eyes locked, as sweat protrudes from his forehead, making his dark hair stick to his face.

"I love you, Skye," he pants. "I fucking love you."

Chapter Forty-Eight

His words heal me, in a subtle way. Though I feel them, I can't return them.

He's forbidden me to speak, and he's in control here.

The misery of the day still lingers, but those words, in the throes of passion, were difficult for Braden.

I know this. I respect this.

He thrusts harshly and stays embedded in me, and as my climax slows, I feel every pulse of his.

He rolls over. Still, I grasp the rungs of the headboard, though I long to curl into his arms.

His breath slows after a few minutes, and he turns to me.

Still, I don't speak.

"We have another serving of dessert," he says.

I don't respond.

His lips curve upward slightly. "You may speak now."

I loosen my fingers from the headboard and wiggle them, gaining circulation. "Yes, we do. Do I get to eat it off you this time?"

He growls. Seriously growls. "Normally I'd take you up

on that, but I have something else in mind. Excuse me for a minute." He rises, wraps a robe around his gorgeous body, picks up the second serving of mousse, and leaves the room.

I smile and stare at the ceiling, the fresh spackle from the now-missing harness still a stark white against the buff paint. Funny that he hasn't painted over that yet.

A few minutes later, Braden opens the door. "Our dinner is here."

Oddly, I'm famished. I haven't gotten any mousse other than what I tasted on Braden's tongue. I rise and find my robe in the bathroom. A look in the mirror is a heinous reminder of the day. My eyes are still red and swollen. How can he stand to look at me?

I erase the thought as well as I can and head to the kitchen to join Braden.

I inhale. Spicy.

"I had Christopher get us Cajun," Braden says. "It won't be as good as yours, but at least we can sort of have the dinner you planned."

The thought of my ruined dinner almost makes me burst into tears again, but Braden's sweet gesture chases the tears away. "That was a nice thought."

"I decided against shrimp étouffée, though. I want the next shrimp étouffée I taste to be yours. I got crawfish étouffée and gumbo with andouille. I hope you like it."

"It smells wonderful. Will the wine you chose still work?"

"Absolutely. It's already opened. Would you like a glass?"

I nod dreamily, and he pours two glasses and hands one to me.

"To…possibilities," he says.

I clink my glass to his and ponder the message of his toast.

Possibilities…

Not probabilities but possibilities.

I like it.

Anything is possible.

Somehow I'll mend my relationship with Tessa. I'll redeem myself after today's half-assed post for Susie. One day I'll prepare shrimp étouffée for Braden without ruining it.

It's all possible.

And tomorrow, I'll be back in New York.

Back in the club.

Where truly, anything is possible.

I follow Braden to the dining room, where the table is still set for the dinner I prepared. He gestures me to sit down. We quietly fill our plates.

The meal is delicious. Probably far superior to what I made. The thought bothers me a little, but only a little.

I'm feeling better.

I'm feeling loved.

Braden is silent as he eats, his gaze never leaving me.

I learned something about him tonight. My sadness gets to him. *Really* gets to him. The thought warms me as well as chills me. I don't want him to ever feel bad, and tonight he felt bad because I did.

He opened up to me tonight, perhaps more so than he ever has.

Much of him is still a closed book, but tonight I got a glimpse of one page, at least.

We clean our plates, and Braden rises, taking them to the kitchen. He returns with the remaining chocolate mousse and a spoon.

He sits. "Come here." He points to his lap.

I warm all over. Have I ever sat on his lap before? I don't

think so. Braden is a wonderful man, but he's not much for offering that kind of solace. The way he comforted me in the kitchen earlier was definitely off-brand for him, as is this.

I don't hesitate. I rise and go to him, eager to please him, even more eager to embrace the comfort of his lap.

I sit down on his hard thighs.

He takes a spoonful of the chocolate mousse and holds it to my lips. "You haven't gotten to taste much of your confection yet. Try it."

I open my mouth and let the creamy mousse sit on my tongue for a moment before I close my eyes and swallow.

"You're a good cook," he says.

"Thank you. I wish you could have—"

He presses two fingers to my lips. "It doesn't matter. You'll make it again sometime. You can make it when we go to New York if you'd like."

New York. Just the thought has tingles rushing through me. "I'd like that."

"We never have to leave the building if you don't want to."

I widen my eyes but then quickly remember that the club is in the lower level of his building. "That would be amazing."

He feeds me another spoonful of the mousse. "I want to give you what you need, Skye, just as you give me what I need."

Control. He needs it, and though I have a limited understanding of why, I still don't know the whole story.

Right now, though, I'm so relaxed, I don't care. I just let the mousse slide down my throat and make me happy.

"Aren't you going to eat any?" I ask.

"I ate an entire serving from your body." He takes a spoonful. "But if you insist."

"You're some kind of wonderful," I say.

He doesn't respond, just feeds me another spoon of chocolate.

Have I made him uncomfortable? He's never told me I'm wonderful. But he has told me he loves me. That's better.

He *is* wonderful, though. No matter what Addison says, no matter what anyone says.

Braden Black is wonderful. And he's mine.

May I be worthy of him.

Chapter Forty-Nine

I text Tessa the next morning.

I'm going to New York with Braden for a few days. She responds succinctly.

Have fun.

Do I respond? I want to tell her how much she means to me, how much I'm aching because things aren't right between us. How I'll do anything to end this "breakup."

But those things don't belong in a text. I should call.

Hmm. Those things don't really belong in a phone call, either. I should go over to see her, but I can't. Braden and I are headed to the airport in a few minutes.

I sigh. A phone call it is, then. Before I can place the call, though, someone calls me.

Betsy.

"Hi, Betsy," I say into the phone.

"Hey, Skye. I'm sorry to bother you so early on a Sunday morning."

"That's okay. What's up?"

"Tessa spent the night at my place last night," she says.

"She's a mess."

My heart sings. Does this mean she's as upset about our break as I am? I hate the thought of her being in pain, but I want her back so badly. "Is she okay?"

"She'll be fine. She drank too much, and then she…"

Worry tugs at me. "What? Then she what?"

"She got some ecstasy from a guy at the club."

My blood runs cold. "What? Tessa doesn't do drugs."

"I know. I tried to stop her."

"Obviously you didn't try hard enough." My words are cruel, I know, but I'm pissed as hell. I'd have been able to stop her.

"Skye, I did. I did everything except knock her unconscious. She was determined. The good news is, I don't think she'll ever do it again. She's fried this morning."

"I'm sorry," I say. "I shouldn't have said what I did. Does Tessa need to see a doctor?"

"I asked, and she said no. She's alert and seems to be herself now. Just tired and achy and feels like shit."

"She responded to my text," I say, "so I guess you're right. She's lucid. I'm coming over."

"No, Skye. She specifically doesn't want to see you."

"I don't care."

"Please don't. It will just make things worse right now."

"Why? Why did she do this? This is so off-brand for her. She likes to drink, no doubt, and overdoes it on occasion, but drugs? She's always said no."

"She's pretty broken up about how things went down between the two of you. Plus Garrett told her yesterday that he doesn't want to get serious with her."

"Why should that upset her? Tessa's never been serious with a guy in her life."

"She was with Garrett. She thought she was falling in love."

She did? How did I not know this about my best friend? Have I been that out of touch?

My heart breaks a little. "Betsy, I'm so sorry."

"It's not your fault. You guys had a fight. It happens. She's feeling left out of this new life of yours."

"Then you're wrong," I say. "It *is* my fault."

"Don't do that to yourself. You didn't intentionally leave her out."

"No," I say, "I didn't, but that makes it almost worse, in a way. I didn't *think*."

"I didn't call to make you feel bad. I just knew you'd want to know."

I sigh. "Yeah. Thanks, Betsy."

"You're going through your own stuff right now. I get it."

"I am, but that's no excuse. As soon as we hang up, I'll call Tess."

"No, don't. Then she'll know I called you, and while she didn't tell me not to, she doesn't want to talk to anyone right now. She made that very clear."

My throat hurts—that feeling when you want to cry but can't. "Not even me?"

"'Especially not Skye or Garrett' were her exact words."

I sigh again. "I've really blown it."

"Like I said, you're going through your own stuff. I didn't call you to put a guilt trip on you. Honestly."

"I know that. It's just… Things have been so out of control. I've had several major life changes within the last month. I'm not trying to make excuses. I just…"

I don't know who I am anymore.

I can't say the words. I couldn't say them to Tessa, and I can't say them to Betsy.

Why is my identity so wrapped up in others all of a sudden?

I'm more than the sum of my parts. Aren't I?

I'm not just Tessa's best friend.

I'm not just Addison Ames's ex-assistant.

I'm not just a budding influencer, the new face of Susanne's discount line.

And...

I'm not just Braden Black's girlfriend.

"It will work out," Betsy says.

Will it?

I'm not sure.

But in a few minutes, Christopher is driving Braden and me to the airport, where we'll take his jet to New York.

Everything will work out once I'm back in New York.

I'll be whole again.

Won't I?

Fuck, I don't even know anymore.

"Tell Tessa..."

"Tell her what?" Betsy asks.

"Just tell her... Tell her I love her. I'm sorry. I've got to go."

"Okay. Don't worry. I'll take care of her. She's going to be all right."

"Thanks." I end the call.

Tessa will be all right. With or without me, she'll be fine. This was just a blip on the radar for her. The Tessa I know will realize she did an out-of-character thing and will vow to never do it again. She'll also realize she doesn't need Garrett Ramirez or any man. That she's just fine on her own.

I've witnessed it. She's pulled herself up before, and she'll do it again.

I just wish I were there to help her through it.

It's what besties do. We help each other. We eat Ben and Jerry's together and commiserate. We tell each other that Garrett Ramirez—or whoever—is a piece of shit who isn't worth our time. We vow never to repeat the ill-advised behavior we engaged in.

We have each other's backs.

Betsy will help her, and Tessa will be fine.

And that's what I want. I want Tessa to be fine, to be happy.

Yes. I want that.

The problem? It's not *all* I want.

Chapter Fifty

Early in the afternoon, we arrive at Braden's Manhattan penthouse.

"When can we go to the club?" I ask.

"Tonight. It doesn't open until eight p.m."

"It's your club, though. Can't we go now?"

He stares at me, his countenance slightly tense. "What are you looking for, Skye? Why is the club so important to you?"

"For the same reason it's important to you," I reply.

He nods. "I think that may be partially true, but you seem to be after something more than just sexual gratification."

"Aren't you?" I ask.

"I like to be in control," he says. "You know that, and playing a scene at the club gives me the control that I like to a greater extent than in a regular bedroom. Though I could easily build my own playroom."

"Why haven't you?"

"Because…the lifestyle is important to me, but it doesn't define me."

"I understand that."

"Do you?"

I nod, swallowing. Do I?

"Because I think," he goes on, "you found something at the club that helps you deal with other aspects of your life."

"So what if I did? Is that bad?"

"No, Skye. Nothing about the lifestyle is bad. But I have no interest in living that way twenty-four seven."

"Neither do I."

"Good. Then we're on the same page."

"How could you think I wouldn't be on the same page? Do you really think I want to spend my life as your submissive day in and day out?"

He shakes his head. "No, I don't think you want that."

"Then why are you—"

"You resisted my control in the bedroom. You still resist my control in other aspects of your life."

"That's true. So why would you think—"

He rubs his jawline. "I don't think that. Trust me on that one. I don't think it for an instant. As to whether it's what you want, we'll find out tonight."

Shivers overtake me, surprising me.

His words are enigmatic. I don't want to be his submissive. I know that as well as I know my own name.

What *am* I after, then?

Why is the club so intriguing?

Many potential answers to my own question exist.

And every single one of them frightens me.

Chapter Fifty-One

No corset tonight. Braden gave me a bustier and black leather miniskirt along with the fishnets, garter belt, and platform stilettos. A much more comfortable ensemble. He also asked that I wear my hair in a high ponytail, which makes me wonder what he has in mind.

Doesn't really matter. I'm already wet and ready.

Last, he places the diamond choker around my neck and eyes me lasciviously. "Nice," he says simply.

My fingers wander to the choker. I did some research on collaring. In the club atmosphere, it means I belong to Braden and everyone else there will respect that. But there's another meaning. A real-life meaning.

Some submissives wear their collars twenty-four seven. They are submissive in real life.

The choker is warm around my neck, almost as if it's burning me. Branding me.

I like the feeling.

Another thing that frightens me.

"What will you wear tonight?" I ask.

"Black pants and a black shirt. My usual."

"That's your usual? Last time, you were bare chested."

"Last time, my favorite black shirt was in Boston. I brought it this time."

"Oh. I see."

"We left quickly in the middle of the night last time," he says.

"I know. And you didn't think…"

"Right. I wasn't sure you were ready for the club. Whether you'd ever be ready for it, actually. As I told you then, I didn't plan to introduce you to that part of my lifestyle quite yet."

Yes, he said all of that then. But the club… It awakened something in me. Something that seems almost as necessary as air.

I clear my throat. "Some of the men wear leather gear."

"They do. I don't."

"Why?"

"I don't find it comfortable."

Is the answer truly that simple?

He continues, "The club isn't a place to play dress up for me."

"Is that what it is for some people?"

He nods. "Dressing in leather with pierced nipples is a fetish for some. It's part of exhibitionism for others. Not for me."

I smile. "Yet you like to dress me up."

His lips curve upward on the left side of his mouth. "Yes, but that's for *my* pleasure. Not for anyone else's. Not even yours."

"It pleases me to look good for you."

"Then I guess it's for your pleasure as well." Braden dons a black button-down, leaving the top two open.

I suck in a breath. God, he's magnificent.

"Are you ready?" he asks, handing me my trench coat.

I nod, squirming against the tickle between my legs.

I'm so fucking ready.

We head to the elevator.

A few minutes later, we arrive at the club.

Black Rose Underground.

"Did you name the club?" I ask.

"Of course. It's my club."

"Where did the name come from?"

"It just sounded good to me."

I nod. I'm not sure he's telling me the whole truth, but I'm so enamored by the club that I let it go.

"Do I have to sign the NDA again?" I ask.

"No. You're good for a year."

Braden signs us in and we enter. It's a little more crowded this evening, maybe because it's Sunday instead of Monday night. Braden leads me to the bar, where he orders two Wild Turkeys. The bartender, a different one this time but still topless, slides the bourbons to us, and Braden hands one to me.

"What would you like to do tonight?" he asks.

I don't hesitate. "I want you to bind me again."

"That would please me, but there's a lot here you haven't seen. I can show you so much more."

"That would be nice," I say, "but maybe another time. I'd like to see the bondage room again. Then I want to go to your suite."

He takes a sip of his drink. "As you wish, Skye." He pulls his phone out of his pocket. "I never showed you this."

I take his phone, and my mouth drops open.

It's a photo of me the last time we were here. I'm bound with the dark-red rope and lying on my side in the semi-fetal position, my eyes closed.

I'm stunned.

And turned on.

"You said I could take photos of you. Cameras aren't allowed in here, but since I own the place, I bend the rules a little. Besides, I have no intention of posting this photo anywhere."

I gaze at my own image, bound and satisfied.

The knot work is simple but beautiful, and the color of the rope against my white skin is lovely in its contrast.

My hair is slightly disheveled, and all I'm wearing are the black stilettos.

And Braden's collar.

But it's the look on my profile that truly draws my gaze.

I look…

Content?

Yes, but more.

Serene?

Yes, but more.

Almost…drunk.

But I'm not drunk. I had one drink that night. Only one, and I don't let myself get too drunk ever.

Then it hits me—the perfect word to describe the look on my face.

Enthralled.

For that's what I truly am.

Enthralled by Braden. In thrall *to* him. In bondage to him. Captive to him and captivated by him.

"What do you think?" he asks.

He's asking what I think of the photo, as a professional. I know this, yet I respond to a different question entirely.

"I see a lot in this photo," I say, "but most of all, I see *me*."

Chapter Fifty-Two

I don't take the time to ponder my own thought, though its meaning seems clear enough. I've been wondering who I am lately, given all the changes in my life.

Yet in Braden's photo, I see *me*.

Is he pleased with my response? He's as stoic as ever, so I'm not sure.

His words from yesterday ring in my mind. *You seem to be after something more than just sexual gratification.* Am I?

Again, I don't take a lot of time to ponder the question, because only one thing is truly on my mind.

"Take me to the bondage room," I say. "Please."

He finishes his drink, sets the glass on the bar, stands, and offers me his hand. "Come with me."

We walk through the same door, into the hall of rooms, and then to the bondage room.

I come alive when we enter, when I gaze at the scenes before us.

"Take it all in, Skye," Braden whispers in my ear. "See. Hear. Learn."

I take the lead as we walk around the room. I don't recognize any of the faces, but then I wasn't looking at faces last time. I was looking at the scenes themselves, the bondage.

Tonight's are similar yet different. Some couples are having sex, others aren't.

The knots in the different colors of rope ensnare me. All so beautiful, some simple, some intricate.

Until one scene totally captivates my attention.

A woman stands, her arms over her head, tied at her wrists, and attached to a pole. She's bound around her waist and breasts, with only her nipples showing. They're plump and taut, and though I've never been interested in women, I wonder what they might feel like against my tongue.

The thought is fleeting, though, because as I rake my gaze upward, I see what makes me quiver even more.

She's bound around her neck, her Dominant holding a chain that's linked to the makeshift collar.

He pulls on it lightly, and she gasps.

Again.

Then again.

Each time she gasps, her cheeks slightly redden.

Then he flogs her bare ass with... I'm not sure what it is. It looks like a ping-pong paddle.

Her ass turns pink, and those nipples, if possible, protrude even farther.

What about this scene speaks to me?

I don't know, but I want to be that woman, and I want Braden to be that man.

This is why I wanted to return to New York. To play out this scene.

"Seen enough?" Braden whispers.

I nod. "Can we go to your suite now?" I whisper.

"Absolutely," he growls.

He leads me out of the bondage room and down the hall, where he enters his code. Once again, we're in his private suite. In one corner stands a pole, something I didn't pay much attention to last time.

This time? I notice.

"Braden?"

"Yes?"

"Can you bind me to that pole? Like the woman we just saw?"

"My knotting is a little different, but yes, I can accommodate you." He unzips my bustier, and it falls to the floor. My breasts are swollen and my nipples already hard and ready.

He pinches one. "Gorgeous."

I tremble, the sensation surging to my pussy. I'm so wet, I must be dribbling down my thighs.

"What about that scene enticed you, Skye?"

I know the answer, but I'm not ready to tell him just yet. "All of it," I say.

He slaps one of my breasts lightly. "Be more specific."

"Her nipples," I say.

"What about them?"

"How her boobs were bound but her nipples were free. They were so tight and hard."

A low groan rumbles from his throat. "And you liked that?"

"Yes."

"What else?"

"Her ass. All red after he paddled her."

Another groan. "Yes. Very nice." He peels my skirt from me and turns me around. "Your ass is prettier than hers. It will be even more beautiful when I make it red." He rips the thong from me so I'm standing only in fishnets and my platform stilettos.

He trails his fingers over the cheeks of my ass. "Is tonight the night?" he asks.

He wants to fuck me there. I've been so enthralled by the bondage that I forgot. The idea intrigues me, but what I really want is—

"Answer me," he commands.

"If you want it to be."

He doesn't reply right away. He's displeased with my answer. He wanted me to be as excited about the prospect as he is.

I'm intrigued but not excited. What excites me is being bound for his pleasure.

And if I'm bound for his pleasure…

"Yes," I say, much more adamantly this time. "Tonight is the night."

This time, his gaze darkens. "Good. Perfect." He turns toward one of the cupboards and opens it. He returns with a bottle of lubricant and a stainless steel anal plug. "I should have made you wear this all day. Hindsight." He lubes up my asshole and gently inserts the plug.

I gasp at the intrusion, but once it's inside, my rim relaxes.

"Tell me," he says, "how you'd like me to bind you."

"Like the woman in the last scene we saw."

He nods and gathers rope from one of the chests. Black this time instead of the dark red. Does the color have significance to him? To me it symbolizes darkness, the underground. I'm following him under this time.

And I can't wait.

"Kneel before me," he commands.

I drop.

"Raise your hands above your head."

I do as he asks, and he binds my wrists tightly with the

rope. I wish I could see him work the knots.

"Now, stand."

I rise, resisting the urge to squirm against the invasion of the butt plug.

He leads me to the pole, where he attaches me with what appear to be carabiner hooks and leather straps. I'm not suspended, but I'm nearly immobile, as moving my feet backward will cause me to stretch to an uncomfortable position.

"Now, face me."

To my astonishment, I can move around. Whatever he attached me to allows this.

"You liked what you saw on the woman's breasts," he says, his voice a rasp. "I'll bind yours even tighter."

My pussy throbs as he pulls a piece of the black rope around the top of my chest. My breasts are full, swollen, and rosy, and my nipples…

I know what's coming, and apparently, so do they.

He continues to wrap the rope, knotting it so quickly that his fingers seem to fly, but when he gets to the swell of my breasts, he pulls two strips down over one breast, using my own flesh as a stop to let my nipples slide through the rope.

The pinch of the nylon rope against my nipple sends surges of electric current through me that land right in my clit. I moan.

I don't speak, though he hasn't forbidden it.

What's happening to me seems too reverent, as if speaking will bastardize it in some way.

He repeats with the other nipple.

This is different than the bondage I witnessed—different tying and knotting—but the result is the same. My nipples are pushing outward and my God, they're hard and straining.

My breasts and nipples now bound, Braden continues

down my abdomen, binding me horizontally until he gets to my belly button. He stops there. "I can bind your legs," he says, "but not this time. I want you to be able to spread them when I take your ass for the first time. Binding your legs will make it more painful for you."

I nearly contradict him, telling him I welcome more pain.

But I don't.

Because talking might bastardize what's happening to me.

"Are you ready, Skye?" he asks.

"Always," I reply, my voice breathy.

I close my eyes, waiting for him to complete the bondage. He'll bind my neck and hold a rope that will allow him to tighten and loosen the collar.

I want this.

I *need* this.

"Turn toward the pole," he says darkly.

I obey, my eyes still closed, the skin on my neck tingling with sharp chills.

I'm ready.

Ready to take this to the next level. And then, once I'm bound, Braden will take my anal virginity.

Yes.

Just yes.

My nipples are straining, the tight friction of the rope deliciously stimulating them. Braden's lips and teeth would be even better, but each time I move, the friction changes slightly, and the stimulation is enthralling.

Yes, my new word.

Enthralled.

I'm fucking enthralled.

Totally under Braden's spell, and when he binds my neck and exerts total control, I'll be home.

Finally home.

The waiting only increases the intensity.

When will he touch the skin of my neck? When will he fit me with a rope collar? When will he pull on it, making me gasp and then releasing, allowing me to breathe in the sweet swell of beautiful air? Then he'll paddle me, make my ass nice and crimson before he fucks me there.

When?

I wait.

And I wait.

Until—

He gently pulls out the butt plug.

I whimper.

"Easy," he says. "I'm going to slide the head of my cock into you pretty quickly. Getting past the elastic rim is the worst part."

But wait…

"Wait!"

"What is it, Skye?" he asks.

"I… You… You didn't paddle me. Like in the scene."

"All right. I didn't realize you wanted to completely mimic the scene."

"Not mimic, but…"

"But what?"

"My neck, Braden. I want you to bind my neck."

He doesn't reply for a moment. A moment that seems like a year.

Finally, he speaks.

"No, Skye."

Chapter Fifty-Three

No?

He won't bind me around my neck?

Why not? I'm showing him the ultimate trust. Giving him the ultimate control. Everything he holds dear.

I don't move. I'm facing the pole, my nipples still strained and aching.

My core is ready to shatter, ready to succumb to the ultimate bondage in this room.

Ready for—

Ready for anything. I open my mouth, ready to shout to Braden that I'll give him what he wants. I'll give him control over every aspect of my life, if he'll only bind me around my neck—

My arms slacken. Braden has unhooked the binding to the pole.

"Turn around, Skye. Face me."

I obey, looking down at the beautiful knotting across my chest.

"Look at me," he says.

I lift my head and meet his gaze. His blue eyes, only a moment ago alive with sapphire flames, now look...

Different.

Not happy. Not sad. Not turned on.

Resigned.

And I don't know why.

He touches the rope around my chest and loosens it.

No. I don't want to be unbound. I *want* to lose control here. I want to go under. All the way under.

I want it because he wants it.

I want it because *I* want it.

"You're not looking at me," he says.

He's right. My gaze dropped to his fingers at the rope. I lift my head and look into his eyes as he finishes unbinding me. The ropes fall to the floor.

Finally, I say, "I don't understand."

He picks up the ropes and brings them to the chest. Then he returns to me, takes my hand, and leads me to the bed. "Sit."

Still naked except for my fishnets and stilettos, I obey.

He sits next to me. "You seem disappointed."

"I'm okay." The lie tastes bitter on my tongue.

"I want you to get dressed," he says. "We're leaving."

"Leaving?"

"Yes."

"But...why?"

"Because I have something to say to you, and I don't want to do it here."

• • •

Back at Braden's penthouse, he seems distant. Finally, he asks me to sit next to him on the couch in the living area.

"I said something to you earlier. Do you remember what it was?"

"You said a lot of things to me earlier, Braden."

He nods. "You're right, but there was something that I said concerned me. That I was worried you were finding something at the club other than pleasure."

Yes, he said that. And I remembered it at the club, but I chose not to think about what his words implied.

"Skye, why did you want me to bind you around your neck?"

"Because it's what happened in the scene."

He shakes his head. "That's not the truth, and you know it."

He's right, and I only realize how right he is in this moment.

He bound me, made my nipples sing, was ready to take my anal virginity and paddle my ass until it was rosy and hot.

He offered me a beautiful scene—a scene any other woman in the club would love.

Indeed, I loved it, too.

But I craved more.

It was the neck binding. The collaring. The leading.

The…

I'm almost afraid to even think the words.

The…choking.

The ultimate loss of control.

I've gone from giving up control to losing control. From craving submission to needing the ultimate mark of it. But what does that all mean?

I lost my job. I lost my best friend.

I've lost control of my own life.

"I won't force you to tell me, Skye, but if you want a relationship with me, you need to be honest."

"I just...wanted it."

"You wanted me to choke you." His statement has no inflection. He's not questioning. He already knows. "Why, Skye?"

"I'm not sure."

"Aren't you?"

"I mean...I have an idea."

"And that idea is...?"

"I wanted to lose control. Completely. Give you complete control. Show you that I trust you."

"I already know you trust me, and you've already given me complete control in the bedroom."

"But I want—"

Braden reaches forward, lightly trails a finger over my forearm. "Giving me control is not about what you want. It's about what *I* want."

I hold back a shudder at his touch. "But—"

"Stop. It's about what you want as well. But it's for me to choose and for you to either consent or decline. Do you understand?"

I nod, swallowing, tears forming and pooling in the bottom of my eyes.

He rubs his forehead. "Damn it, Skye! Say yes or no."

"Yes, I understand. Of course I understand, Braden."

"Do you? Do you really?"

Before I can answer, he continues.

"Because I don't think you do. You don't understand *me*."

I lift my eyebrows, my eyes turning to circles, the tears still threatening. "I don't understand you? How am I supposed to understand you when you keep things from me?"

I expect him to flare up, lose his temper.

Instead—

"Point taken," he says, even-tempered. "So let me enlighten you about something."

"All right. I'm listening."

"I told you once that I only have one hard limit."

I nod.

"It's neck binding. Breath control. Choking. I won't do it. Ever."

Oh? What are your hard limits?

I only have one.

What is it?

I don't talk about it.

Don't you think I should know? So I don't bring it up?

Trust me, Skye. You will never *bring it up.*

Braden was wrong. I brought it up. Why did he think I wouldn't?

Control. It's the ultimate loss of control, and he assumed I'd never go there.

"Choking is taboo," I say. "You told me once you love the forbidden."

"I do."

"Then why?" I ask. "Why won't you do this?"

"Why? Perhaps I'll tell you why…as soon as you tell me why you feel you need it."

"I…don't know."

He inhales. Exhales. Inhales again. Is he thinking about how to reply to me? Is he angry? Sad? Does he feel anything at all?

Because I can't tell.

"For God's sake, Braden," I finally say. "Can you show me some emotion for once in your life?"

He cocks his head as his nostrils flare. "You think I don't

show you emotion?" He stands. "How can you say that? I've shown you more emotion than I've ever shown anyone. Anyone, Skye. If you don't know that, you should."

He's right. I'm not being fair. He showed me a ton of emotion last night when my dinner burned and I lost it. "Braden—"

"No. You don't talk. Not until I'm done. I told you who I was. I told you I wasn't wired for relationships. But I made an exception for you. I made that exception because I love you, Skye. I wasn't looking to fall in love. I knew it would put a dent in my life—"

I can't help responding. I'm torn in half, and I'm angry. "A dent, Braden? I'm a fucking dent?"

"Shut up! Just shut the fuck up, Skye. I will have my say, and then you can have yours. If you're brave enough."

"Brave enough? What's that supposed to mean?"

"You know exactly what it means, and if you interrupt me again, this discussion is over."

My lips tremble as I nod. I force the anger to dissipate.

He clears his throat. "I made an exception for you. I decided to have a relationship—or try, at least—but I fear this little experiment of mine has failed."

Little experiment? I'm a damned experiment? I want to yell, scream, tear out his hair. Punch his smug face until it's bruised and battered.

I want to cry, sob in his arms, and tell him I'll do anything to please him.

I want to beg him to take me back underground, tie me up, choke me.

I want to bare my soul, confess my love, tell him I'll do anything… Anything…

But I sit quietly. I sit quietly because I'm afraid. I'm very afraid of where this is leading.

If you're brave enough...

I've lost so much already.

"The club is about pleasure," Braden says.

"I know that. I get pleasure there."

"You do. But you get something else, as well. Something that's important to you, and that's what you need to face before we can continue in a relationship."

I finger his collar still around my neck. "Braden, please..."

"I love you, Skye." He tunnels his fingers through his hair and then rubs his forehead. "I love you more than I ever thought I was capable of loving another human being. But you want something I can't give you. Something I'll never be willing to give you."

I gulp. "I can live without the choking."

He trails a finger across my forehead and down my temple. "Can you? Because this isn't just about the choking. It's about more than pleasure. More than pain. More than my dominance over you and your submission to me. You're punishing yourself, Skye, and I can't be a part of it."

I shake my head vehemently. "But you... You punish me all the time!"

"That's *my* prerogative. Not yours."

"I get that. And you're wrong. I love everything we do. You know that. I'm not punishing myself. Why would I do that?"

He kisses my forehead.

A kiss goodbye?

That's what it feels like, and a vise clamps around my chest so hard that I think I might actually die right here on this bed. Die of a broken heart.

He wasn't sure I was ready for the club. I remember, watching his demeanor when he told me about his lifestyle here in New York, that he seemed to feel like he was making a mistake. That it was too soon for me.

How can I convince him he's wrong? That I need this as much as he does?

Maybe more?

Maybe more...

Oh God. It's the *more* that's the issue.

That vise around my heart? I don't feel it now. I'm numb. Completely numb. The irony of the situation is not lost on me. After my conversation with Betsy, I rushed into Braden's office, afraid he'd end our relationship if I refused to do something he wanted.

In reality? Our relationship is ending because he refused to do something I wanted.

"Why would you punish yourself?" Braden finally says, staring past me and out the window. "That's a question *you* need to answer."

A sob lodges in my throat.

I want to answer. More than I've ever wanted anything, I want to open up and give him what he's asking for.

But I can't, because I don't know.

I'm lost. So lost.

And I'm about to lose the man I love.

Braden and Skye's story reaches its thrilling conclusion! Be sure to preorder *Follow Me Always*, available May 25, 2021.

A Note From Helen

Dear Reader,

Thank you for reading *Follow Me Under*. If you want to find out about my current backlist and future releases, please visit my website, like my Facebook page, and join my mailing list. If you're a fan, please join my street team to help spread the word about my books. I regularly do awesome giveaways for my street team members.

If you enjoyed the story, please take the time to leave a review. I welcome all feedback.

I wish you all the best!

Helen

Facebook:
Facebook.com/helenhardt

Newsletter:
Helenhardt.com/signup

Street Team:
Facebook.com/groups/hardtandsoul